SUMMER at PRIMROSE TOWER

Annie Robertson

SUMMER at PRIMROSE TOWER

WELBECK

First published in 2022 by Welbeck Fiction Limited, an imprint of Welbeck Publishing Group based in London and Sydney.
www.welbeckpublishing.com

A CIP catalogue record for this book is available from the British Library

Paperback ISBN: 978–1–78739–768–2
Ebook ISBN: 978–1–78739–769–9

Printed and bound by CPI Group (UK) Ltd., Croydon, CR0 4YY

For Dani and Lesley,
friends and neighbours

PROLOGUE

'You did the right thing, love,' said Irene, placing her hand on Jennie's back. Even through the layers of thick clothing and her yellow waterproof coat, Jennie could still feel her touch, full of support, full of love, full of Mum.

'I hope so,' said Jennie, her voice as brittle as the twigs that snapped under her wellies. She couldn't tell if she felt frail because of shock or hurt or confusion, or a combination of all three, but she did know it felt better to be out in the woods of the Brompton Manor estate. The first bursts of spring were pushing through the undergrowth, fighting for life.

'If you ask me, you're better rid of him,' said her dad, Tony, bringing up the rear in his navy anorak and Dunlop wellies.

'Thanks, Dad,' she replied, her voice catching. Out of everyone, her dad was the one she felt worst for. He was the one who'd gone to the church to tell everyone the wedding was off, he was the one left out of pocket.

'I still can't get my head around it fully, if I'm honest,' said Irene, watching Bruno, their family's black Labrador, rooting around in the ferns up ahead.

Even Bruno's been out of sorts the last twenty-four hours, thought Jennie.

With all the comings and goings – Jennie and her sister, Claire, in the house; Jennie's boss, Dorothy, dropping off the bouquets and corsages; all the outfits hanging about the place – Bruno had been banished to the kitchen. And then there was the feeling of desolation in the house when she'd called the wedding off. All the phone calls that had to be made. Everyone's heads full of thoughts but barely anyone saying a word. Bruno hadn't been fed until long past 9 p.m., everyone too befuddled to remember him.

'I should have made the decision months ago,' said Jennie, taking the left fork in the path, as she'd done so many times over the years – family outings on Christmas Day to walk off lunch, leisurely New Year's strolls while making resolutions with Claire, Easter egg hunts arranged by the family who owned the estate, summer fetes, and Halloween ghost trails. She knew the estate as well as her parents' back garden: it was like an old family friend who she knew would always be there for her, in good times and bad.

'Why didn't you, love?' Irene asked, her grey-blue eyes searching her daughter's. Jennie could see the hurt caused by keeping her feelings from her mum, in a way she never usually did. It was as if that betrayal hurt Irene more than Jennie calling off the wedding.

Tears pooled in Jennie's eyes, and though she tried to hold them back with a finger, they splashed out like heavy raindrops and flooded down her cheeks.

'I thought he was feeling nervous, you know? When I first applied for the apprenticeship, he told me then that we'd be over if I got it, but I thought he was just worrying about the prospect of me going to London. And I never thought for a moment that I'd get it, that I'd actually have to tell him I was going,' she said, recalling how she'd dreamt of the Sarah Cunningham apprenticeship for years, but had only recently found the confidence to apply. 'I figured they'd choose someone else, and Stephen and I would go back to normal. We'd get married. I'd keep working at Dorothy's. Maybe along the way we'd have kids,' said Jennie, though expressing those thoughts out loud made them seem preposterous now. Laughable, really. *What is it they say . . .?* she thought. *What a difference a day makes . . .*

'When I told him I'd been accepted, he said I had to choose – the apprenticeship or him – and I just knew,' she continued, replaying the moment in her head when she'd naively snuck round, the night before the wedding, to tell him she'd got the position, and how his heart-shaped face and round dark eyes had sharpened when she'd told him.

It was the same look he'd get whenever he was in a mood and likely to fly off the handle, and she'd always modified her behaviour to bring him round. But the night before the wedding she didn't. That night she held her ground. 'It was clearer than anything has ever been. How could I possibly spend my life with someone who didn't support me in the one thing I love most?'

'You've wanted to be a florist since you were knee high to a grasshopper,' said Tony, and Irene laughed, lines crinkling round her eyes.

'Do you remember the endless daisy chains, the pressing of pansies, the countless Flower Fairies books? You've always been flower daft,' said Irene. And Jennie thought of the little Ragged Robin flower fairy, and how her mum's slight face and short hair weren't so dissimilar.

'And Stephen never understood that fascination,' replied Jennie, a knot of guilt in her stomach at not telling them about his ultimatum, the threat that came when she wouldn't relent: 'I'll make sure you never make a success of yourself,' he'd said, looming over her with a look in his eyes that suggested he was conjuring up all the ways he might bring her down. It took Jennie back to early on in their relationship when he'd told her he wouldn't take her out if she didn't change her dress, and she'd thought it was just a bit of healthy possessiveness. And then a couple of years later, when she'd mentioned wanting to set up her own business, he'd encouraged her into buying the house instead, bamboozling her with facts and figures about 'growth and investment', and how it was definitely in both their 'best interests' to buy. She felt so foolish that it was only when one hundred and fifty people were preparing to attend their wedding that she figured out she couldn't possibly spend the rest of her life with him.

'Better to realise now than five years down the line,' said Irene, and again that twist of guilt for not telling her parents the whole truth, the way she had throughout her life, even when it was raw or embarrassing, like teenage crushes gone wrong, or having to tell her dad about her first period when her mum was at work. But with this, with Stephen's threat, she wanted to protect them. *It's the last thing they need on top of everything else,* she thought – *all the cancellations, the deposits lost, the endless questions from guests. I owe them that.*

'You move to London and make a name for yourself, show him what he's missing,' said Tony, still bristling with pride about his daughter's plans, despite the cancelled wedding.

'It's just an apprenticeship, Dad. I'm not going off to be the Queen's florist,' she said, secretly thrilled that he was as pleased as she was, maybe more so.

'Your dad's proud of you, love. He's been googling Sarah Cunningham Flowers night and day since you applied. He can't believe his daughter's been selected by such a prestigious florist.'

'I can't believe the scale of some of those events. What sort of money must people have?' he whistled, genuinely awestruck, blissfully unaware of life beyond Gloucestershire and Brompton Marsh, where he'd lived all his life.

'A *lot*. More than we will ever know, that's for sure,' laughed Jennie, loving that her dad had somehow managed to retain such innocence despite being in his fifties.

'If you do well, Jennie, you'll be set for life.'

'I'll be happy being set for the next four weeks. I still need to figure out where to live until the apprenticeship begins,' she said, knowing there was no way she could return to the house she'd shared with Stephen.

'Stop with us, love. Your dad and I already talked about it. We'll be glad to have you back home.'

'Are you sure?' she asked, dreading even having to pop by the house to collect her things, not that there was much; the place always had felt more Stephen's than hers. They'd bought it a couple of years ago, a new build on the edge of the village. Stephen had insisted on something secure, even though Jennie had fallen for a pretty little flat in the centre of town with a tiny shop below and an outbuilding that would have been perfect for a flower business. But Tony had backed Stephen up, both man-splaining that a new build would be, 'low maintenance' with 'low bills' and 'low risk', so Jennie had gone along with it, even though it was more expensive, and all her savings were required to secure it.

'Of course we're sure,' said Irene, as the path changed from the mulch of the forest floor to the gravel paths of the estate.

'Thanks, Mum,' said Jennie, opening the gate to the walled garden where her parents peeled off to look at the hellebores. Jennie followed Bruno, who'd trotted up ahead towards her favourite sight, the gardener's cottage, with its symmetrical twelve-pane windows, the white paint peeling to expose the weathered wood. Jennie had lost count of how many times she'd sat in the garden, drinking in the scent of the rambling roses and honeysuckle. And each year she watched as another pane was lost in the enormous glass house that lined the wall opposite the cottage, and the roses grew woodier, and the brambles more invasive. And she'd lost count too of how many times she'd dreamt of owning the cottage, of restoring it to its former glory and running her own business, *Jennie Treloar Flowers*, from the garden. In more fanciful moments she'd even designed the branding, imagined a little vintage van emblazoned with her logo and pictured herself driving it through the countryside. But she knew it was nothing more than a fantasy, something she'd never be able to afford, even if she did acquire the skills at Sarah Cunningham's. The dream of an apprenticeship with Sarah was enough for her.

Jennie came round from her reverie when she noticed Bruno being joined by a greying border terrier, and not far behind him an elderly woman, tiny in stature, in a tatty work jacket, large enough for a man.

'Hello,' said Jennie, as the woman passed.

'Lovely day,' she replied, stopping, her hands crossed behind her back pensively.

'It won't be long until the daffodils are in bloom,' said Jennie, noticing the grey roots of the woman's straggly short hair. 'There's always such a lovely show this time of year.'

'The snowdrops have been glorious,' replied the woman, her gaze cast down.

'Always a treat,' Jennie smiled, wondering how frequent a visitor the woman was to the garden. 'It looks as if the groundsmen are busy,' she added, nodding to a man in the far corner of the garden lugging huge bags full of garden waste out of the gate.

'It's a full-time job.'

'Must be,' she agreed. 'I fantasise of something similar one day – tending to roses, growing my own blooms for bouquets.'

The woman smiled at her, a smile that Jennie couldn't quite decipher – either wistful or faintly humorous, as if she were being a little too fanciful for her liking.

'Anything is possible, with hard work and a little luck on your side,' she smiled, before bowing her head, her hands still clutched behind her back, and walking away. And even after she was far out of sight, there was something about her presence, something almost magical, that left Jennie wondering if a little luck of her own was about to come her way.

1

Jennie rang the round, pewter doorbell of Sarah Cunningham Flowers and waited, drumming her fingers nervously on her denim skirt. Her nerves had begun around 5 a.m. when she was awoken by the rumble of an early morning tube train, and it had taken her a moment to establish what the noise was and why her stomach was doing somersaults. And then it came back to her: her move the previous day from her mum and dad's to a bedsit in Primrose Hill for the three-month apprenticeship, starting today.

When no one answered, she cupped her hands and peered through the glass door to see if anyone was there, but the shop was empty. She was about to ring the bell again when a middle-aged woman came through from the back. Tidying her loose blond curls, Jennie pressed her delicate pink lips together, and stood a little taller as the woman reached up to unbolt the door.

'Jennie?' asked the chestnut-haired woman, opening the door then wiping her hands on her black apron.

'Yes.' She reached out and shook the woman's warm hand.

'I'm Sarah.'

Jennie hesitated for a moment, waiting for her to elaborate, 'Sarah, the shop manager,' or 'Sarah, I clean out the buckets and strip the stems,' but when more wasn't forthcoming, Jennie asked, 'Sarah Cunningham?'

'Of course!' she laughed heartily, welcoming Jennie into the shop. Its slate floor felt solid beneath Jennie's rose-pink Converse trainers, and the scent from the flowers took Jennie's breath away. 'Who were you expecting?'

An entire rank of underlings, thought Jennie, looking around in awe. It was too early for the flower van to have arrived but still, on two sides of the shop, there was an impressive array of blooms, sitting on elegant black dressers. Jennie noticed that the flowers were grouped by colour, not type, which highlighted tone and texture.

'I wasn't expecting you to be on the shop floor,' said Jennie, catching sight of her wide blue eyes in the dresser mirror.

'Best place for me,' said Sarah, going behind the long, black wooden counter on the left-hand side of the shop and picking up a couple of pewter buckets, which matched the doorbell. Jennie noted that detail was clearly paramount to Sarah. 'Grab that one for me, will you?'

Jennie took the bucket and followed Sarah through to the back of the shop and into the workroom.

'This is where all the real work happens,' said Sarah, putting down the buckets and gesticulating at the large room, its whitewashed brick walls diametrically opposed to the shop in every way. Four large workbenches filled the centre, a row of Victorian scullery sinks sat against the left wall, at the back an open door led to the office, and the remaining two walls were lined with shelves and stashed full of everything from oasis to stem strippers.

'You'll start out front in the shop, doing hand-ties and arrangements for local footfall. Once you've proved yourself there, you can start back here, helping with the events.'

Jennie's heart skipped a beat at the mention of events. For years she'd been following Sarah on Instagram, gasping daily over breathtaking images taken at events ranging from corporate entertainment to celebrity bashes, and even a minor royal wedding – the type of occasions that left her dad speechless. With over 200,000 well-heeled followers, it seemed anyone who was anyone in London wanted Sarah Cunningham flower designs at their event.

'So,' said Sarah, washing out a bucket at the scullery sinks. 'It's clear from your application that you've got the skills.' Jennie recalled the process of applying for the position – forms to fill in, two references, a portfolio of her work, and a short statement on what she felt she could bring to Sarah Cunningham Flowers, something she'd agonised over for weeks during her lunch breaks, so that neither her old boss, Dorothy, nor Stephen would find out. 'But what the apprenticeship is really about is whether or not you have creativity and individuality. We're always looking to develop our brand, so a copycat isn't what I'm looking for.'

'I hope I'll be able to demonstrate both those things,' said Jennie, aware that she sounded horribly wooden and formal. She hoped Sarah wouldn't think her designs would turn out to be as rigid.

Sarah took down an apron from a peg by the sinks and handed it to Jennie. 'I'm sure you will,' she said kindly. 'And don't worry, there will be plenty of help along the way.'

'I'll do my very best,' Jennie said, putting the apron over her cropped sweater and tying a knot at the front of her slim waist. Her eyes fell on the embroidery. *Sarah Cunningham Flowers* was stitched on the black fabric in pewter thread, and a flutter of delight danced inside her as the realisation of her dream hit home.

'I expect nothing less,' said Sarah. 'Have you settled into the apartment?'

It had been less than twenty-four hours since Jennie had arrived in the city. The flat was tiny with a small wet room in one corner, and a kitchen in the opposite corner which was just big enough to accommodate a cooker and sink with a cupboard below, and two units above. There was no work surface, so anything she wanted to prepare had to be done on a tray on her knee or on the small coffee table next to the two-seater sofa bed. It was a far cry from the familiarity and cosiness of her family home.

'Just about. I brought some things from home to make it feel more like mine,' said Jennie, who'd Facetimed her mum as soon as she'd arrived and laughed about how miniscule it was. It made their home on the cul-de-sac look positively palatial.

'It's small, so it doesn't take much to cheer it up.'

'Exactly!' Jennie knew the flat would soon feel like home – all her bits and bobs, things that hadn't fitted in to Stephen's 'minimalist' aesthetic, had been packed away in her old bedroom and were already doing the trick – even if she was feeling a bit lost in London. The city felt a long way from Brompton Marsh, where everyone spoke to everyone whether they knew you or not.

But then again, thought Jennie, *sometimes everyone speaking to everyone isn't such a good thing*. Jennie had learnt from experience that the local grapevine meant everyone knowing your business, and when you were the subject of gossip, as Jennie had been after ditching Stephen at the altar, village life could feel pretty claustrophobic. *Perhaps being in the city isn't such a bad thing after all, even if it does feel a bit lonely and overwhelming at the moment.*

'So,' said Sarah, going back through to the shop with Jennie, where she presented her with a broom and changed the Closed sign to Open, 'we have three rules when serving customers: one, always learn their name; two, treat each person as if they're about to spend ten thousand pounds, even if they only spend ten; three, the customer is always right.'

'Got it,' said Jennie, who, wanting to show willing, began sweeping up the remains of yesterday's stems.

'And here's your first of the day,' said Sarah, opening the door with a smile. 'Good morning, Kat. How are you?'

'I'm well, thank you, Sarah,' said Kat, a girl around Jennie's age, early thirties, with jet-black hair in a short, sharp asymmetric cut, one side long and angled across her face, the other side shaven.

'Kat, this is Jennie.'

'Hi,' said Jennie, putting aside the broom.

'Is it your usual?' Sarah was already pulling out dark anemones in purple and red.

'Yes, please.' Kat's hair fell over one eye, which was painted with thick, black liner.

'Jennie, why don't you choose something for Kat that will complement her selection.'

Jennie, recognising that this was her first test, came out from behind the counter to assess Kat, not so much that

Kat would notice, but enough that Jennie might pick up on her character and taste. She wore black skinny jeans and a black T-shirt with rolled-up sleeves, which exposed her brightly coloured tattoos of skulls, serpents and lilies. She held her chin down, but whilst her body language was guarded, and her clothing gender-neutral, there was something about her that was innately warm and feminine, much like her choice of anemone.

'I think the black calla lily,' said Jennie, taking three stems from the bucket on the dresser. Sarah passed the anemones to Jennie to group together, who formed them effortlessly into a posy, even though her fingers were trembling.

'What do you think?' Sarah asked Kat.

'I like it,' she replied with a shy smile.

'I do too,' said Sarah, indicating to Jennie that she might wrap them, before saying goodbye to Kat and heading out back.

'Is today your first day?' Kat asked quietly, as Jennie meticulously tied and trimmed the posy, and wrapped it in Sarah's elegant, matte black paper. She'd hoped her shaking hands weren't visible to Kat.

'Is it that obvious?' laughed Jennie. She finished the arrangement with pewter ribbon. The bow was puffier than she'd usually make but she knew that was down to nerves, and she had a feeling Kat wouldn't mind.

'No, no,' said Kat in a way that suggested she'd like to retract the comment, anxious not to have offended Jennie. 'It's just, I haven't seen you before.'

'Are you a regular?'

'I come in when I can. Flowers are a treat, not a necessity, not like for some around here.' She rubbed her knuckles over her dark, red lips, and looked out the window to the passing residents of Primrose Hill.

'You don't live locally?'

'Kind of,' she said, trying to remove cash from her back pocket. 'On the other side of the hill, the estate – the poor man's Primrose Hill.'

Jennie smiled at Kat's self-deprecation and wondered if the 'poor man's Primrose Hill' just meant another extremely expensive London neighbourhood. 'I'm not from round here.'

'I can tell,' giggled Kat, placing her money on the counter. 'You ask too many questions!'

'Sorry,' said Jennie, blushing and feeling suddenly conscious of her country ways.

'Don't apologise, it's sweet. Makes a change. When did you arrive?'

'Yesterday,' she said, handing Kat the posy and processing the transaction on the till.

'Wow, you are new!' She took the posy and hesitated before asking, 'Would you like me to show you the sights?

16

I wouldn't mind, it's not often I get a chance to do the tourist stuff.'

'That would be great,' said Jennie, delighted by the offer, and hoping everyone she'd meet at Sarah Cunningham Flowers would turn out to be so nice.

*

'Jennie, can you come through to the office?' asked Sarah, on Friday afternoon.

'Sure,' said Jennie, happy to have the opportunity to sit down for five minutes after an exceptionally busy first few days.

The shop had rarely been empty all week, and, at the times when it had been, there was tidying and cleaning to attend to or the phone to answer. Sarah had watched intermittently but for the most part Jennie was left to her own devices, to create hand-ties and arrangements with flowers she'd never used before, flowers that didn't fall within her previous boss's standard weekly order. Dorothy, the owner of Brompton Floristry, where Jennie had worked since leaving college, had been stuck in the 1980s with pink carnations, white chrysanthemums and red roses. Now Jennie had at her fingertips stems of orchids, delphiniums, hydrangeas and bells of Ireland, to name but a few; in short, everything she'd ever wanted.

'Fiona, cover the shop, will you?' asked Sarah.

'On it,' answered Fiona, Sarah's student 'shop girl' who worked the busy days, sweeping the floor, cleaning buckets and doing the lunch run. And all while looking effortlessly cool in her high-waisted jeans, granny cardigans and big wire-rimmed glasses.

'Take a seat,' said Sarah, as she poured Jennie a coffee from the filter machine in the corner of her office, which was almost the only thing not buried in a mountain of paperwork. It amazed Jennie that Sarah could run a successful business in such a disorganised fashion.

'Customer feedback is good,' she said, handing Jennie a coffee. 'And passing trade has been higher than usual this week. I think word is spreading that there's someone new in town.'

Jennie smiled modestly, believing Sarah probably said the same to all her apprentices at the end of their first week.

'Your skills are excellent, and I can see that you have creative flair,' she said, trying to find a space for her mug amongst the mess on her desk. 'I'm very pleased.'

Jennie watched as Sarah rummaged for something, lifting pieces of paper and empty coffee cups. 'I don't usually ask apprentices to get involved with events so early on but, for you,' she said, finding what she was looking for, 'I'm going to make an exception.'

Feeling a surge of excitement, Jennie placed her hands under her thighs to stop them from shaking. She'd dreamt of this moment for years – helping create a Sarah Cunningham event – and now, here she was, her dream playing out in real life. Sarah pulled her glasses down from the top of her head, where they'd been acting as a hairband, and read the hand-written note in front of her.

'The Arbuthnotts,' she read. 'Dinner party for twenty, a week tomorrow.' She looked up expectantly. Jennie hoped Sarah didn't expect her to know who the Arbuthnotts were; she smiled and nodded in an ambiguous manner that might pass as impressed or excited. 'I'd like you to work on this. They're *extremely* important clients, very influential.'

'I'd love to,' said Jennie, thrilled at the opportunity to assist Sarah. She hoped if she did well that it might not be too long until she had the chance to do an event all on her own rather than just assisting, though she knew she had many more skills to learn before she could be trusted with that level of responsibility.

'The Arbuthnotts, and their contacts, account for a large percentage of the business, so it's important we get this right.'

Sarah went on to list exactly what the Arbuthnotts required for their dinner party: a centrepiece running the length of the table, napkin rings, two standing arrangements, two smaller arrangements, a large arrangement for the entrance hall, and five vases for the living room.

'That's a lot for a dinner,' said Jennie, thinking she'd done weddings back home with less.

Sarah returned to her notes saying nonchalantly, 'Quite simple by their standards.'

There had been moments like this throughout the week when Jennie had had to pinch herself, to remind herself that she really was working for one of the most distinguished florists in the country, and prestige brought wealth. There was the middle-aged American woman who came in and spent over a thousand pounds on a whim because 'I need cheering up', the elderly English gent who asked that a member of staff be dispatched to his house twice a week to refresh the arrangements, and the wife of a diplomat who required a different arrangement in their entrance hall every evening. It was a world away from Dorothy and Brompton Floristry, where the most they did was drop bouquets at people's front doors, or position flowers at weddings. And here, in Sarah's office, was another pinch-herself moment, a dinner party for which the flowers alone would cost more than Jennie used to earn in a month, and certainly far more than the tiny hourly rate she was receiving for the apprenticeship.

'The house is on Cornwall Terrace, overlooking the park – the usual decor: marble floors, taupe walls and a stash of modern art.'

'Ah-huh,' said Jennie, nervous excitement bubbling in her stomach.

'The dinner is informal, the caterer is doing a seasonal spring menu, quite light, so you need to keep that in mind when you're designing the arrangements. The flowers need to be there by 10 a.m. sharp, so let's make sure everything is ready by 9.'

Jennie furrowed her brow and waited for Sarah to correct herself – surely she meant to say 'when *we're* thinking about the arrangements' – but she didn't.

She can't be suggesting I'm to create and develop the designs myself.

Sarah, noticing Jennie's pensiveness, glanced up from her paperwork. 'Everything okay?'

'Y-yes,' she stammered, trying to remain composed, trying not to burst with fear and excitement at the prospect of doing her own Sarah Cunningham event. 'You'd like me to work on this alone?' she asked, hoping she hadn't misunderstood but also worrying that she wasn't really up to the challenge so soon.

'You don't feel I'm asking too much of you, do you?'

'No!' said Jennie quickly, hoping very much that Sarah hadn't noticed the change of pitch in her voice, which would almost certainly give away her concerns.

2

'I never imagined the city to be so beautiful,' said Jennie, who held tightly to the handrail in a pod of the London Eye.

'It's good to be reminded,' said Kat, standing by Jennie's side, both of them looking down at Big Ben and the Houses of Parliament, which to Jennie appeared to be made out of matchsticks. 'When you've lived here most of your life you lose sight of its beauty.'

'I guess that's true of wherever you live,' mused Jennie, thinking of home and of how its soft, honey-stone beauty was, more often than not, lost on her. The tourists that lined the narrow streets throughout the year served only to annoy the locals rather than remind them of how lucky they were to live in such a romantic setting.

'Where is it you're from?'

'A little village in Gloucestershire – Brompton Marsh,' she replied, looking north to locate Regent's Park and Primrose Hill beyond. It amused her how quaint Brompton

Marsh now felt in comparison to the vast urban sprawl laid out beneath her, even the grounds of the manor house estate would look small next to the royal parks.

'Have you lived there all your life?'

Jennie nodded, and gulped back an unexpected wave of homesickness. Until she'd left, she hadn't quite realised how integral her community and surroundings were to who she'd become. Now, surviving without them, it felt sometimes as if she was breathing with only half a lung.

'Do you miss it?'

'I miss the familiarity of it, the rhythm of village life . . .' she answered, drifting into thoughts of how she missed her family home, and being able to pop down the road to the corner shop where Janette and Trevor would share the village gossip, even if she was now part of it; and she missed walking Bruno in the grounds of the Brompton Manor estate, set amidst the gently rolling countryside, which enveloped the village like a warm, comforting hug. 'But I needed to get away,' she said, coming out of her daze when an image of Stephen, the night before their wedding, his eyes full of wrath, popped into her head.

'Can I ask why?'

Given that the two of them were in a capsule with fifteen or twenty other people and their every word could be overheard, Jennie only offered a vague reply, 'Let's just say the apprenticeship couldn't have come at a better time.'

'Fate lent a hand?'

'You could say that,' she said, her voice trailing off, her mind meandering to thoughts of Stephen, and of how her life might have turned out if the apprenticeship hadn't come up when it did. It struck her hard that she had almost willingly walked into a life of compromise, devoid of understanding. The thought sent a cold shudder down her spine.

'That's Buckingham Palace over there.' Kat pointed to the building and its grounds. 'And St James's Park beside it.'

Jennie looked to where Kat was pointing, a red rose tattooed on her knuckle, glad that she was sensitive enough to steer the conversation in a different direction.

'I can't get over how much greenery there is, and how much wildlife must live among it all,' said Jennie, hoping she'd find time soon to explore the city's green spaces.

'There's always a park to escape to, or some tree to hide under,' said Kat absently.

'Are you often in need of a tree to hide under?' Jennie asked, not quite able to read Kat's distant expression.

'More often than I'd like,' she replied, moving to the bench in the centre of the pod.

Jennie joined her, the bodies of the other passengers partially obscuring their view of St Paul's Cathedral. 'Is there something in particular that's troubling you?'

'Nothing that every other person hasn't been through at some point in life.'

'A break-up?' enquired Jennie.

'One that's on the cards, at any rate,' said Kat, her gaze far away across the city.

*

'What did you need to get away from?' asked Kat, after she and Jennie had left the London Eye and found a riverside table outside a canteen near the Royal Festival Hall.

'My relationship.' Jennie paused, checking in with herself to decide how much to divulge to a near stranger. But there was something about Kat, and her aura of vulnerability, despite her edgy appearance, that made Jennie feel comfortable sharing her story. 'I was with a guy, Stephen. We were together for five years, engaged. But when I told him I'd applied for an apprenticeship in London, he told me if I got it, we'd be over.'

'You're kidding?' said Kat, her dark brown eyes wide in disbelief.

'Nope,' Jennie laughed lightly, heartened by Kat's incredulity. 'Not kidding.'

'Was this a while before the wedding?'

Jennie sucked her mint pressé through a straw. 'Three months. But he was convinced I'd choose him over my career, and I, naively, thought he was just feeling insecure, a bit threatened, you know, that eventually he'd be supportive of my ambition.'

Kat shook her head, her hair falling over one eye. 'How long before the wedding did you find out you'd got the position?'

'The night before.'

'No way!' she said, fully engrossed in the drama of it all. 'What happened?'

The image of Stephen, his eyes boring through her, came rushing back to Jennie. 'I went round, told him I'd got it, fully expecting him to be happy for me. I thought he'd tell me we could work around it.'

'But he didn't?'

'Nope. Instead, he told me to choose: him or the apprenticeship.'

'Shit. How did he take it when you told him you were choosing your career?'

'He threatened me, told me he'd make sure I never made a success of myself,' said Jennie, who'd been relieved every day since that the threat had so far been hollow.

'My God! He threatened you? Had he done that before?'

Jennie circled her straw in her drink. 'Maybe not full-on threats, but little things, you know: what clothes to wear; what food to eat, who not to see. The night before the wedding was the climax, I guess,' she said, thinking back to how their relationship had begun.

They'd met at the village pub, The Fox and Hounds. Jennie had been there with some old school friends; Stephen was on a work night out. When they ordered the same drink at the same time, Stephen had asked Jennie her favourite flavour of crisps, and they'd laughed in amazement when they'd both said 'prawn cocktail' in unison. She'd liked his soft features and well-groomed hair, but more than that she'd been flattered by how attentive he was, and when he'd asked her out, she'd said 'yes'. After that, it wasn't long until they were spending days together at a time, and then weeks. 'He was always keen to keep me close. When we moved in together and the spark began to wear off, he wasn't that keen for me to go out; he always said he preferred us just spending time together.'

'Sounds claustrophobic.'

'It was, sometimes. I guess we fell into a routine over the years, and I didn't notice things slipping away. I'm thankful that he responded the way he did the night before the wedding, at least he left me without any doubt. In that moment, I just knew.'

'Good for you.'

'Yeah,' sighed Jennie. 'I just wish I'd realised how wrong he was for me in time to cancel the wedding properly, to let people know, to spare my parents the cost and embarrassment.'

'Did everyone arrive dressed to the nines, with gifts, the lot?'

Jennie dipped her head in shame, thinking of all the friends and family she'd inconvenienced. 'That's the bit I feel worst about. If I'd thought for a moment that he was serious in his threat, I'd have gone out of my way to cancel everything months before the wedding.'

'Who stood up on the day and told everyone what was happening?'

'My poor dad.' Jennie squirmed at the memory of telling him, recalling how she'd thought he'd be devastated by the financial ramifications when in fact all he'd cared about was her welfare, even if he had been a bit stunned for a few weeks after. 'He had to go down to the church and tell everybody I wasn't coming. I can't imagine how he must have felt.'

'Shit, that's bad.'

'Tell me about it,' winced Jennie. 'I've never felt so awful in my life.'

'But surely people could see it wasn't your fault.'

'I don't know . . . I never told anyone about Stephen's ultimatum, not even my parents.'

'What did you tell them?'

'That he wasn't supportive of my career. They didn't need to hear the rest, that there was a threat hanging over me; they'd become good friends with his parents, and I didn't want to ruin that for them.'

'Jeez, you're nice.'

'Maybe, or perhaps I was just in shock,' said Jennie, who'd asked herself many times why she hadn't realised earlier how unsupportive and damaging he was of her and her dreams.

'Well, Stephen's loss is London's gain,' said Kat, raising her glass.

'Thanks, Kat,' said Jennie, realising this was the first decent chat she'd had with a girlfriend, other than her mum and Stephen's mother, in years. The thought made her both happy for where she was now, and sorry for all those friendships she'd missed out on, all the girls she'd known from school and the women she'd met through the flower shop. She often wondered how their lives had turned out, hearing snippets from Janette and Trevor, or seeing them in a far corner of the pub. Jennie wished she could go back and make changes, stand up a bit more to Stephen, or at least move forward and forge new friendships of her own. Even if everything else were to fail, she knew she could get through it if she had friends by her side. 'Anyway, that's enough about me, what's going on with you?'

'What I'm going through is pretty minor compared to what you've been through,' said Kat.

'I doubt that.'

'My partner, Lauren, she's convinced I'm seeing someone else.'

'How come?'

Kat shrugged. 'I've no idea. All I have to do is mention another woman and she's instantly paranoid that person is more interesting, more alluring to me than she is.'

'How does she feel about you being out with me?'

'I haven't told her. I said I was going out for a walk to look at the spring flowers.'

Jennie liked the fact that it sounded plausible to Lauren that Kat would do such a thing; Jennie had often escaped Stephen's darker moods with a walk through the woods of Brompton Manor, spotting the bright shoots of spring bulbs bursting through the dark winter undergrowth, the vibrant green of summer leaves, or the carpet of leaves in autumn, and on towards the walled garden, where she could sit for hours, dreaming her life away. 'Are you thinking of ending the relationship?'

'It can't continue the way it is,' said Kat, her eyes cast towards the river. 'But we live together, so it's not quite as simple as just calling it off.'

'Ah,' said Jennie, understanding Kat's predicament. 'Something else we have in common.'

'How long had you been living together?'

'Two years. We'd bought a house. Now he's buying my share. It's meant to be settled soon but until it is, I'm skint.'

Kat offered a sympathetic look. 'What a muddle we make of love.'

'Indeed we do,' reflected Jennie, thankful that the worst of her break-up was over, and sympathising with Kat being on the painful precipice of hers.

As they waited for their food to be served, Kat pulled out a vintage black compact inlaid with a deep red rose.

'That's beautiful,' admired Jennie.

'It belonged to my grandmother,' Kat explained, just as Jennie's phone rang. She excused herself to pop to the toilet.

'How's it going, love?' asked Irene, and Jennie could tell immediately that she was still concerned about how her daughter was getting on in the 'big city', as they called it; she'd telephoned twice a day since she'd moved, sometimes three.

'Really good, Mum. Sarah's asked me to do my first event.'

'No way. That's fantastic, love!'

In the background Jennie could hear horse-racing on the telly, and she imagined her dad, who'd bet on the horses as long as she could remember, sitting on the sofa beside Irene. He'd always hoped for a big win to buy all the things he could never afford for his family on his modest income as a school janitor. 'Anyone famous?'

Jennie laughed. While her dad had become fixated on speculating about the cost of the events, her mother was more interested in the 'celebrity clients'. It was all she'd talked about for weeks.

'Just some rich family doing a dinner party, nothing to get excited about.'

'I expect Sarah wants to give you a few trial events before unleashing you on the celebs!'

'Sure, Mum,' humoured Jennie. 'What's going on at home?'

'Oh, not much. Same old, same old. Your dad ordered a new top box for his scooter at the beginning of the week so that's all he can talk about. I had a doctor's appointment yesterday. That's about it.'

'Are you okay?'

'I'm just a little tired, nothing to worry about.' Jennie detected her mother's trivialising tone, the one she used when she wasn't ready to talk about something, so Jennie changed the subject.

'How's Bruno?'

'He's fine. He found a dead pheasant in the woods this morning. I had to get your dad to wrestle it off him.'

'Nice,' chuckled Jennie, enjoying hearing about the minutiae of home. It reinforced just how much she missed it.

'And I bumped into Tracy at Sainsbury's.'

Her mother's comment hung in the air for a moment longer than it should have done, Irene uncertain if she should have mentioned the meeting with Stephen's mum,

Jennie not sure how to respond. She hadn't seen Tracy since the week before the wedding, and though she'd meant to write, or call round, she hadn't been certain what to say. Somehow the days and weeks had passed, and then the time hadn't seemed right, and the moment was lost.

'How was she?'

'Okay, I think. Difficult to say.' Jennie could tell by the tightness in her mother's voice that she wasn't telling the whole truth.

'Mum?' she probed.

'I think she misses you, but she's too proud to say.'

A pang of sadness hit Jennie at how she missed Tracy too. In some ways she'd been closer to Tracy than to Stephen. They'd spend many an evening sitting on the sofa, wine glass in hand, putting the world to rights. And Jennie certainly felt worse for Tracy in the break-up than she had for Stephen, particularly since she hadn't spoken to her.

'I said we should meet up, have a chat, you know, over a bottle of wine,' said Irene.

'That's a good idea.'

'You wouldn't mind?'

'Why would I?'

'Well, you know—'

'Mum, what's between Stephen and me is just that; don't let it get in the way of your friendship with Tracy – that's really important to me.'

'Okay, love, if you're sure.'

'I'm sure,' she said, feeling that familiar knot of guilt for not having told her mother about Stephen's threat.

Jennie was quiet for a moment, wondering if Tracy had mentioned Stephen. Although Jennie knew she'd made the right decision in calling off the wedding and she couldn't forgive him for threatening her, she couldn't quite shake off all the feelings she'd had for him over the last five years.

'She said Stephen's doing okay, in case you want to know.'

'Right,' said Jennie, trying to sound casual, amazed by her mother's capacity to read her mind even over the phone. 'That's good,' she continued, attempting to sound pleased for him, when in fact she wanted Stephen to be hurting, to feel guilty for how he'd behaved, to experience some trace of regret that would prove their five years together hadn't been a complete waste of time. And while she didn't want his apologies, and she certainly didn't want him back, she did need to see something that told her he'd loved her – that she hadn't been so foolish as to almost marry a man who hadn't.

3

Jennie stepped back from the pedestal arrangement she was working on for the Arbuthnotts' dinner party and thought for a moment. 'There's something about this that isn't quite right.'

'It looks great,' reassured Louise, a forty-something mum who worked part-time for Sarah. She'd gone out of her way, since Jennie began, to make sure she had everything she needed and knew what she was doing. 'It's easy to lose the overall effect when you're working so close to it.'

'I'm not sure that's it,' she pondered. Jennie was used to losing sight of things; this felt different, as if the creative whole wasn't coming together.

She was trying to create a sort of Jackson Pollock effect – as if the flowers had been tossed up and then frozen in mid-air as they fell. For the most part it was working, her palette of primary and secondary colours – cornflowers, foxtails, narcissi, poppies and buddleja – was vibrant, but the pedestal, a black cast-iron stand with three scrolled feet, spoilt the illusion. Jennie felt it was too formal and old-fashioned for what she was trying to achieve.

'I need a different stand, something that will blend in with the surroundings in the house. What did Sarah say?' Jennie wiped her hands on her apron and referred to her notes on the workbench. 'Either marble or taupe.'

'I don't think we have anything like that,' said Louise, pulling her ash-grey hair into a twist and securing it with a pencil. 'You'd need to order something in.'

'I haven't time for that,' frowned Jennie. 'They have to be ready by nine tomorrow and delivered to the Arbuthnotts' by 10 a.m. sharp.'

Louise dunked a biscuit in her cup of tea. 'The flower market opens at 4 a.m., you might find something there.'

'But I don't have a car,' she said, worrying about how to get to the flower market at such an ungodly hour.

'Sarah won't mind if you take a cab and charge it to the company.'

Jennie assessed the remainder of the work to be done, and figured she needed about three hours to complete the task. 'If I finish the rest of the arrangements now, get up at three and take a taxi, I could be back by six to finish everything in time.'

'Sounds like a plan to me,' said Louise, her dunked biscuit breaking into her tea. She fished it out with a finger and dumped it in the bin. 'Just be sure to be back in plenty of time. Sarah's a stickler for punctuality; I've seen too many apprentices be shown the door for not completing work on time, and I wouldn't want you to be one of them.'

*

At 3.30 a.m. the next day, with Louise's warning ringing in her ears, Jennie – showered and dressed – stumbled into the cab, which smelt heavily of watermelon air freshener that did nothing to mask the odour of sick that permeated the upholstery. Jennie had a feeling that the driver, who had to look up the location of the flower market, was more accustomed to taking home late-night revellers rather than early morning workers. But, despite the cab, it was thrilling for Jennie to travel through the city at the break of dawn, to see deliveries being made, roads being swept, and tourists heaving suitcases into taxis on their way to the airport for early flights.

It was even more thrilling for her to arrive at the flower market, a place she'd wanted to visit all her life. The sights and smells of the massive warehouse full of flowers blew her mind. Wholesalers from Britain, Holland and beyond brought their products here to sell to florists between four and ten in the morning. Jennie loved that she'd stepped in from the mostly sleeping city to a vibrant hubbub of activity where no one seemed to notice or care that the rest of the city was still asleep.

So as not to waste time and risk not meeting Sarah's 9 a.m. deadline, Jennie had studied the layout of the market online. The flower vendors were in one section, the sundry suppliers in another. She wove her way through the endless crates of blooms, all as fresh and full of vitality as if they were still growing in the ground, towards the sundry suppliers where she spent almost an hour looking for a suitable stand. In the end she settled for one in taupe, which, she hoped, would blend in with the walls of the Arbuthnotts' entrance hall and dining room that Sarah had described.

At the exit to the market, the clock read 5.13 a.m. Jennie felt confident that she'd be back at the shop by five thirty, leaving her plenty of time to complete the arrangements without Sarah ever knowing of the rush to meet the deadline.

It was then Jennie realised there wasn't a cab in sight.

'Crap,' she muttered, cross with herself for not having thought to book a return ride, having assumed there'd be a rank of taxis nearby. Hastily she looked around for a notice board that might have the number of a local cab firm. There wasn't one.

She took out her phone and searched for taxi companies in the area but, it being so early in the morning, no one picked up.

Scanning the parking lot, she prayed a taxi would materialise but all she could see were endless vans emblazoned with flower company names from across the country. Despite the urgency, she still found a moment to imagine the vintage van of her dreams with her own logo sitting in the car park, but her daydream was quickly broken by a voice from behind her.

'Do you need help?' asked the voice.

Jennie turned to discover a man, similar in age, of medium height and build with short brown hair; a cowlick curled above his brow.

'No thank you. I'm waiting for a black cab.'

'You'll struggle to find one at this hour,' he smiled, clutching several wraps of white anemones with jet-black pistils. 'You might be better off calling an Uber.'

'Thanks,' she said shortly, not wanting to strike up a conversation. Back home such openness was normal, but here in the city, it felt out of place.

'Sorry, I should have introduced myself, I'm James,' he said, with no trace of an accent, and she noticed his eyes were periwinkle blue. 'Would you like me to order you an Uber? I don't mind. I wouldn't want to leave you standing here in the cold,' he said, performing an exaggerated shiver.

Jennie felt her lips twitch into a smile. 'It's kind of you, but no. Thank you.'

'Okay. Well, I tried,' he shrugged, a glint in his eyes.

As he walked away, Jennie found herself drawn to his confident gait, and the pull of his sweater across his strong shoulders.

When he got to his car, he called back to her, 'Are you sure? Last chance.'

'Positive,' she smiled, though part of her wanted to accept.

'Okay then, nice meeting you,' he sang, getting into his car and giving her a wave, Jennie kicking herself as he did so.

'Uber,' she said distractedly, when he'd driven off and was out of sight.

Living in the Cotswolds, where she had her own car, she'd rarely had cause to use a taxi service. It was gone five thirty by the time she'd signed up, downloaded the Uber app and ordered. And then it didn't show up for another half hour.

'Regent's Park Road,' she said to the driver, shoving the plinths into the boot while trying not to fixate on the fact that it was already six o'clock and she was cutting it perilously fine. She figured if they were back by six-thirty, although it would be tight, if she worked quickly, she could still get the pedestals done without Sarah knowing of the hurry.

'Traffic's bad,' said the driver, a thirty-something guy with a hooked nose, nine o'clock shadow, and a strong Cockney accent.

'How bad?'

'About as bad as it gets.'

Jennie hoped the driver was one of life's pessimists and that actually it wouldn't be quite as bad as he made out but, by the time they hit the river, she accepted he was right.

'Is there another route?' she asked, desperately trying to ignore the fact that her phone read twenty past six and they were going nowhere.

'All the routes will be as bad as each other. There's been an accident at Victoria, it's gridlock.'

She wondered if she'd be quicker on foot, but the plinths were heavy and there was no way she could walk the five-mile route carrying the three of them. And besides, given her lack of London knowledge, she'd probably get lost. She drummed her fingers anxiously on the window ledge.

The driver looked at her through the rear-view mirror. 'You in a hurry?'

'You could say that,' she said tersely, thinking of what Louise had told her. She was only too aware of how important it was to make a good first impression, to make it look as if her work was effortless. Anything less than her best and she faced the very real possibility of kissing goodbye to her apprenticeship. The prospect of heading home to Brompton Marsh with her tail between her legs, and giving Stephen the satisfaction that she'd failed, didn't bear thinking about.

'Don't worry, love. I'll get you there.'

They sat in traffic, listening to Capital FM, inching slowly forwards. When Jennie saw the sign for Victoria Station it was already quarter to seven. Even if they did make good progress from here, she feared she wouldn't complete the arrangements in time. *Maybe with a bit of adrenalin behind me I can do it*, she thought, but she knew it wouldn't be her best work, and she knew she couldn't risk delivering anything but her best for Sarah.

'That's been the cause of the delay,' said her driver, pointing to a bus with a bike under its front wheel. 'I guess someone else won't be arriving on time this morning either.'

Jennie stared out the window, mystified by the commuters hurrying past the crash, barely acknowledging the fate of the cyclist. In Brompton Marsh an incident like that would be the talk of the village for years. She couldn't fathom how people could just walk by, without so much as a backward glance. Her own stomach felt tight, and her head light at the sight of it.

After what felt like aeons standing still, the traffic began to move more steadily but it was after seven and already the morning rush hour had begun. Even the sights of Hyde Park Corner, the hotels of Park Lane and the department stores of Oxford Street failed to lift Jennie's crumpled spirits. It was twenty past seven when they reached the more familiar surroundings of Regent's Park, and Jennie, reconciled to her fate, began to imagine life back home: Stephen gloating; Dorothy preening, Janette and Trevor spreading the gossip faster than wildfire.

'I hope your day gets better,' said the driver as he helped Jennie remove the plinths from the boot.

'Thanks,' she muttered. 'But I reckon it's about to get a whole lot worse.'

Putting the key in the lock of the shop door, she wondered how she was ever going to complete the work in the space of an hour and a half, and was surprised to find the door already open.

'Hello?' she called, entering the shop, keys between her teeth, two large pedestals under one arm and a third under the other.

Someone called, 'Jennie?' from out back and a moment later Sarah appeared. Jennie's heart dropped when she saw the anger etched on her brow. 'What's going on? Why aren't the flowers ready?'

'I'm so sorry,' said Jennie, terrified that Sarah would fire her on the spot. She could feel her hands trembling and her heart racing. 'The pedestals weren't right, so I decided to go to the market this morning to make sure I had something that was suitable and then get back to finish the work, but then there was an accident and the traffic was gridlocked . . .' Jennie was aware that she was jabbering. 'I promise I left enough time, I was up at 3 a.m.,

43

I never thought for a moment it would take two and a half hours to find a cab and travel five miles.'

'Welcome to London!' said Sarah, not unkindly, lifting the plinths through to the workroom, where she rolled up her sleeves. Jennie was mystified that Sarah appeared not to be firing her, but helping her.

'I wouldn't usually make such last-minute changes,' Jennie continued to blether, hoping to convey her good intentions. 'I just so wanted to get it absolutely perfect for you and your clients.'

'Your attention to detail hasn't gone unnoticed,' said Sarah, going to her office and returning with a cup of coffee for them both, which Jennie received more gratefully than Sarah could ever know. 'Now, let's get this job finished before the clients kick up a fuss.'

*

Jennie stared in amazement as Sarah pulled the van up in front of the Arbuthnotts' house. It was like something out of a Regency romance – a crisp white facade, colonnades, arched windows, marble steps and black railings – about as far from the chocolate-box cottages of Brompton Marsh as Jennie could get. As she slid down from the seat of the van onto the pavement, staring up at the palace of a house in front of her, she felt a small sense of achievement.

The last two weeks had been such a whirlwind of activity that Jennie had had little opportunity to stand back and reflect on her dream come true. But here, in front of the Arbuthnotts' home, she had a 'pinch-yourself' moment: her dream of working for Sarah Cunningham really had come to life.

'Jennie!' called Sarah, bringing Jennie back down to earth. 'Grab that, will you? Ring the bell and start taking things in.'

'Me?' she asked, surprised that Sarah would want the apprentice being the face of the company.

'Who else?' asked Sarah, picking up vases, her bum at Jennie's eye-level.

In the large side-mirror of the van, Jennie tightened her ponytail, ran her tongue over her teeth, and straightened her apron before ascending the front steps of the house.

On ringing the bell, she didn't hear it chime. She pressed it a second time, still nothing. She was about to press it a third time when the large black front door was opened by a maid in grey uniform with a white frilly apron, with a little white headdress pinned to her short, dark hair.

'Good morning,' said Jennie. If it weren't for the fact the maid's uniform was knee-length, rather than floor length, Jennie might have been forgiven for thinking she'd entered the pages of a Jane Austen novel.

'Yes,' replied the middle-aged woman guardedly in a Spanish-sounding accent.

'Sarah Cunningham Flowers,' said Jennie, feeling she was stating the obvious given that she was standing beside a large floral display.

'This way.'

The maid opened the door fully to allow Jennie into the large entrance hall with its marble floor, sweeping stone staircase and enormous chandelier.

'Wait here,' she said, pointing to the base of the stairs, where Jennie stood as instructed. She looked at the height of the ceilings, the scale of her place, and imagined her dad tutting about the cost of the upkeep. She could hear him whistling and see him scratching his head in bemusement. 'Lady Arbuthnott said you may position them as you feel correct,' said the maid, on her return.

'Thank you,' said Jennie, who hadn't realised the Arbuthnotts were titled – working for a lord and lady made her stomach churn even more excitedly.

'We've to position them ourselves,' she told Sarah at the van.

'Of course,' laughed Sarah. 'You didn't expect Lady Arbuthnott to do it herself, did you?'

'No!' said Jennie, trying to cover her lack of experience. She didn't mention that back home she was used to handing flowers over at the front door to the intended recipient, who was always delighted – or leaving them on the step and scarpering. She'd never had to position arrangements in a customer's home in her life.

'So, let's get to it before a traffic warden books me.'

Sarah and Jennie set up a relay system, Sarah handing things out of the van, Jennie taking them up to the entrance hall. When the flowers were all in, Sarah went to park the van round the back, giving Jennie time to admire her work. The plinths really did blend in seamlessly with the colour scheme of the hall, and they worked beautifully with the Arbuthnotts' modern art collection. Jennie allowed herself a quick pat on the back.

'Come on then,' said Sarah on her return, picking up a pedestal and carrying it through to the dining room, which was situated to the left of the entrance. 'There's no time to stand around gawping.'

'Right,' said Jennie, picking up another arrangement and following Sarah's lead.

'I think they want them here.' Sarah pointed at the two back corners of the dining room with its dark wood floor, taupe velvet curtains, long table with puce velvet chairs, and matching floral rug. Everything oozed opulence.

'Do you think the colour scheme works in here?' asked Jennie uncertainly, concerned that the subtle, muted shades of the dining room didn't lend themselves to the Jackson Pollock effect.

'Definitely. It's as if you've brought in two spectacular pieces of modern art. I wish I'd come up with the design myself.'

'Thank you,' said Jennie, trying to contain her delight.

'Can you find the maid and ask where she wants the box of napkin rings?'

Jennie took the box and went into the hall in search of the maid, but as she did the front door opened and a tall, striking woman in her late twenties entered.

'Oh-my-God!' she yelled, before her key was even out of the door. She walked straight up to Jennie's pedestal arrangement and exclaimed dramatically, '*Who* is responsible for these flowers?'

Jennie wasn't certain if the woman liked them or loathed them, but before she had the chance to say anything the woman turned to her, clocked the napkin-rings in the open box and asked, 'Did you do these?'

'Yes,' replied Jennie nervously.

'My God,' exclaimed the woman. 'You're amazing! I've never seen anything like them in my life. You absolutely have to do my birthday party!'

It took Jennie a moment to compute what had been said but when she did, she heard the woman saying, 'Forgive me, I'm George.'

Jennie puzzled for a second over the name of this slender, pretty woman with her oval face, bee-stung lips and elegant nose.

The woman, recognising the confused expression on Jennie's face, said, 'Georgette, but everyone calls me George.'

'Jennie.' She attempted to shake hands while holding the napkin box.

'Do you work for Sarah Cunningham?'

'Yes,' said Jennie. 'Well, sort of, I'm her new apprentice.'

'God she's great,' said George, pulling her tan leather gloves off with her teeth. 'But these are different from her usual work. Are these your designs?'

'They are.'

'Darling, you just *have* to do the designs for my party, I insist.'

Before Jennie had time to say that George should probably speak to Sarah, the front door opened, distracting them both, and a man entered.

'What do you insist on?' he asked George, and Jennie, doing a double take, suddenly clocked that it was the man from this morning, James. He flashed her a smile that seemed to spread from one side of his face to the other, his blue eyes twinkling. 'Nice napkin rings!'

'Thanks. Nice anemones,' she said, too flustered by the shock of the co-incidence to mention their earlier encounter. She wondered if he'd bought the flowers for George, and if they were a couple.

'This is my friend, James Cavendish,' said George, introducing them both, neither one of them mentioning that they'd already met. Jennie latched onto the word 'friend'. James locked eyes with Jennie and didn't let go, but she quickly glanced away, unnerved by the feeling that James was reading her every thought. And since most of those were about how hot he was, she really wasn't keen for him to know them. 'Jennie's responsible for these amazing flowers, she's Sarah's apprentice. Aren't they incredible?'

'They are. The cornflowers are stunning.'

Jennie was impressed that James should call a flower by name. He smiled at her, teasingly, she thought, with that rich guy confidence. She puffed a little breath in an effort to dislodge a hair that was sticking to her nose, unable to recall a time that she'd felt this naked when fully clothed.

'James, why don't you go put those flowers in water,' suggested George, when she clocked his smile.

'On it,' he said, brushing past Jennie, his sweater grazing her arm, causing a rush of tingles to shoot through her body in a way she hadn't experienced in very long time.

Sarah, Jennie and George sat in the 'principal drawing room', which had five huge windows commanding views of the lake in Regent's Park. They were brought coffee and macaroons by the housekeeper, who served them without speaking a word, and whom Jennie instinctively thanked when neither George nor Sarah had done so, then spent the rest of the time fretting that she might mark the pale linen upholstery of the sofas with her perma-green florist's fingers.

'The party is next Saturday night at Annabel's, in the private room. It's my thirtieth, so I want it to be fabulous.'

'Annabel's is a members' club,' said Sarah, for which Jennie was thankful, since she'd assumed it was a friend's house. 'The private room is red, and lined with bottles of wine, their red seals pointing out into the room.'

'It sounds wonderful.' Jennie made notes as Sarah spoke, keen to avoid any more slip-ups.

'It is,' said George, flicking her long, brown hair to one side. 'We're having dinner for immediate family and closest friends followed by a party for a few hundred.' Jennie loved the way George was so nonchalant in describing a party for so many. *Back home a party this big would only be for a wedding, or a funeral*, she thought.

'And what do you have in mind for the flowers?' asked Sarah. 'Table decorations, entrance flowers, anything else?'

'Corsages would be fun, just for me and a few close girlfriends.'

As Jennie made notes, she thought the scale of things wasn't so different from what she'd just prepared for

George's parents' dinner party. If Sarah was willing to allow Jennie to do the job on her own, she felt she could manage this time, assuming she didn't have another pedestal disaster.

'I want it to feel light and youthful, in contrast to the old-fashioned feel of the room. And I definitely don't want red. There's a lot of red already.'

'Got it,' said Jennie, underlining 'no red' twice in her notepad.

'Jennie will come up with designs and samples for you to look at early next week,' advised Sarah, putting down her teacup and getting up.

'Very good,' said George, standing and shaking Sarah's hand. 'I'll expect something as spectacular as the ones downstairs.'

As Jennie shook George's hand and said goodbye, she hoped she'd be able to rise to the challenge and that there wouldn't be another near disaster, because although Sarah had been gracious enough to overlook this one, another would *surely* spell the end of her apprenticeship.

4

'It almost feels as if we're inside the whale,' said Jennie, her eyes roaming the main hall of the Natural History Museum, where the skeleton of a blue whale was suspended above them.

'What do you mean?' asked Kat, from where they were sitting on the wide steps.

'Don't you think the ceiling arches look like rib bones?'

Kat laughed and broke open her packed lunch. 'I see what you mean, though the thought would never have occurred to me!' she said fondly, looking at Jennie as if she was something of an enigma. 'How was your big event on Friday?'

'Not bad,' replied Jennie, touched that Kat should remember the dinner. 'Actually, because of it I've been given another party to do.'

'Great!' Kat said, stuffing a stray piece of lettuce into her mouth. 'What is it?'

'A thirtieth birthday.'

'Is it for anyone I might have heard of?'

'She's called George Arbuthnott.' Jennie said 'George Arbuthnott' as if trying out a phrase in a new language for the first time.

'Oooh,' cooed Kat, impressed. 'That's a big deal. Even I've heard of George Arbuthnott.'

'You have?'

'She's from old money, but she made a name for herself a few years ago as an influencer.' Kat pulled out her phone and within moments was showing Jennie George's Instagram account.

'How many followers?' she asked, staring in astonishment at the figure at the top of her page. 10.7m.

'Crazy, right?' said Kat, scrolling through the grid of photos, one of which Jennie recognised immediately as the Arbuthnotts' dinner party, her flowers framing the shot. A little tremor of delight shot through her body. 'Definitely lives the Chelsea life, rather than the Essex one, like me.'

Kat had told Jennie at the South Bank how she'd grown up on the outskirts of London, 'an Essex girl, for my sins' with her single mother, who remarried when Kat was ten. Throughout her teens she was obsessed with getting as far away from home as possible, so she'd flung herself into studying languages at school and then at university. During a gap year she'd been a TEFL assistant in Brazil, then after university she trained as a TEFL teacher before working in six different countries, including Mongolia, Bolivia and Namibia – 'more because I liked the sounds of their names than because I knew anything about them'. Jennie was awestruck by Kat's experience, and by her current job teaching English to new arrivals in the UK. It made her realise how little she'd done with her life, and strengthened her resolve to change that.

'Sarah must be pleased.'

'She did seem to be,' said Jennie, still thrilled that George had loved her designs. She was conscious of the fact that if they had bombed, Sarah might have thought twice about keeping her, particularly after the pedestal hiccup.

Kat offered Jennie a crisp. 'You know George Arbuthnott has a reputation for being quite tricky, right?'

'Really?' asked Jennie, taking a crisp. She still knew nothing about her, other than what Kat had mentioned, and the fact her parents seemed to have an exceptionally nice house and *a lot* of money. 'She seemed pleasant enough.'

'They teach you how to be "pleasant" at finishing school, even if you're Cruella de Vil.' Kat cocked a pencilled-in eyebrow.

Jennie laughed. 'Her friend seemed nice too.' *And handsome*, she thought. Not that she imagined for one moment that he was interested in her.

'It's easy to be nice when you're loaded.'

'Well, all I have to do is arrange some flowers. How hard can it be?' she said, pinching another crisp.

'For someone like me, extremely hard!'

'But for someone like me, it should be simple,' she said, hoping she wouldn't be proved wrong. 'How was your week?'

'Not so great,' said Kat, putting down her homemade sandwich in its beeswax wrapper. 'Lauren and I broke up. She moved out.'

Jennie scanned her friend's face for any trace of how she was feeling. 'What happened?'

'She found the tickets for the London Eye in the pocket of my jeans,' replied Kat, holding Jennie's eye.

'And she didn't know that we'd been together?'

'I knew if I told her she'd assume I'd been out on a date with you, she would never have believed we're just friends.'

'Even if she knew I was straight?'

Kat scoffed lightly at Jennie's naivety. 'I told her; it didn't make any difference.'

'How do you feel?' she asked, concerned that she was the source of tension between Kat and Lauren, especially when there was no truth in Lauren's suspicions.

Kat shrugged and took a drink from her can of Diet Coke, her chunky skull ring clinking against it. 'I think it's for the best. The trust hasn't been there for a while, but

I can't pretend I'm over her. She's one of the best friends I've ever had.'

Jennie's thoughts turned to Stephen, whom she could never have described as a best friend – there hadn't been enough balance in their relationship for that, it was always his way or the highway. And she wondered if she'd ever have a relationship that felt like a friendship, or have enough trust in anyone to even begin one. 'How long were you together?'

'About three years. It feels terrible her not being in the flat. It's so quiet.'

Jennie sat for a moment, trying to imagine Kat at home alone, with only her misgivings for company. 'Was it just the mistrust on her part, or were there other problems, too?'

'At first it was only that, but it seeped into every aspect of our life and chipped away at our friendship. We'd been through so much together – me coming out, her mother dying – but one way or another she built up a picture in her mind of me fancying anyone but her, which wasn't the case at all. Paranoia is a weird thing.'

'You miss her?'

'Very much. Do you miss Stephen?'

'Not really,' shrugged Jennie, hardly having had time to think about him over the last couple of weeks. But there were times, particularly in the evenings, when she'd wished she had someone to chat to and curl up beside – despite all that had happened, habit led her to think of him then.

'We should do something to cheer ourselves up,' said Kat, brushing crumbs off her black jeans and galvanising herself into action. 'What never fails to make you happy?'

Jennie didn't have to search long for the answer. 'Ice cream!'

'Then I know just the place!'

*

Jennie couldn't get enough of the fact that whatever her heart desired, London had it at pretty much any time of day. The ice-cream parlour Kat had taken her to was kitsch-tastic. From the lemon-and-white striped walls to the colourful leather stools at the counter, and the little booths to huddle in, it was perfection. As was the enormous sundae parked in front of her.

'Stephen would have a fit if he could see this. He hated me eating junk, in case I got fat.'

'What a charmer!' laughed Kat, and Jennie had to stop herself from spitting out ice cream when she laughed, too.

'There's no way I can finish all of this,' she said, delving deeper into the hot fudge sauce, cream and pecans.

'Bet you another you can!'

'Deal!' she giggled, watching Kat set about her mint-choc-chip extravaganza in its pretty cut-glass dish.

'We've established ice cream makes me happy, what about you?' asked Jennie.

'Flowers,' replied Kat, without stopping to think. 'If I could buy fresh flowers every day, I would.'

'Sounds like you should have been the florist, not me.'

'You don't love flowers?'

'I do,' said Jennie, who couldn't imagine her life without them. 'Just not as much as ice cream!'

Kat and Jennie chatted away contentedly for a while, enjoying their sundaes, until Kat's phone interrupted them.

'It's Lauren,' she said, looking at the screen, uncertain whether to answer.

'You should talk to her.'

Hesitantly Kat swiped her finger, her nail a deep red, across the screen.

'Hi . . . not bad . . . just out with a friend . . . Jennie . . . yeah . . . it's not how you think . . . she's new in town.' Kat offered Jennie an apologetic look, 'it's really not like that, you can't keep—' then moved from the booth to outside. Jennie watched as she paced back and forth in front of the parlour window until she suddenly stopped and looked at her phone.

'She hung up,' said Kat, returning.

'Ouch. I take it she wasn't happy about you being out with me.'

'You could say that.' Kat pushed her sundae aside. 'God it's exhausting.'

'Do you want to go see her, see if you can talk some sense into her?'

'I doubt it would work. She wants to get back together and if I go to her, we'll inevitably end up doing something we regret and making things even more complicated.'

'The passion's still there?'

Kat nodded. 'I've never fancied anyone as much as Lauren.'

'You sound caught between a rock and a hard place,' said Jennie, not quite knowing the feeling. For all she'd found Stephen attractive, it was never in a raw, sensual sort of a way, not even in the beginning when she could stare at him for hours and watch him sleep. The truth was, she wasn't sure that instinctive, animal magnetism really existed, other than in the movies.

Kat rubbed her brow. 'If it wasn't for the jealousy, we'd have had the perfect relationship. I just don't know how to manage that part of her.'

'If she could sort out the paranoia, you'd get back with her?'

'For sure.' Kat looked as if the weight of the world was on her shoulders. 'In a heartbeat.'

5

The second hand of the workroom clock ticked past ten. Jennie stared at it, wondering why George hadn't arrived to discuss the mock-ups for her birthday party.

'Don't worry, she'll be here,' said Louise, who'd developed a knack of knowing when Jennie was overthinking.

'Why's she so late?'

Louise stabbed another white rose into a large ball of soaked oasis, which was to adorn the top of a stone urn in someone's conservatory. 'Because she's an Arbuthnott.'

'What does that mean?'

'It means, if she's booked to see you at 9 a.m. but fancies turning up at eleven, that's what she'll do. They're used to people accommodating their every whim. When you have that much money, the world generally stops for you.'

'Right,' said Jennie, more used to the 'if I'm free, I'll help; if I'm not, go somewhere else' approach at Dorothy's.

Just then Sarah popped her head round the door to tell Jennie that George had arrived. Jennie inhaled deeply, put down the wire she'd been fiddling with, and went out front to greet her.

'Hi, George,' she said brightly.

'Hi,' answered George, who had a less exuberant air about her than on their previous meeting, her eyes more stormy grey than piercing blue. She followed Jennie through to the workroom, looking at her phone as they walked.

In the workroom, Jennie offered George a stool, which she looked at, with its glue stains and little bits of foliage stuck to it, and chose to stand.

Fair enough, thought Jennie. *If I were wearing designer white jeans and a camel sweater, I probably wouldn't sit on it either.*

'So, these are the designs,' said Jennie, showing George the three final sketches on her workbench, alongside the mock-ups. 'Obviously the sample pieces are not to size.'

George squinted at them, her head cocked to one side, but said nothing.

'I worked to your brief of light and youthful, avoiding reds,' Jennie continued nervously.

'They're not what I want.'

Out of the corner of her eye, Jennie clocked Louise, who raised her eyebrows as if to say, 'it's bloody typical'.

'Okay,' said Jennie, disappointed but determined to create something George was happy with. 'Do you have something more specific in mind? Is it the colour palette, flower choice or structure you don't like?'

'I don't know,' she sniffed, turning her attention back to her phone, which she held as if it were surgically attached to her palm.

Reaching for her notepad, and ready to start afresh, Jennie gathered all her floristry know-how, determined to produce whatever George wanted. 'But the brief is correct, yes?'

George nodded, a manicured finger scrolling over her phone.

'I chose lots of whites and yellows to create the lighter tones you were after.'

'I don't like the daisies,' she said, snapping off her phone and dropping it into her Mulberry tote.

'That's fine,' said Jennie, pleased to have something constructive to work with. 'There are lots of other small-headed white or yellow flowers that we can use instead. And because you asked for youthful, I kept the structural component quite light and loose. Do you like that?'

'It's too informal for Annabel's.'

Louise cleared her throat and rolled her eyes, and Jennie resisted the urge to return the gesture. She now knew what Kat had meant by the Arbuthnotts being 'tricky'.

'Something tighter, fuller perhaps?' Jennie asked.

'Maybe,' sighed George.

'I tried to create a youthful feel by mixing up a lot of different textures and shapes that you might not usually find together or which, traditionally, are considered clashing. And I also moved away from traditional geometric designs.'

'Which I don't like.'

Tapping her pencil lightly on her notepad, Jennie considered how to create the feel George wanted within the confines of her dislikes. 'So, perhaps a design that combines light and youthful with slightly more traditional aspects?'

George rolled her head slowly, as if trying to rid herself of a crick in her neck. 'I might like to hear Sarah's ideas.'

'Sure,' said Jennie, hoping that Sarah's standing might sway George into seeing the designs differently.

She went to find Sarah and the two women returned to George, who looked thoroughly out of place amongst the chaos of the workroom.

'George,' said Sarah, shaking George firmly by the hand and moving her glasses to the top of her head. 'How are you?'

'In a bit of a muddle, darling. These aren't what I had in mind at all.'

Sarah looked at Jennie's work, not for the first time; she'd already given the designs the all-clear. 'What is it you were hoping for?'

Jennie stood back, waiting to hear if George could articulate her thoughts any more clearly to Sarah.

'Something more—' George paused, searching for the words. Jennie hung on her silence. In the end she shrugged and, gripping tightly to the straps of her tote, said, 'I don't know. You're the florist, darling.'

'Jennie, can you remind me of the brief?'

'Light and youthful, with no red.'

'I never said no red,' interjected George.

Jennie was about to reach for her notebook when a discreet but firm hand on her back from Sarah reminded her of what she'd been told on her first day – the customer is always right.

'George, would you like red?' Sarah asked appeasingly.

George thought for a moment before saying, 'Yes. Red is exactly what I'd like.'

'And might I suggest that traditional with a twist would suit the environment of Annabel's, and be more to your taste?'

'Yes.' George flicked her hair assertively, as if the idea had been her own.

Sarah pulled her glasses back down and cast Jennie a look that said, 'some customers just need a bit of *handling*', which Jennie was rapidly learning for herself.

*

'You sound tired, love,' said Jennie's mum, later that evening. 'Have you been working too hard?'

'Only out of necessity,' replied Jennie, looking at the picture next to her bed of her mum, dad and sister, Claire. The photo was taken about ten years ago, on the day of Claire's graduation. She was the only person to graduate in their family. Her mum had straightened her hair to an inch of its peroxided life, and her dad wore a bright Pringle sweater under a navy blazer, which Jennie couldn't remember seeing him wear before. Claire looked the picture of happiness, youth and hope, and Jennie was trying to mask her tipsiness after a celebratory lunch. It felt like yesterday yet also a lifetime ago. Now Claire was living in Stroud with her husband, busy juggling a career in HR with motherhood. If they were lucky, they saw each other twice a year despite not living far from one another. 'George changed her mind about her birthday party flowers, so now I've got to come up with something completely different at the last minute.'

'You'll manage.'

'I hope so,' she replied, not wanting to tell her mother that she'd spent the afternoon coming up with new designs but by six o'clock she still didn't have anything she was happy with. Louise had suggested heading home for a rest, ordering a pizza and starting again in the morning, and though Jennie rarely gave up until her work was completed, for once she felt it was the right decision.

The sound of the receiver muffled for a moment as Irene told Tony to turn down the television, and Jenny recalled all the times they'd sat as a family, her dad fawning nightly over Alex Jones on *The One Show*. She wished she were there with them.

'Are you feeling any better?' asked Jennie, reaching for a slice of her freshly delivered pizza.

'I'm not sleeping all that well, but it's quite normal at my time of life, nothing to worry about.'

'What did the doctor say when you saw her?'

'That she'd arrange for me to see the gynae-thingumybob.'

'Gynaecologist?'

'That's the one.'

'Why?'

'Jennie,' her mum laughed tightly. 'All these questions. There's nothing wrong. The doctor said it's just precautionary. Don't worry. We're not.'

Though Jennie wasn't convinced, for her mother's sake, she let it lie. 'Just make sure you tell me what the consultant says when you see her.'

'Of course, love,' she said, and Jennie heard her swallow and position a glass on the side table next to her seat on the sofa.

'Are you having a glass of wine?'

'Tracy brought it over on Friday night.'

Jennie had forgotten about their plans to meet up with Stephen's parents, it knocked her for a moment. 'Did Alan come over too?'

'Mmm,' replied Irene. 'We had an Indian takeaway and played Cranium. You should have seen Tracy trying to mime *An Affair to Remember*.'

'Positively pornographic!' called Tony.

'Did it feel weird?' she asked, wondering if the dynamic between her parents and Stephen's had changed after the wedding was called off. She hated the idea that she might have been responsible for fracturing her parents' friendships. Tony and Stephen's dad, Alan, had become scooter buddies over the years, and her mum and Tracy often went to the outlet village, from where they'd come back with bags of stuff, their nails done, and all the gossip caught up on. Once a month they'd all have dinner at the pub.

'Not after a glass of wine or two. By the end of the evening, we were all quite merry.'

'Your mother almost snogged Alan.'

'Mum!'

'Your dad's exaggerating, as usual. We just had a cuddle.'

'Really?' Jennie was surprised but pleased to hear that it sounded as if any wounds had healed.

'Why should our friendship suffer just because you and Stephen decided not to marry?'

'I agree,' said Jennie, glad to hear her mum say so.

'We told them all about how well you're doing in the big city. I forwarded her the link you sent to that Instagram page. She couldn't believe you were doing an event for someone with so many followers, a celebrity, well, not as we know them. What do they call them, love – influencers?'

Jennie rolled her eyes. 'Right, influencers. It's a big thing, Mum. People make a lot of money from having so many followers.'

'It's a lot of old bollocks if you ask me,' said Tony, in the background, which made Jennie laugh.

'She was really impressed, love. A bit tongue-tied, really.'

'Mum, they probably don't want to hear how I'm doing. I did jilt their son at the altar.'

'Stephen only has himself to blame for that, love. Your intentions were perfectly clear when you applied for the apprenticeship. And besides, between you and me, Tracy thinks you're too good for him.'

'No, she doesn't! No mother thinks anyone is too good for their own child.' Jennie was incredulous that her mother could believe such a thing, but she recognised how like Tracy it was to say it, anyway.

'You may be right, love, but the point is, she doesn't harbour any ill will towards you, or us. She understands you wouldn't have been fulfilled, and ultimately both yours and Stephen's happiness would have been compromised, and the marriage would have failed. It was better you called an end to it when you did.'

'Though a little earlier would have been preferable,' said Tony wryly. 'Before I paid the deposit on the venue, the church, the cars—'

Jennie heard a muffled cry from her dad, which she guessed was the result of her mother throwing a cushion to shut him up.

'The money, as he knows, isn't important,' said Irene. 'What's important is that you're happy.'

'Thanks, Mum.'

'Are you happy, love?'

Jennie thought for a moment about how she was beginning to feel settled in London and was making friends. 'I am. I just hope I can make George happy too,' she said, wondering if anyone, particularly her, was capable of doing so.

6

Outside the flower shop, the following morning, was the biggest flower truck Jennie had ever seen; it was at least twice the size of the one she was accustomed to at Dorothy's. Climbing its side steps she entered another world: floor-to-ceiling shelves lined both sides of the refrigerated lorry, and on them lay the flowers on their sides. Every millimetre of space was lined with blooms in every conceivable shape, shade and scent.

'You see something you like?' came a voice.

Jennie turned to be greeted by a tall, fair-haired man. He, like the truck, was enormous.

'Henrik,' he said, reaching out a hand as large as a plate.

'Jennie. Sarah's apprentice,' she explained, shaking his hand, surprised by his gentle grip.

'Nice to meet you,' he smiled, putting his hands into his little money apron. It took Jennie a moment to place his soft vowels as a Dutch accent. 'What can I get you?'

'That's a good question,' said Jennie, attempting to take everything in, feeling like a child in a sweet shop. 'I'm doing a thirtieth birthday party. The brief is red, traditional but with a twist.'

'So, we start with the red rose, yes?'

Henrik stood to reach for the large-headed red roses, which were at the top of the rose section; Jennie would have needed the stepladder to reach them herself.

'Maybe some different sizes?' he suggested, collecting more red roses with medium, small and spray heads.

'It's still pretty traditional despite the different sizes,' remarked Jennie.

'So, we do something different with the foliage?'

She thought for a moment, casting her eye around the truck. She was loath to put dark foliage with red roses – it was so mainstream, so predictable, even if George probably would like it. Jennie wanted that twist, something that would make the arrangements stand out as a Sarah Cunningham design.

'I love those deep red hydrangeas,' she said, pointing to the column of shelves housing the hydrangeas, and the dark burgundy ones in particular, that stood out from amongst their paler counterparts.

'They would make your design more modern.'

'And if, like you say, I do something different with the greenery—' said Jennie, moving to stand in front of the foliage section. For all that Henrik had – salal, eucalyptus, ruscus, ferns and banana leaves – nothing jumped out at her.

'You could use a green flower instead of a leaf – carnation, chrysanthemum, hypericum, alchemilla.'

'All a bit too obvious.' Jennie thought further. 'What about green hellebore?'

'We have that.' Henrik pointed down to where it was located.

Jennie took a wrap off the shelf and positioned it next to the rest of the flowers, which Henrik was holding.

She smiled, satisfied.

'You like?' he asked.

'A lot,' said Jennie, relaxing, able at last to see a plan coming together.

Henrik placed the wraps by the till. 'Do you need anything else?'

'Yes,' she remembered, clicking her fingers and pointing. 'Glassware for the table decorations. Something reasonably low so that it doesn't interfere with eye contact.'

'I have just the thing,' said Henrik, going to the sundries section at the cab end of the truck and returning with what looked like an old-fashioned bon-bon dish.

'Perfect.'

Henrik processed the order and asked Jennie to sign, which she did, with a gulp. The flowers she'd chosen, just to create sample pieces, amounted to almost the same as Dorothy spent on flowers each week at Brompton Floristry.

'Let me help you,' said Henrik, picking up the armful of wraps and carrying them down the steps, where Louise was waiting to come on board. He handed Jennie his card, their fingers brushing as he did. 'And if you need anything else, just give me a call.'

'I will, thank you,' she replied, returning his smile, wondering if he was this kind to everyone.

*

'I can't believe he gave you his number,' teased Louise, a little later, sitting at her workbench while putting the finishing touches to a bridal bouquet, a pearl-tipped pin gripped between her teeth.

'He just gave me his card in case I needed something,' said Jennie, quite enjoying the idea that Louise thought it might have meant something more.

'If I wasn't married, I know what I'd need from him!' she laughed, removing the pin from her teeth and pushing it firmly into the bouquet.

Jennie laughed too. It had been a while since she'd had any male attention, other than James's, and she wasn't sure offering to call someone a cab really counted, and there was no doubting the fact that Henrik was *all* male. She couldn't remember meeting anyone as tall and broad as he was. 'How long have you and Sam been married?'

'Twelve years.'

'Was it love at first sight?'

'Hardly,' said Louise, who turned her attention to taking the wraps off the flowers before stripping the thorns and leaves from the stems. 'I thought he was an arrogant arse for the first ten years of knowing him.'

'How did you meet?' Jennie asked, between a mouthful of cold pizza left over from the night before, and wiring roses for a corsage.

'He was a friend of my sister's from uni. Actually, he dated her for a bit before we got together.'

Jennie, shocked by the revelation, swallowed her mouthful of pizza rather more quickly than felt comfortable. 'For how long?' she asked, thumping her chest in discomfort.

'Almost a year.'

'And your sister didn't mind when you guys got together?'

'They were young, it was never going to be anything long term, and we didn't get together until almost ten years later.'

Jennie thought of Claire's ex-boyfriends and wondered how her sister would feel if Jennie took up with one of them. She wasn't convinced Claire would be as accepting as Louise's sister.

'How did that come about?'

'He was at my sister's thirtieth. He'd grown up since I last saw him. We had a cheeky fumble outside the pub and the rest, as they say, is history.'

'Did you date for long before he proposed?'

'A couple of years, then we married a year after we got engaged, and Aubrey came along three years after that. Not the most romantic story you'll ever hear, but it's ours.'

'I think it's extremely romantic,' said Jennie, thinking of what her granny used to say – what's meant for you won't go by you – and wondering if she'd already, without knowing it, met the person she might spend the rest of her life with. The thought sent a fuzzy little sensation down her spine, even if her list of male acquaintances was woefully short and, therefore, her choice of prospective partners narrow.

By mid-afternoon Jennie had developed George's table pieces and a scaled-down pedestal piece, while Louise tidied and assisted where necessary. By six o'clock the pieces were finished, and Jennie sent pictures of them to George's phone.

'She'll definitely be happy with these,' said Louise, admiring Jennie's creations.

'You think?' she asked, concerned about George's unpredictability.

'Definitely. Why don't you call it a night? You look tired.'

'I can't go until I've placed the order with Van Beek's,' sighed Jennie, aware that if she didn't place the order with the wholesaler tonight the flowers wouldn't arrive by Saturday morning.

'I can do that for you,' said Louise, sloshing out buckets. 'Just leave it on my desk and send me a message when you get the all-clear from George.'

'Would you?' asked Jennie, thrilled at the prospect of an early night after another long day on her feet.

'Sure. What are friends for?'

Jennie reached for her coat, more grateful than Louise could know, not only for offering to order the flowers but also for the blissfully casual mention of friendship.

7

When Jennie arrived at work early on Saturday morning, she felt energised and ready for the task ahead of preparing George's birthday flowers, which she'd approved at the eleventh hour.

'Morning,' she sang to Louise, who was checking the order from Van Beek's, already lying on the workroom floor ready to be prepped. 'These look stunning.'

'They sure do,' said Louise, busy ticking the order off the list on her clipboard.

'Except . . .' said Jennie, taking a closer look while removing her coat.

'What?'

Jennie scanned the flowers on the floor. 'I don't see the hydrangeas.'

Louise flicked through the pages on her clipboard. 'Hydrangeas aren't on the list, only hyacinths.'

'What?' Jennie reached out for Louise to hand over the paperwork.

'See?' said Louise, pointing with her pen to the alphabetical list of flowers. 'Hyacinths.'

'Please tell me there hasn't been a cock-up,' whispered Jennie, looking at Louise, who was now crouched down beside the flower heads, searching. She dug out a wrap from the bottom of the pile and held them up.

'Red hyacinths,' she announced.

Jennie's heart sank.

'They're beautiful.'

'They may well be,' said Jennie, a deep pool of regret welling in her stomach for not placing the order herself. 'Only they're meant to be hydrangeas.'

'Oh God, you're kidding?' said Louise, only just registering the gravity of the mistake; the colour drained from her rosy cheeks. 'I must have read hyacinth where you'd written hydrangea. Jennie, I'm so sorry.'

Jennie rubbed her temple, trying to figure out what to do. 'It's my fault. I should have printed the list in block capitals. My handwriting's appalling.'

'I feel awful. I can't apologise enough,' said Louise, reaching out to rub Jennie's arm.

'Not a problem,' she said, trying to think on her feet. 'I can strip and cut the hyacinths to size and adapt the designs. It'll work.'

'I'll help in any way I can,' said Louise, muttering about how cross she was with herself, and frantically trying to make order on her workbench.

'Louise, it's fine,' reassured Jennie, who knew exactly how she was going to rework her designs.

'It's just so bloody typical of me.'

'I'm sure it's not,' laughed Jennie.

'I'll bet it is,' chimed in Sarah, arriving in the workroom.

'You don't even know what I've done.'

'No, but I know you well enough to know you're capable of whatever it is.'

'Harsh,' said Jennie, enjoying the banter, recalling how she and Dorothy often used to work in silence, with only the local radio for conversation. Working with Louise, Sarah, and Fiona, at the weekends, was a breath of fresh air in comparison.

'What's happened?'

'Jennie needed hydrangeas for her designs, and I ordered hyacinths.'

'It's really not the end of the world, Louise,' said Jennie, rhythmically stripping the stems of leaves. 'If my handwriting was better . . .'

'You're lucky she even remembered to place the order. It wouldn't have been the first time she's forgotten,' said Sarah, hanging up her coat.

'It happened once,' cried Louise, outraged.

'Three times,' asserted Sarah, holding up three fingers. 'The Buckshaw and Harrison wedding. Simion Awards. And the Oldfield funeral.'

'Ouch,' winced Jennie, when Louise had no defence.

'And it's not just work,' she confessed. 'When Aubrey was a baby, I left him in the supermarket car park, and I've lost count of how many times school have called me to remind me to collect Ellie. Sam says it's like living with a concussed hamster.'

'Well, that's bloody charming!' laughed Jennie.

'He has a point,' Sarah added dryly.

'There's no denying it. My memory is appalling.'

'If she wasn't such a bloody good florist, I've have got rid of her years ago,' smiled Sarah. 'Now, enough chit-chat. Let's get these flowers ready. The last thing we want is for George Arbuthnott to have something to gripe about.'

*

Despite Louise's mistake, the arrangements worked out beautifully and were more than ready in time for the party. Jennie was in the process of taking them from the van to the private room at Annabel's when she heard George shriek.

'What *is* that smell?'

At first Jennie thought someone had burnt something in the kitchen or there was a toilet blockage, but when she heard, 'I *loathe* the stench of hyacinths!' She froze where she stood on the staircase.

A split second later and George sped past her. 'Sarah!' she called. 'Sarah!'

'She's at the van,' mumbled Jennie, watching George's double-denim-clad figure disappearing down the stairs. The lingering scent of her Le Labo Santal 33 perfume took Jennie straight back to sitting on the couch with Tracy, going through perfume samples she'd brought back from her job at a cosmetics counter.

Outside the entrance, on Berkeley Square, Jennie found George ranting at Sarah, her hands squarely on her hips.

'She doesn't like hyacinths?' asked Jennie, joining Sarah after George had left.

'Apparently not.' Sarah sat at the back of the van, patting a space next to her for Jennie to join her.

'I'm sorry, Sarah. Louise took the blame for ordering the wrong flowers but if I'd written it more carefully the mistake wouldn't have happened.'

Sarah pinched the bridge of her nose, where her specs had left little imprints. 'It's unlucky.'

'I can take them out, substitute them with more spray roses – I've plenty left, and we've still got time.'

Sarah looked at Jennie, the lines between her eyebrows deeply furrowed. 'I'm afraid I'll have to ask Louise to do that.'

Though Jennie instinctively knew what this meant she still found herself asking, 'Why?'

'George is insisting I let you go.'

A moment's silence fell between the two women as Jennie tried to grasp the magnitude of what Sarah was saying, but somehow it didn't quite sink in.

'If I don't, not only will she tell her parents not to use the company again, she'll also tell those in their circle, and hers, not to use me again. And, like I said before, the Arbuthnotts and their friends account for a large percentage of our income, possibly 40 or 50 per cent.'

Jennie nodded numbly.

'I really am sorry, Jennie. You were the first apprentice I've had since Louise that I had any real intention of taking on in a permanent role.'

Sarah's attempt to soften the blow only made it harder as the news hit Jennie like an Arctic Truck.

'But my hands are tied. Without them and their contacts it could spell the end of the company.' She paused. 'And it's not something I'm comfortable with, but the truth is, in this part of the world, it's not *what* you know but *who* you know.'

Jennie swallowed hard.

'You can keep the apartment until you've found somewhere else to go,' Sarah continued, putting her hand on Jennie's back. 'But after that, I'm sorry to say, we must sever our ties.'

'Thank you for the opportunity,' Jennie said quietly, glancing up to meet Sarah's eyes, which was difficult. 'I hope the incident doesn't affect your business.'

'That's kind of you,' said Sarah, giving Jennie a side-on squeeze and a quick peck on the hair.

'What's going on?' asked Louise, arriving at the van, stretching for her bottle of cola in the back. 'Have I missed something?'

'You could say that!' said Sarah, getting up to give them some space.

Jennie filled Louise in on the news.

'I don't know what to say,' she said, her wide eyes conveying her shock and regret. 'It's my fault, not yours.'

'It's okay,' said Jennie, wiping away a tear with the heel of her hand. 'It was a mistake.'

'Let me talk to Sarah,' she said getting up, but Jennie caught her by the arm before she could go any further.

'It won't make any difference.'

'Maybe not, but I won't be able to live with myself if I don't try.'

'George won't care whose mistake it was. She wants my head gone, so that's what Sarah has to do. I get it.'

Acceptingly, Louise shrank down beside her. 'I'll miss you!'

'I'll miss you too,' said Jennie, disappointed to be losing a budding friendship.

'If there's anything I can do to help, *anything at all*, just call me.'

'Thank you,' said Jennie, hugging her again. 'I'll do that.'

*

Jennie slung her bag over her shoulder, put her head down and walked, uncertain of where she was going. *Right now,* she thought, *it doesn't matter.* As far as she was concerned, she could keep on walking until she reached Brompton Marsh where her parents would welcome her home with open arms. *I could hide myself away for a bit,* she thought, *away from Dorothy and Stephen and the rest of the village, who'd almost certainly add this to their list of things to gossip about.*

As she hurried along the pavement, her mind awash with thoughts, someone coming in the opposite direction got in her way.

'Sorry,' she mumbled, attempting a sidestep to get past, but the other person did the same and they wound up blocking each other again. 'Sorry,' she repeated, this time glancing up.

'Well, hello,' said the man brightly, with a broad, open smile. 'It's Jennie, isn't it?'

'Yes,' she said, instantly recognising James with his lively blue eyes.

'James,' he prompted.

'George's friend?' she asked, trying to play it cool, though her insides were dancing. It was impossible to forget someone so obviously comfortable in his own skin.

'That's right,' he smiled. 'How are you?'

'Good,' said Jennie, then shook her head. 'Actually, not so good. But probably best you ask George about that instead of me.'

'She's upset you,' he said, more a statement than a question, as if it were something he expected of her.

'I suppose *I* upset her first,' said Jennie, not wanting to complain to him about his friend, even if she had just got her fired.

'You must forgive her. She worries about getting things wrong and people thinking badly of her. It's part of her job, keeping up appearances. She's been stressing about this party for weeks, months – hell, probably a good part of her adult life!'

Jennie laughed lightly and tried to imagine what it must be like living life through the lens of Instagram. 'I'm sure Sarah and Louise will fix the problem and George will be fine again.'

'Whatever it is, I'm certain she overreacted, she does that when she's stressed. Don't worry about it, okay?'

'Sure,' said Jennie, disarmed by the tenderness in his eyes, and how like sapphires they were as they sparkled. 'I have to go.'

'Of course,' he said, with a slight shake of his head as if trying to cast aside an unhelpful thought. 'It was very nice to see you again.'

'And you,' said Jennie, somewhat cheered by the encounter. 'Enjoy the party.'

As she walked away, she had a feeling that James was still standing there. Turning to check, she found him watching her. For a moment she thought he was going to call out, as he'd done at the flower market but, in the end, he simply offered a wave and headed off in the direction of Annabel's.

8

Jennie returned to the shop to collect her personal items, going straight to the workroom where she sat at her bench. Still stuck there with Blu Tac were the sketches for George's designs, flower heads and foliage lay scattered around her stool on the floor, and an un-drunk cup of tea, one she'd been too busy to drink, had formed a skin on the surface.

'What might have been,' she muttered, pulling off the sketches and taking out her phone to call Irene. As the dial tone rang she looked round the room, hoping to capture the scent and feel of her dream, before returning to the reality of being unemployed and imminently homeless in London.

'Hiya, love,' her mum answered, a supermarket Tannoy sounding in the background. 'Is everything okay?'

'Not really,' mumbled Jennie.

'I can't hear you very well, love. Speak up.'

Jennie ran a hand over her forehead.

'Jennie?' The voice on the Tannoy stopped. 'What's wrong?'

'Sarah had to let me go,' she said, her voice cracking. Vocalising what had just happened made it suddenly real, and it felt as if she'd been slugged in the gut.

'What? You're joking.'

'Nope,' said Jennie, feeling bad that she was turning her mother's morning on its head. She figured this was the last thing her mum would have been expecting when she strolled into Sainsbury's with her trolley and shopping list to do her weekend shop.

'What happened, love?'

'There was a mix-up with a flower – Louise ordered hyacinths instead of hydrangeas. Turns out George hates hyacinths, so she insisted Sarah fire me.'

Irene was quiet for a moment. 'That doesn't make any sense.'

'No, not to you and me, but to someone like George Arbuthnott, it makes perfect sense.'

'It must be a mistake. Sarah will sort it,' said Irene, as if Jennie had simply had a telling-off from her teacher, and after a word from Mum, it would all be resolved.

'I don't think so, Mum. George is a really important client,' she said, though she wished her mother was right. 'I guess if you hate hyacinths, you don't want your ten million followers seeing them. I think it really is over.'

'Right . . .' said Irene, lost for words. 'What will you do?'

'I don't know.' Jennie rolled a red rose petal absently between her thumb and index finger. 'I have no job, and no place to live. There's not much I can do.'

'Get on the next train home, love. I'll collect you from the station. What do you want for supper?'

Jennie laughed, despite herself. Her mother had always used food to cheer her up – warm milk and cookies when she fell and scraped her knee, rice pudding when she fell out with her 'best friend' from school, or homemade pizza when boys didn't fancy her back. But for once Jennie wasn't certain she wanted her mother to fix things, and she certainly didn't want her parents to have to deal with another disappointment or embarrassment.

'I need to pack, Mum. Sort a few things out,' she said, knowing she couldn't possibly stay in the apartment now that she'd lost the apprenticeship, despite Sarah suggesting otherwise. 'Let me call you in a little while.'

'Okay, love. Don't worry, Dad and I will look after you, everything will be fine.'

'I know, Mum,' said Jennie, thankful for her mother's optimism and unfailing support, particularly after the wedding debacle. 'Would you mind not telling anyone about this, not just yet anyway? I could use some time to let it sink in, figure out what to do next.'

'Of course, love. Mum's the word!'

After finishing the call, Jennie looked round the workroom one final time, taking a mental snapshot of what might have been and something to which she would always aspire – a hugely successful floristry business that employed a growing team, though she knew the odds of her achieving that were now even more miniscule than before. In the shop she was relieved to find Fiona still busy. Without saying goodbye, she stepped outside, closing the door behind her. She was about to cross the road to head back to the bedsit when she heard her name being called. She turned to find Kat hurrying up the pavement towards her.

'Hi,' said Jennie, pleased to see a friendly face.

'Are you leaving for the day?' asked Kat, glancing at her phone to check the time.

'Actually, I'm just *leaving*.' Jennie's voice broke. She blinked away a tear, which didn't go unnoticed by Kat.

'What's happened?'

Jennie swallowed hard. 'Long story.'

'Why don't you tell me about it over a bite to eat? The pub on the corner does good mains and great puds! And a drink on a Saturday afternoon is a must, right?'

Jennie had no real desire to head back to the flat – and a drink, after the morning she'd had, sounded exactly what she needed.

*

'Louise must feel awful,' said Kat, after Jennie had told her the story of the hyacinths, and they were settled at a table in the pub on the corner of the hill.

Jennie took a long suck of peach Schnapps and lemonade through a straw. 'I feel bad for her. If it weren't for the fact I'm about to be homeless, I might almost feel worse for her than I do for me.'

A waiter arrived with calamari for Kat and Jennie to share. 'What happened to your flat?'

'It was part of the apprenticeship, a temporary arrangement. Sarah said I could stay as long as I needed, but I can't, it wouldn't be right.'

'I might be able to help,' said Kat, helping herself to the squid.

'You know of somewhere?'

'My place,' she suggested, watching for Jennie's reaction.

'Really?' Jennie tried to rein in her enthusiasm, not wanting to appear too desperate.

'The room Lauren used as her study is free,' said Kat, skewering more squid.

'Have you got used to her not being there?' asked Jennie, having to restrain herself from saying, 'when can I move in?'

'Not really. Having someone fill the room might help alleviate the loss.'

'You don't worry about what Lauren might feel?'

Kat shook her head. 'I think in her heart of hearts she'd rather I had a friend move in than a complete stranger.'

'And you don't know anyone else who's looking?'

'Only you!'

'It sounds great,' said Jennie, but then a realisation dawned, which dampened her enthusiasm. 'But without a job I've no money for rent. All my cash is tied up in the house I bought with Stephen, and until he's sorted that out, I've nothing to fall back on.'

'When do you think it will be sorted?'

'It's meant to be just another couple of weeks.' Suddenly, without the small stipend that came with the apprenticeship, two weeks seemed like a very long time.

'I can help you out for a bit,' shrugged Kat. 'My flat is owned by the council, so I'm not meant to sublet anyway. It would be a perfect solution.'

Jennie twiddled the straw in her drink. 'That's really kind, but I couldn't live with you without contributing something.'

'You can help out with bills for the first few months. I'm sure it won't take long for someone with your skill to find a job.'

'Thanks,' said Jennie, thinking about the prospect of an 'ordinary' florist job. 'I was spoilt at Sarah's.'

'There are so many florists in London, I'm certain you'll find something that suits you, even if it's not around here.'

The waiter cleared the plates and brought the burgers they'd both ordered.

'The truth is, now that I've worked for Sarah, everywhere else would feel like a come-down. If I'm honest, what I'd really like is my own business . . . but I know it's just another dream. Ultimately, I'll just have to take what I can get,' said Jennie, unable to resist eating a fat chip with her fingers. No situation was ever too grave for Jennie to resist chips.

'Why does it have to be a dream? The Sarah Cunningham dream came true, and you've been a florist long enough to know how to run the business side of things. The experience at Sarah's would make you really desirable. You could use the money from your house to set it up,' said Kat, as if it was easy, squirting ketchup all over her fries.

'In case you hadn't noticed, the Sarah Cunningham dream has turned into a nightmare, and besides, I wouldn't have enough.'

'Why not?'

Jennie wiped her fingers on her napkin. 'I'd need premises of my own, equipment, sundries, even the cost of initial flower stock would be a lot.'

'You could work from home,' Kat said, pointing a chip at Jennie. 'That would reduce the cost.'

'Home is Brompton Marsh, and Brompton Marsh already has a florist. I'm not sure the village could cope with me setting up in competition; I've caused enough gossip around there lately. And I doubt my parents would want me running a flower shop out of the garage.'

'You could work from my home,' ventured Kat.

'That's really kind, but there's no way I would put that on you,' replied Jennie, though inwardly she loved the idea.

'Why not? I'm offering! This way you don't need a shop, you can buy everything you need and promote yourself for private events. Isn't that what you love doing most? Isn't that the big dream?'

Jennie began to think about the suggestion seriously. It wasn't beyond her skillset to set up a little website and generate some interest on Instagram, even if she wouldn't ever get close to either Sarah or George's number of followers. And the money from the house would be enough for equipment, stock and sundries. So long as she could get a deposit for flowers up front from clients, the idea wasn't inconceivable.

'So?' asked Kat.

'You should take some time to think this through,' said Jennie, wanting to give Kat the opportunity to retract her offer.

'There's no need. It's a win-win situation. I get a flatmate I like and trust, you get a place to work and stay until you've got some income. Come on. How about it?'

Jennie paused, looking at Kat in amazement. Was it really possible that in the space of half an hour her life had gone from upside down to landing firmly on her feet again and now being about to take a stab at launching her own business? *It might not be in the grounds of Brompton Manor*, thought Jennie, *but it's a start*.

'Only if you're absolutely certain,' she said, with an inflection that told Kat 'now's your last chance to back out'.

'I've never been more certain of anything,' replied Kat, raising her drink towards Jennie.

'Then, yes. Thank you!' said Jennie, chinking her glass against Kat's, excited about how one small gesture could change the direction of her life in an instant and bring her one step closer to her dream.

9

After a leisurely lunch, Jennie returned to the bedsit to pack, and Kat dashed home to pick up her car. By late afternoon, all of Jennie's belonging were stashed in Kat's Ford Ka, and they were on their way to her flat.

'You mustn't get your hopes up,' said Kat, as she drove up past the park. 'It's home, but it's not glamorous.'

Kat crossed a busy junction and indicated left, turning into a street that had beautiful old Victorian detached homes on one side and a 1970s estate on the other.

'This is it! Primrose Tower,' she said, parking the car in a space only just bigger than a wheelie bin. Jennie peered out of the car window, looking up at a tower block, which loomed some twenty storeys above her.

'Looks great,' she said, and she took off her seatbelt, hoping that she sounded more enthusiastic than she was feeling. Despite the valiant efforts of some colourful window boxes on the small balconies, it was poles apart from the characterful cottages of Brompton Marsh.

'It's a good location,' said Kat, in much the same way people say, 'she's got a good personality' when asked if someone's pretty.

Jennie got out of the car. 'Which floor are you on?'

'Seventeenth. If you're lucky the lift will be working. If not, by the end of the day you'll have thighs of steel.'

Laughing, Jennie followed Kat down the concrete walkway that led to the entrance. Kat held open one of two heavy double doors, next to which was a tired old sign that read 'Primrose Tower'. Inside was a large, dimly lit lobby with a red concrete floor, walls of dingy cream covered in graffiti tags, and large boarded-up windows.

'What's behind the chipboard?' Jennie asked.

'Empty shops. A community room. Stuff like that. I don't think any of it has been used in a very long time,' she answered, calling the lift. 'Hi Omar,' she waved, and a janitor, steadily mopping the floor in the far corner, looked shyly in their direction. He put Jennie in mind of her dad, and she pushed away a longing to rewind time and be at her old home in Brompton Marsh, before all the upset with Stephen. It had taken them a year to make the house theirs, spending most weekends decorating, visiting furniture stores and taking endless carloads of stuff to the dump. Even though Stephen had made most of the decisions, choosing minimalist 'man furniture' over her preferred country cottage style, she had enjoyed the project, and never once imagined that only a year later she'd have moved out and back in with her parents before moving to London on her own.

'Don't worry, the apartments are much cosier than the communal areas,' said Kat, calling the lift.

'I'm sure,' said Jennie, catching the janitor's eye, who looked quickly away.

'The lifts smell a bit,' said Kat, as they listened to the grinding of the elevator descending towards them. 'But don't let that put you off.'

'Something told me not to expect velvet seats and an operator!'

'Or muzak!' laughed Kat as they stepped into the lift, which smelt of stale beer. 'The closest we get to elevator music around here is the teenagers with phones on full volume.'

The banter between the two of them made Jennie feel less like a fish out of water and by the time the lift creaked to the seventeenth floor she was feeling much more encouraged and looking forward to seeing Kat's apartment.

As the lift doors opened, a woman, olive skin, dark eyes, tall and heavily pregnant, was waiting to go down.

Jennie greeted her with a 'Hello.'

The woman didn't respond, staring straight through both of them.

Typical Londoner, she thought, still very much in the village mode of saying hello to anyone and everyone.

Kat walked over to the corner of the lobby and turned the key in the lock of her front door. 'Welcome home!' she sang.

Inside, the flat was comparatively bright and airy, the opposite of the communal spaces, which were badly lit and void of anything other than the odd fire extinguisher and empty notice board.

'Bathroom on your left,' said Kat, flicking the light on.

'Nice cactus collection!' Jennie admired the three long shelves of cacti that sat above the bath.

'Just be careful when you're showering, a spike in the wrong place can really hurt!'

'Noted.'

Next Jennie popped her head round the door of Kat's room, which was an elegant shade of green, with a bold floral bedspread.

'Beautiful,' said Jennie, surprised that Kat, so gothic in her attire, would have such a contrasting interiors style.

'And this will be your boudoir.' Kat opened the door next to her own bedroom with a flourish to reveal a plain room, empty other than a wooden single bed, a white MDF chest of drawers and a built-in mirrored wardrobe.

Despite its functionality, Jennie immediately recognised the potential of the space.

'Great view,' she said, looking out over the neighbourhood, Primrose Tower casting a long shadow in the lowering sun.

'Wait till you see the one from the living room.'

Kat led Jennie into the next-door room, the living room, which flowed through into the kitchen.

'Wow!' whistled Jennie, when she saw the view extending over Primrose Hill, Regent's Park and the city in the distance. 'That's spectacular.'

'People pay millions for that view, but here it's ours for one hundred pounds a week.'

'Incredible,' said Jennie, still staring out of the window.

'So, do you think you could be happy here? Is there enough room for you to work?'

Jennie pulled herself away from the view over the city below and looked around. The living room was big with a dining area and table from where she could work, and the proximity of the kitchen made it ideal for water and buckets. Feeling invigorated and hopeful she smiled and said, 'I think it'll be perfect.'

*

It didn't take long to ferry all of Jennie's belongings from the car to the lift to the apartment. But when they were finished and her things lay littered on the bed and floor of her new room, she collapsed on the sofa from exhaustion.

'Takeaway?' asked Kat, a little later, pouring Jennie a glass of white wine.

'Good plan.' Jennie would rather have gone hungry than venture out to the supermarket and then cook a meal.

'What's your preference?' asked Kat, handing her a collection of menus.

'Indian.'

'My favourite too,' said Kat, flicking through the menu.

A half-hour after the meal arrived the girls had devoured all of it bar one onion bhaji and a small piece of naan bread. The foil trays lay scattered on the coffee table, the plates smeared with sauce, a half-empty bottle of Pepsi stood without its cap, both girls too full to move from their spot on the sofa to replace it.

'May every day be as gluttonous as this,' laughed Kat, raising her glass.

'Indeed,' said Jennie contentedly.

Jennie's eyes were closing when a scream jolted her out of her sleepiness.

'What was that?' she asked, sitting up quickly from where she'd been slouched on the sofa.

'Not sure,' replied Kat unperturbed, clearly accustomed to all sorts of odd noises from the people living above, below and next to her. But Jennie was unsettled by the noise and continued to listen. After a moment she heard another sound, except this time it was more of a groan.

'Did you hear that?'

Kat nodded, eyes closed, still unconcerned.

It was only the third scream that brought Kat out of her food stupor.

Sluggishly she suggested, 'Maybe we should investigate.'

'Really?' asked Jennie uncertainly, her imagination in overdrive. She had images of going out to the lobby to find someone who'd been stabbed lying in a large pool of blood. Back home when Jennie read of knife crime in the city it seemed remote, almost otherworldly, but now it felt like a very real and present danger.

In the hall, there was no stabbing, just the olive-skinned woman they'd seen earlier, sitting close to the lift shaft, clutching her belly. Kat went straight to her and crouched down, Jennie loitering behind.

'Are you okay?' asked Kat.

The woman released a bovine cry, her hands grabbing her belly.

'It's okay,' reassured Kat. 'We'll get help. What's your name?'

The woman looked at Kat, terror in her amber eyes.

'No English,' she managed to say before screaming again.

'I'm Kat,' said Kat, tapping her chest to demonstrate that she was saying her name.

She then pointed enquiringly at the woman, who responded 'Zaynab,' between pants.

'Hi Zaynab.' Kat put her hand on her shoulder. 'It's okay. We'll get an ambulance.'

Kat looked at Jennie to suggest she call 999. But Jennie, stunned by the situation, just looked on blankly.

'Jennie, call for an ambulance,' pressed Kat.

'Right,' said Jennie, shaking herself out of her daze and fumbling with her phone. 'What's the address?'

Kat gave Jennie the address and then, once they were assured the crew was on its way, said, 'I need to get Mary.'

'Who's Mary?'

'She lives on the nineteenth floor. She's a nurse; she'll know what to do.'

Before Jennie could say 'I'll get her', Kat ran out of the stairwell door, leaving Jennie alone with a woman who didn't speak a word of English and who was about to give birth on the lobby floor.

*

Kat returned with Mary, a statuesque Black woman in her sixties, her hair tight and short. It probably only took Kat two minutes to fetch her, but it had felt like two years to

Jennie. The only experience Jennie had of childbirth was what she'd seen on *One Born Every Minute*, and even that she struggled to watch.

'It's okay,' she'd repeated endlessly, crouched down beside Zaynab. She'd tried several ways of communicating that the ambulance would be there soon, acting as she might with a frightened toddler rather than a fully grown woman. She made the *nee-naw* sounds, attempted to indicate flashing lights by whirling a finger over the top of her head, and at one point she even pretended to drive frantically towards a hospital. By the time Kat got back, Jennie wasn't certain who was more exhausted – herself or Zaynab.

'Who have we here?' asked Mary, assertive but friendly with a clipped accent that Jennie couldn't place. 'How far apart are the contractions?' she asked Jennie.

Jennie shook her head, uncertain of the answer.

'How often does she scream?'

'Every thirty seconds or so.'

Mary lifted Zaynab's dress over her knees, calmly and professionally without a hint of panic, and demonstrated very clearly the sort of breathing Zaynab needed to use. 'Baby's almost here. Jennie, fetch hot water and towels.'

'Sure,' said Jennie, dashing back to the flat and into the bathroom where she threw open the cupboard doors in search of towels. In the kitchen she filled a baking bowl full of warm water and returned to the scene as quickly as she could, spilling water as she hurried.

But when she arrived back, clutching towels and bowl, the ambulance crew were already there with Zaynab in a wheelchair, a mask over her mouth.

'Is she okay?' asked Jennie, putting down the things and following everyone into the lift.

'She's fine,' said Mary calmly, though her eyes were wide with the immediacy of it all. 'Let's just hope she can hold on till we get there.'

*

'Who's the next of kin?' the midwife asked as soon as they arrived in the maternity unit of St Mary's Hospital. The three women exchanged blank looks.

'We found her in the lobby of our block,' explained Kat. 'All we know is that her name is Zaynab and she doesn't speak English.'

The midwife looked at Zaynab, now lying on the ambulance gurney, as if searching for clues. 'She's wearing a ring, which suggests a husband.'

Kat pointed to the ring and gestured to Zaynab, 'Who?'

'Mohammed.' A wan smile grew on Zaynab's lips, in spite of the pain.

Once more, Kat used body language to enquire, 'Where?'

'Syria.'

'Telephone?' asked Kat, showing Zaynab her phone.

Zaynab shook her head. Kat, nodding in quiet understanding, glanced over to the midwife.

'No contactable next of kin,' wrote the midwife, completing the paperwork. 'We'll take her to room six.'

It was agreed on the way that Kat could stay as translator, Mary as nurse, and Jennie as a friend. In the room, Zaynab was transferred to a bed, her back propped up with several pillows, her feet positioned near her bottom, and examined.

'Baby's already crowning,' said the midwife.

Jennie was well aware from where she was standing at the bottom of the bed that the baby was crowning. Mary, on Zaynab's left, leant down to look, Kat, on Zaynab's other side, remained by her head; both women held tightly to Zaynab's hands, and bore the pressure every time she yelled.

'Can you tell her to push?' the midwife asked Kat.

Kat used her hands and breath to perform the action of pushing. Zaynab pushed. Jennie saw the baby move fractionally forward, exposing a mass of black hair. When Zaynab pushed again the baby's mucus-covered face, grey and crinkly, emerged. Jennie, never having seen a newborn baby in the flesh before, did not realise its colour was wrong. It was only when the midwife called for the doctor that she realised something wasn't right. As she dialled,

Zaynab pushed again and the baby inched further forward, exposing the umbilical cord wrapped tightly round its neck.

'Doctor's on his way, just to be safe,' reassured the midwife, returning to where Jennie stood. 'Cord round the neck is more common than you'd think.'

Jennie, feeling faint, took a seat in the corner, where she put her head between her knees. She heard Zaynab push twice more, the midwife announce the baby's arrival and, at the same moment, the doctor arrive.

'Let me look it over,' he said. Jennie looked up to see the doctor take the baby to one corner where he tended to it, his back to the room. Jennie, like everyone else, held her breath waiting to hear the baby's first cry.

From her bed, Zaynab, beneath her breath, uttered what sounded to Jennie like a prayer. Beside the bed, Mary continued to hold Zaynab's hand. Kat wiped the hair from Zaynab's face and squeezed her shoulder.

Despite all that was happening, it felt to Jennie as if a silence hung over the room; she was certain she could hear her own heartbeat.

Not a moment too soon, the silence was punctured by the baby's cry. Everyone gasped. Tears burst from Jennie's eyes, Kat beamed, Mary thanked the Lord, and Zaynab took her baby from the doctor, visibly shining, and gazed into its eyes.

'It's a boy,' said the doctor. Zaynab checked beneath the baby's blanket and her eyes brimmed with tears.

'Mohammed,' she said, kissing the baby's forehead for the first time, her tears spilling over his brow.

It was only as Jennie brushed away her own tears that she realised that the doctor standing beside Zaynab was James.

'James!' she whispered, stunned by this second co-incidence. In all her wonderings about him, she'd never once imagined he was a doctor.

'Jennie!'

'What a surprise,' she said, curious to know why he wasn't at George's party. 'Shouldn't you be somewhere else?'. The event she'd been fired from this morning felt like a lifetime ago.

James grimaced. 'We had a bit of a spat. A sick colleague was the perfect excuse to get away.' He removed his gloves and motioned with his head for her to follow him outside.

In the corridor he explained that George had been riled when he'd challenged her decision to have Jennie fired, and they'd fought.

'I'm sorry about that,' said Jennie, flattered that he should have defended her.

'Don't be. I was tired, having got up early to get her the birthday flowers she wanted from the market, and I was listening to her ranting about something as inconsequential as one wrong flower—' Jennie's brow knitted together. 'Not to say that flowers are unimportant, I know they are—'

Jennie chuckled, enjoying seeing him backtrack. 'It's okay. I do realise flowers aren't quite as important as delivering babies!'

'Right,' he laughed, his blue eyes dancing with hers. 'Anyway, I saw something today that didn't sit comfortably with me. She's a great friend, an old friend, but sometimes she crosses the line.'

'Has she calmed down?'

'I've no idea. She's either extremely drunk and forgotten all about it, or extremely drunk and bitching about me to anyone who'll listen.' James rubbed his face wearily. 'I feel rubbish confronting her on her birthday like that, but somebody had to, right?'

Jennie, uncertain how to answer, evaded the question. 'But you're okay?'

'Delivering a baby safely into his mother's arms gives me some sense of perspective.'

'I guess being an obstetrician does that,' Jennie smiled.

'For sure.' He paused, his gaze resting on Jennie's for a moment. 'How about you? What will you do next?'

Jennie explained about bumping into Kat, the turn of events, and how she might try setting up on her own.

'Good for you,' he beamed, and she couldn't help but be drawn in by his enthusiasm; she liked his infectious, upbeat disposition, it was refreshing. 'It was great to bump into you again—'

'And you,' said Jennie, wanting to return to Zaynab but at the same time feeling a pull to stay with James. 'I should go,' she said, indicating to the room behind her.

'Of course, but—' he paused, as if searching for the right words. 'Perhaps I could grab your number, arrange to see you some time? Make up for what happened with George.'

'I'd like that,' said Jennie, thrilled at the offer, but uncertain if he was asking by way of an apology, or something more.

10

After the birth, and once Zaynab was settled, Kat, Mary and Jennie had travelled home in Kat's car, animatedly recounting the events of the evening. When they arrived back, Kat had invited Mary in for a glass of fizz. It wasn't until two in the morning that the high of the birth began to wane and they decided to call it a night.

'Who was that?' Jennie asked blearily, the following morning, as Kat put down her phone on the kitchen table.

Kat rubbed her eyes and sighed. 'Lauren.'

'How's she doing?'

'Not great – she found out you've moved in.'

'She hasn't taken it well?'

'That could be the understatement of the century.'

'Would it help if she met me?' asked Jennie, sitting down with a bowlful of Kat's muesli, still to do her own shopping after the move the previous day.

Kat shook her head. 'I doubt it, but thanks for the offer,' she said defeatedly, sounding exhausted by it all. 'What are your plans for today?'

'Once I've organised my room, I thought I might create a website,' said Jennie, hoping she was up to the task. Stephen, who worked in IT, had bored her rigid one night on how to build a basic website when he'd decided they should have their own domain, for reasons she could no longer remember. She wished now that she'd had both eyes on what he was doing rather than just one. 'How about you?'

'I have to catch up on some work, but this afternoon I'll pop by the hospital, I thought I'd offer to teach English to Zaynab.'

'That's such a great idea,' enthused Jennie, wishing she could offer something as practical. She couldn't help feeling her job as a florist, for all she loved it, didn't really hold such value.

'Do you want to join me?' asked Kat, getting up to put on some toast.

'Sure,' replied Jennie, who was keen to see Mohammed again – he and Zaynab had been her first thought when she'd woken up. 'I still feel bad that we had to leave her there on her own last night; a visit this afternoon would be lovely.'

The morning flew past and by lunchtime, Jennie had her bedroom feeling as much like home as she could hope for.

Her rosebud bedclothes were in place, the photo of her family was by her bedside, and her clothes were neatly stored in the wardrobe.

As she sat down to lunch in Kat's simple white kitchen, she heard a knock at the apartment door. Peering through the spy hole, she saw a small woman of Indian descent.

On opening the door, Jennie discovered that the woman stood little more than five foot tall, with an iron-straight dark bob, and was surrounded by plastic laundry bags from which spilled baby paraphernalia.

'Kat?' asked the lady in a gentle, well-spoken voice.

'Kat's at work, I'm afraid. I'm her flatmate, Jennie.'

'I'm Prisha,' said the woman, extending her hand with a slightly toothy smile. 'I live next to Mary on the nineteenth floor. She told me about last night's excitement and that Kat might accept a few donations on Zaynab's behalf.'

'I'm sure she would,' said Jennie delightedly, looking at what Prisha considered to be 'a few' donations. There was enough to kit out several nurseries, let alone one.

'I can't believe you brought this all down by yourself,' exclaimed Jennie, lifting two of the bags, which weren't light.

'I'm strong; I have six children. My family call me The Mule!' she said, picking up the other two bags and bringing them into the flat.

Jennie laughed while trying to stop a bright red potty from escaping her clutch.

'Zaynab will be grateful for this,' she said, while surveying the bags in the hall. 'Would you like a cup of tea?'

'I'd love one.'

Prisha took a seat at the table as Jennie rifled through the cupboards, full of Kat's crockery and pots from her travels, looking for where she kept the mugs and teabags.

'So, Mary is your neighbour?' she asked, having successfully found what she needed and put on the kettle.

'She is, she moved in when her boys were young. Must be over thirty years ago now.'

'How long have you lived here?'

'All my life.'

'Really?'

'I was born in the flat.'

'It seems like this tower's seen its fair share of births. You know Zaynab came close to delivering her baby in the lobby last night?'

'My mother had me on the bedroom floor. If you look closely, I think you can still see a mark!'

Jennie laughed, enjoying Prisha's unexpected company. To be sharing a cup of tea with a neighbour was more than she'd done in her two years at the house she'd owned with Stephen, who hadn't been keen on visitors, particularly unexpected ones.

'So your parents lived here before you?'

'They still do, with us,' answered Prisha.

'Gosh, six children, you and your parents?' Jennie tried to imagine three generations of her family all living in her parents' home in Brompton Marsh. It was hard enough when it had just been the four of them, with teenage tantrums, only one loo, and netball kit clogging up the hall. She couldn't imagine adding a set of grandparents into the mix.

'Until not long ago my mother's parents lived with us too.'

'Gosh,' whistled Jennie.

'It's busy,' said Prisha, accepting her tea and biscuits. Jennie took this to be an understatement.

'How old are your children?' she asked, joining Prisha at the round table.

'My eldest is seventeen, a girl, and about to graduate high school, then I have a sixteen-year-old boy, fourteen- and twelve-year-old girls, a nine-year-old boy and a six-year-old girl.'

Jennie couldn't keep up. 'That sounds like a lot of work!'

Prisha cupped her hands round her mug and blew gently.

'It was, and sometimes still is, but this year is the first that they're all in school full-time, so it's much easier. It really does seem like only yesterday that I brought Aanya back from the hospital. The lift was broken, and I had to walk up nineteen floors, can you imagine, straight after childbirth? It took me the best part of an hour.'

'I really can't,' said Jennie, who, after last night, had a newfound understanding of how brutal the experience could be.

'It certainly wasn't the easiest start to motherhood, but things got better, and I had a lot of help from my family and childhood friends in the tower. Nowadays I have more time for myself, even with caring for my parents.'

Jennie took a custard cream and dunked it in her tea, which made a thought of Louise pop into her head. 'Are they unwell?'

'Just the usual complaints of the elderly, nothing too serious.'

'That's good,' she said, successfully removing her biscuit from the tea before it dissolved in the hot liquid.

'And what about you? How long have you been living here?'

Jennie looked at the kitchen clock. 'Less than twenty-four hours.'

'What a welcome you've had – it's never quiet in the tower!' giggled Prisha joyfully.

'I'm beginning to see that,' said Jennie, hearing the front door open and Kat call her name.

'In the kitchen,' she replied.

'Zaynab's home,' Kat called back, picking her way through the bags in the hall, muttering, 'what is all of this stuff?'

'She's back already?'

'I know, it's crazy.'

Kat arrived in the kitchen to find the two women sitting at her table. Jennie introduced Prisha and explained about the donations.

'Brilliant! Zaynab will be delighted,' said Kat. 'Why don't you come meet her and the baby? You can give the things to her in person.'

*

'Zaynab, it's Kat,' she called, entering Zaynab's flat, which had the same layout as her own, but that's where the similarities stopped. Jennie saw, through the bedroom door, that all Zaynab had in the way of possessions was a single divan bed with an inadequate blanket. There were no pictures on the walls, no furniture in the hallway; it was all-but empty.

In the lounge she found Zaynab sitting on a tired, brown velour sofa, with Mohammed in her arms and Mary sitting beside her. Jennie gave a little wave, uncertain if Zaynab would even remember her from the night before.

'Zaynab,' said Kat. 'You remember Jennie? And this is Prisha – she's brought you some things for the baby.' Kat pointed to Prisha, the belongings and the baby.

'Yes, thank you,' said Zaynab, in fractured English, nodding courteously to both women.

Zaynab's voice sounded different to Jennie today. Last night she had made only the most elemental, guttural sounds before the birth and, afterwards, the soft, lilting coos of an exhausted new mother. Today her voice did not sound strong; to Jennie it sounded laced with fear.

'You're welcome,' said Prisha, going straight to Zaynab and Mohammed. Mary moved up to make space. 'What's his name?'

Zaynab looked to Kat for interpretation.

Kat pointed to herself and said, 'Kat,' then to Zaynab saying, 'Zaynab' and finally at the baby with a questioning expression.

'Mohammed,' said Zaynab, smiling and kissing the baby's forehead.

'After her husband,' said Mary, who pointed to the only picture in the room, of a handsome, kind-looking man in a red T-shirt.

'Where is he?' Prisha asked, turning to Kat.

'Syria,' Kat replied. Then in a quieter voice she said, 'Though we're not sure if he's alive.'

Prisha nodded and squeezed Zaynab's hand. Although Zaynab couldn't understand what Kat had said she'd heard the name of her country and the tone in which it had been said. A look of despair washed over her face. Prisha reached to the bag closest to her and took out a small, soft white bear.

'For Mohammed,' she said, placing it beside the baby's cheek.

Zaynab smiled weakly.

The five women sat quietly for a moment, Zaynab, Mary and Prisha on the sofa, Kat and Jennie sitting beneath them on the floor, all looking tenderly at Mohammed.

'When I had my first son back in Nigeria the whole community pulled behind us. Neighbours brought enough food to feed a small nation, friends handed down clothes and supplies, my mother and grandmother were there to offer advice. At no point did I feel as if I was on my own. We must help this girl in the same way that I was helped.'

'Agreed,' replied Prisha. 'I had similar support, I'd have gone mad without it. Let's start by unpacking all of these bags and setting up the nursery.'

Jennie, glad to be of use, picked up two of the bags and took them to the little room, which in Kat's apartment was Jennie's room, but in Zaynab's was to become the baby's. She opened the door to find a bare, white space with only a small empty cot in it.

'She'll need curtains for naptime,' said Prisha, following in behind with more of the bags. 'I might have something we can use.'

'I'll get to work on putting things away,' said Jennie, and she opened the sliding wardrobe door to see how much storage space there was.

Prisha put down the bags and began rummaging for curtains and bedding, while Jennie folded clothes and sorted them onto the shelves of the wardrobe.

'Anything I can do?' asked Kat from the doorway. Jennie could hear Mary in the kitchen making tea and, from the living room, Zaynab singing gently to Mohammed.

'She'll need a changing table. Could you look for one on Gumtree or eBay?' Prisha asked.

'Sure,' said Kat, taking out her phone from her back pocket. Within minutes she was messaging someone about picking up a table later that day.

In the space of an hour, Prisha had made up the cot with some small sheets, a beautiful patchwork blanket, an infant sleeping bag with yellow giraffes, and a few soft toys. Above the cot hung a mobile with jungle creatures, on the wall was a cross-stitch Noah's Ark, a fleecy rug adorned the floor, and Prisha had secured a blackout blind to the window. In the wardrobe, Jennie had organised the Babygros, tiny cardigans and bootees, spare bedding, and a little basket of nappies, wipes and lotions for under the changing table.

'It's come together really well,' said Jennie, as both women stepped back to admire their handiwork.

'Let's show Zaynab.'

Jennie fetched Zaynab, who, walking slowly and tentatively after the delivery, followed Jennie through from the living room. Outside the closed door, Mary took

Mohammed, and Jennie indicated to Zaynab to cover her eyes. When Jennie opened the door, Prisha called, 'Surprise!', her arms wide. Zaynab, taking her hands away, stepped into the room and, after a momentary look of amazement, her face lit up.

'Good?' asked Kat, her thumbs up.

Zaynab took a second look around before saying, 'Yes' and then promptly burst into tears.

'It's okay,' soothed Prisha, coming to comfort her, nestling her small frame against Zaynab. 'We'll take care of you.'

'Yes, we will,' said Kat, standing on the opposite side of Zaynab and putting her arm around her. Jennie stood watching Kat and Prisha comforting Zaynab, and Mary doing the same for Mohammed, and couldn't help wishing she had more to offer. The only thing she could think to do was to go back to the flat, select some flowers from one of Kat's arrangements, and position them in a vase.

After a short time, Jennie returned and placed the display of daffodils on the nursery windowsill. It was a far cry from the gigantic baby bouquets in pinks and blues with balloons and teddies she was used to creating, but there was something about the arrangement's seasonal simplicity that suited the occasion, serving as a token of congratulations for Zaynab, and as a welcome to the world for Mohammed.

11

'How's that gorgeous little baby?' asked Irene, who'd called every day since Mohammed's birth, almost ten days ago. Jennie knew her mother was really checking in to see how she was doing and using her passion for newborn babies as a convenient excuse. Sometimes Jennie couldn't help but think her mum had missed her calling, that she should have been a midwife rather than a school catering assistant.

'He's fine, Mum.'

'And Zaynab?'

'We're doing what we can to help.' Jennie poured herself a bowl of muesli in the kitchen. 'Prisha's taken on the role of surrogate granny, showing Zaynab how to change nappies, how to bath him, different breastfeeding positions, stuff like that. And Mary's looking after her social needs, making sure all the right services have been notified.'

Jennie heard her mother open the window and spray the furniture polish, talking to Jennie as she went about her usual Monday-morning ritual of cleaning the house from top to bottom.

'It must be so hard. No family, no money for childcare, not being able to speak the language. She must feel very isolated.'

'We're rallying round,' she said, closing the fridge door with her shoulder. 'Kat's been teaching her some English while Mohammed's sleeping, and I've been running errands for her when I can – making sure the fridge is full and that she's got baby supplies.'

'If someone had told you when you moved to London that you'd be buying nappies a month later you'd have laughed!'

'You're not wrong,' she said, taking a mouthful of cereal, creating a natural lull in the conversation.

'Have you had time to try and find a job?'

Jennie had been wondering how long it would take her mum to get round to asking.

'I've set up a website, and put up some adverts around Primrose Hill.'

'Have you had any responses?'

'A bit of website traffic. It'll take time.' Jennie didn't like to say that responses to her ads had been non-existent, and she'd had no visitors to her website, other than the ones she suspected of being the ladies from the tower having a nosey. 'Have you been to see the gynaecologist yet?'

'Not yet, love, and don't go changing the subject. You need to think about what your next step is. You know you can always come home. I'm sure Dorothy would welcome you with open arms. I've heard the new girl she's taken on isn't up to much.' Jennie heard the under-stairs cupboard latch twang open, her mother take out the hoover, and then a pause as she caught her breath.

As her mother plugged in the hoover, Jennie imagined returning to Brompton Marsh, her tail between her legs, and walking back into Brompton Floristry to ask for her old job back. It was more than her pride would allow.

'The truth is, Mum,' she said, stirring the milk, 'until the money comes through from the house, I'm going to have to sign on. Stephen should have it all settled by the end of the week, but just in case there's a problem I thought it best. I've an appointment at the job centre this morning.'

Irene paused before saying, 'There's no shame in that, love.'

'I know. It's just not what I had in mind when I arrived.'

'Everyone has setbacks. See it as a temporary fix.'

'You're right. It'll give me some time to set up an Instagram page and hopefully get some customers that way.' Jennie thought about how different life was now to when her parents were starting out when you simply answered an ad in the local newspaper. She admired her mum for being so understanding.

'That's the spirit! I'm sure there are plenty of people in Primrose Hill looking for a florist.'

'Right,' agreed Jennie, who knew her mother must be right, she just wished she knew how to find them.

*

'Can you confirm your name and date of birth?' the job centre advisor asked Jennie, not looking away from his computer screen.

'Jennie Treloar. 10th of March 1990,' she replied, her hands crossed neatly on her lap, her ankles crossed beneath the chair, her posture poker straight.

'Thanks,' mumbled Kieran, who was so thin and pimply he looked as if he hadn't yet graduated high school. He stared blankly at the screen, confirming the answers Jennie had already given online. 'No partner, no current employment, previous employer Brompton Floristry.'

'That's correct.' Jennie knew he didn't intend to make her feel even worse about herself, but he did sound like a judge reading the petty crime record of a wayward teenager.

'Any savings over sixteen thousand pounds?'

'No,' said Jennie. All her money – thirty thousand pounds that she'd managed to save over ten years at Dorothy's – was still tied up in the house. Stephen had put down almost double that, and it was his salary that had secured

126

the mortgage, a detail he was never slow to remind her of. She wished now more than ever that she'd invested her money in a business years ago, rather than ploughing it into the house with Stephen.

'No work or benefits claimed outside of the UK during the last four years?'

'No.'

'And you're not an asylum seeker?' asked Kieran, at last looking up at Jennie to confirm this.

'I'm not.' Jennie thought of Zaynab and of how difficult it must have been for her to navigate the immigration system with no English and little understanding of the process.

'Fine,' he said, mindlessly tapping away at his keyboard as Jennie scanned the contents of his desk – yellow stickies round his computer screen, his phone with an R2D2 cover, and a key to a Vauxhall car with a Darth Vader keyring. 'What kind of work are you looking for and where?'

'Florist. In London.'

'Anything else?' he asked, still typing.

'Floristry is all I know.'

'Would you be willing to retrain?'

'I'd rather not. Flowers are my passion.'

'Passion doesn't pay the rent,' he muttered, not glancing up from his computer.

'Not always, but I'd like to try,' she said, battling Kieran's attitude. She wondered about a system that nurtured people's passions, and the impact that might have on society as a whole, instead of the grinding mechanism that they currently had.

'Oooh-kaay,' Kieran sang, but Jennie refused to be rubbished by his scepticism. Her parents had instilled in her from an early age that if she worked hard she would be rewarded, and part of working hard was being determined and focused, not flitting from one thing to the next. Kieran's attitude only made her want to succeed all the more at setting up on her own. As far as she was concerned, signing on was a stopgap until the funds came through from the house and money began to trickle in from the business.

After Jennie had shown her P45 and passport she was dispatched, reminiscent of a chicken awaiting decapitation, to the next advisor.

Pauline, a portly woman in her fifties, who wore a skirt and top that looked as if they had been made out of lilac and grey bedclothes, had clearly been in the job several decades longer than Kieran. Her whole demeanour spoke of utter disillusionment – from the straggly greying hair that hadn't been combed in weeks to her lackadaisical typing.

'What salary do you expect?' she asked, taking a slurp of tea from a stained mug, which read Bite Me.

'Upwards of twenty thousand pounds.'

Pauline sucked in a whistle and shook her head.

'It's what I earned in my last job,' Jennie explained. Her salary at Dorothy's had gone up incrementally by five hundred pounds a year from fifteen thousand to twenty thousand. She felt the least she could expect in London was the same.

'I'll put it down, pending review.'

Pauline pushed back her wheelie chair towards the printer. As Jennie waited, she looked around at the various posters on the walls – Career Fair, Try Something New, Your Career Starts Now! She spotted one with a family, the woman in a headscarf holding an infant. Refugee Integration Loans, it said. When Pauline returned Jennie asked her about it.

'They're to help pay for things that enable easier integration into a new society,' she told Jennie.

'Like what?'

'Housing deposit, training courses, work equipment, that sort of thing.'

'Is there a form I can take for a friend of mine?' she asked, hoping that even if she couldn't stop her own life from falling apart, perhaps she could do something to make Zaynab's the best it could be.

12

'I'm not sure there's any point in going,' Jennie said to Kat on Thursday evening. James had texted her on Monday to arrange dinner, which Jennie had been fretting about since. 'I think he only asked me because he feels guilty about how George treated me – a sympathy date, you know?'

'So, don't go,' shrugged Kat, who was lying on the sofa in her 'Not A Morning Person' pyjamas, watching some loud family entertainment show on the television. It wasn't quite the response Jennie was hoping for; she'd been looking more for a pep talk to build up her confidence, not casual disinterest.

'But it's always good to get out, right, meet new people?' she pressed, not wanting to be needy but requiring a little reassurance that it wasn't a complete waste of time.

'Sure,' said Kat, who was focused entirely on the telly and eating a carton of ice cream, which she was holding in her hand with an oven glove.

'So, I should go?' Jennie pressed, wondering why Kat was quite so distracted.

'Yup, you should definitely go.'

'Even though I'm not really sure if it's a date or not? It may just be an apology because his friend got me fired.'

'Jennie,' said Kat, turning away from the telly and throwing a cushion at her. 'IT-IS-A-DATE. SO JUST GO!'

Not wanting to poke the bear any further, and remembering that her mum had been adamant that it was a date too when she'd first told her about it, Jennie went to her bedroom and flung on her fanciest pair of jeans, which showed her bum off to its best advantage, and a pretty floral blouse, too. Her mum had taught her to always present herself well regardless of the occasion – Irene always looked immaculate even in her dinner lady uniform. At the bathroom mirror she applied a skim of mascara and lip gloss, rubbing her lips together then fluttering her eyelashes to help them dry. As she did, a sudden kaleidoscope of butterflies flitted through her stomach. She hadn't had dinner alone with a man other than Stephen in over five years, probably more, given the dearth of interest there'd been pre-Stephen. The last time she'd really dated was during her college year, when no one had any money, and dates usually revolved around drinks at the pub, or a movie. Standing in front of the mirror she wished she'd had more experience over the years, and that her confidence hadn't been so badly eroded by Stephen.

'Are you done?' Kat asked playfully, appearing in the bathroom doorway, wanting in for a pee.

'Absolutely,' said Jennie, giving her cheeks one last plump in the mirror. Kat was already undoing the drawstring of her pyjama shorts.

'Have fun!' she sang, pulling down her bottoms and sitting on the loo before Jennie had even left the room.

*

'I love this place,' said James enthusiastically, after they were seated in the atrium at the centre of the restaurant, the fading evening light casting soft shadows on the tablecloth.

'I can see why,' she said, looking around the busy restaurant, anything to avoid the immediate intimacy of the small table and how good James looked in his crisp white shirt and jeans, which, Jennie had noticed on the way in, showed off a very pert bum.

'The meatballs are ridiculously good,' he said, as he handed Jennie a menu with a twinkle of delight. Jennie admired how unselfconscious and at ease he was with himself. It was worlds away from the imposter syndrome she was desperately trying to quash and conceal. As a child she never went to restaurants with her parents, other than the pub beer garden, and Stephen rarely took her anywhere, other than the pub, and the local Italian on her birthday. Next to James, she suddenly felt very unworldly.

'Then that's what I'll have,' she said, relieved not to have to focus on ordering. She was so flustered by James's proximity, and her mind preoccupied with how good he looked and trying to act as if she belonged, that she wasn't certain she'd have the capacity to make a decision about food.

'Me too, and shall we have a bottle of the house red?' he asked, beckoning over a waiter.

'Sounds good to me,' replied Jennie, liking that he'd asked.

As he ordered, Jennie repositioned her blouse, which had a habit of slipping down and exposing too much of her slight cleavage.

'It was good of you to come, I wasn't sure you would,' said James, after they'd made slightly nervous small talk about their days, or at least Jennie had been jittery, James didn't seem to suffer from nerves at all.

'Why not?' she asked, liking that he'd shown some insecurity, wondering if it implied that he might be interested in her after all, as Kat had said.

'Because of how George treated you,' he explained, as Jennie leant back to allow the waiter to pour the wine. 'I was worried you might find me guilty by association.'

'After what you did for Zaynab? Hardly!'

'How is she?' he asked, his voice immediately adopting a professional tone, which Jennie liked. Talking about Zaynab felt like more neutral territory, giving Jennie the feeling that she was on solider ground. She told him about the progress Mohammed was making, and the support his mother was receiving from the ladies in the tower.

'Sounds like you and the others are great neighbours,' he said, sampling the wine, his eyes watching Jennie over the top of the glass.

'I guess,' she replied, her own eyes flitting over everything from the silverware to the tealights, anything other than James's gaze, which she found impossible to read. It felt as if he was looking straight into her heart, but she convinced herself otherwise, unable to believe he could possibly be interested in someone like her. 'I'm not sure yet if I'm really part of the group. I've only just moved in.'

'Oh?'

'After things ended with Sarah, I had to find a new place. My flat was part of the apprenticeship.'

'Oh God, now I feel twice as bad. Dinner is *definitely* on me!' cried James, their starters of aubergine and feta arriving.

'I shouldn't worry too much, I've done my fair share of moving recently. If floristry doesn't pan out, I think I could start up a removals company!'

James laughed, allowing Jennie to relax a little.

'Why all the change?' he asked.

Usually, Jennie wouldn't launch into her private life with someone who was almost a total stranger, but there was something about James and his open, thoughtful nature that made her want to confide in him. She found herself wondering if it was an innate quality or something he'd developed during his medical training. After a large mouthful of red she said, 'I left my fiancé the night before our wedding.'

'Seriously?' he said, his eyes widening. 'What happened?'

Over her starter Jennie recounted the story. 'I'm not sure Brompton Marsh has ever known such scandal!'

'Sounds like you've been put through the mill,' said James, a small pause falling between them. He smiled at her, his eyes full of warmth and affection, and Jennie fought to fight just how much she fancied him.

'How about you?' she asked, fiddling with her napkin as the waiter removed their starters and brought the mains. 'Is there someone who's put you through the wringer?'

'To be honest, because of the nature of my work, most of my relationships haven't gone past six months. I was seeing someone recently, but I called it off when someone else caught my eye.'

'It must be hard switching jobs and locations all the time, on top of all those hours,' she said, reaching for her glass of water, trying desperately to conceal how foolish she felt for even imagining he might have been interested in someone like her. *Of course there was someone else who caught your eye*, she thought.

'I can't pretend it's easy, but it'll get better,' he said, tucking into his food. Despite herself, she couldn't help but admire the way he ate with abandon, without worrying about splattering his face or clothes with sauce as she was prone to doing. 'It's not long now until my consultancy exams. After that I can take a permanent position and settle down a bit more.'

'That's good. And nothing came of the other girl?' she asked coolly, impressed at her ability to make out that her gut wasn't twisted in disappointment.

James cast her a puzzled look.

'The girl who caught your eye,' she prompted, wondering jealously who the lucky woman might be.

'Right,' laughed James, almost cryptically. 'No, nothing's come of that, yet.'

After a short pause between them where it seemed to Jennie as if James was leaving something unsaid, James said, 'You know, my sister, Fran, is getting married next month. She saw the flowers you did for the Arbuthnotts' dinner, and the ones at Annabel's, and she's asked if you'd be interested in talking to her about her wedding flowers.'

'Seriously?' said Jennie, only just containing a mouthful of red wine.

'Absolutely. Are you interested?'

'James, are you kidding? Of course, I'm interested. This is precisely the sort of thing I've been hoping for.'

*

'Did you have fun?' Kat asked, still on the sofa when Jennie returned home, a little after eleven.

'Definitely a sympathy date,' said Jennie, taking off her shoes, exhausted by the evening – she felt as if she'd done three spinning classes in a row. After the mention of his sister's wedding, she'd been left wondering if it hadn't even been an apology dinner, but more of a business meeting. 'But his sister's getting married and she wants to chat to me about the flowers so that makes up for things. I'm meeting her tomorrow.' James had called Fran at the end of the evening and made the arrangements then and there, before walking Jennie to the end of her road. When they reached the row of Victorian houses, she made her excuses and left, not waiting for an uncomfortable goodbye. When he was out of sight, she walked towards the tower, happier messaging her mum to let her know that it hadn't really been a date after all than lingering uncomfortably around James.

'Well, that's some good news at least,' said Kat, snapping off the telly, and Jennie noticed Kat's face was blotchy from tears, her dark eye make-up smeared.

'What's up?'

Kat slumped further down the sofa, rolling her head back against the cushion. 'Lauren stopped by.'

'It doesn't look as if that was a good thing,' observed Jennie, sitting on the armchair next to her.

'No,' exhaled Kat. 'It was exhausting. She's still adamant that you and I are more than flatmates. And when I told her you weren't paying rent, she hit the roof.'

Jennie saw the look of distress on her friend's face and wished there was something she could do to make things better for her. 'I should be able to pay you some rent tomorrow when the house money comes through, perhaps that will ease Lauren's mind.'

'Won't you need all of that to cover the cost of flowers for the wedding?'

In all her excitement at the prospect of a wedding gig, Jennie hadn't had the chance to consider the practicalities of it. Kat was right. A wedding would require a huge number of flowers and sundries, it might even require an assistant or two, all of which required money, and while it was standard to take a deposit for a wedding, it wasn't standard to ask for the full cost up front.

'It won't use up all of it, not by a long way, and besides, Fran would pay a deposit,' said Jennie, hopeful that was the case, but not entirely certain.

'You should double-check with Stephen that the money's coming.'

Agreeing with Kat, Jennie hurriedly wrote Stephen a message.

Is the house money coming through tomorrow?

He replied immediately, which surprised Jennie; she wouldn't have been at all surprised if he'd chosen to ignore her and only have dealings via their lawyers. He always was cautious about money. Jennie had had to check with him whenever she wanted to spend more than ten pounds on herself. She couldn't wait to be financially free of him.

'He says it is,' she read, putting down her phone.

'That's good.'

'So, I can pay you some rent. That might help Lauren feel a little more comfortable.'

'You don't have to worry about the rent, or Lauren, for that matter,' said Kat, getting up and stretching, the piercing in her belly button riding up above the top of the pyjama shorts.

'It'll make me feel better if I do.'

'Before I forget,' said Kat through a yawn, ignoring Jennie's protests, 'Prisha said she wants to talk to you about her daughter's prom. Not sure what exactly. I think she's with Zaynab tomorrow morning if you want to pop in.'

'I'll do that,' said Jennie, excited to find out what Prisha might want, and glad to have something to think about other than her disappointment over James.

*

Prisha was holding Mohammed against her shoulder when she answered the door to Zaynab's flat the next morning. She put a finger to her lips, indicating for Jennie to come in quietly.

'Zaynab's sleeping,' she whispered.

'Okay,' Jennie whispered back, placing her hand on Mohammed's back. His infant eyes, wide and slow, searched for the source of the touch.

The two women tiptoed past Zaynab's bedroom and into the lounge where Prisha handed Jennie Mohammed. She took the baby awkwardly, at first holding him at arm's length and then attempting to nestle the tiny bundle in the crook of her arm. Whichever position she tried, she could not achieve the comfort and ease with which Prisha had been holding him.

'It takes practice,' smiled Prisha, not offering to take him back and instead opening the ironing board and turning her attention to a basketful of laundry.

'I guess so,' said Jennie, attempting to find a comfortable position on the sofa whilst trying not to disturb Mohammed, a task far harder than it looked.

'I was hopeless with my first. It's hard to believe she was born seventeen years ago. It feels like yesterday. Those first few years are such a blur. It's exhausting,' said Prisha, who was busy ironing a tiny Babygro.

'But you did it six times,' said Jennie, unable to imagine having even one child.

'I suppose you forget the worst of it. And then you start forgetting the good bits too and another child reminds you of them. Before you know it, they start going to nursery and school, and the house feels empty and another feels like a blessing, not a chore.'

'And then they're seventeen and graduating high-school . . .'

'And choosing a dress for the prom,' smiled Prisha, folding the Babygro into a perfect square. 'It's hard to believe my own school dance was more than twenty years ago.'

'What did you wear?'

'I wanted to wear a spaghetti-strap dress with a cowl neckline, I had it all picked out. It was deep red and very hugging,' she recalled dreamily. 'But my father had a fit and said I had to wear a sari or else I couldn't go. I can still remember so clearly getting ready in my room, wishing I could slip on that dress on my own, rather than have my mum fussing over my sari. When my date buzzed for me, Dad made him climb all nineteen floors to come get me – he told him the lift was broken, even though it wasn't! The whole experience was mortifying, but the thing that I remember most was longing for that dress. If I'd been more rebellious, I'd have bought it and put it on in the school loos, but I didn't have that sort of courage.'

'Sounds like that dress still haunts you.'

'It's the reason I wanted Aanya to have the dress of her dreams.'

'Has she chosen it already?'

'She chose it months ago. Now she's all about the finishing touches – the shoes, bag and make-up – and she wants flowers in her hair, and a corsage.'

'Sounds like she's got it all sorted,' said Jennie, allowing Mohammed to suck on her bent finger.

'I don't suppose you'd be able to help with the flowers?'

'I'd love to,' said Jennie, thrilled at the idea of being able to help Prisha when she'd been doing so much for Zaynab.

'We'd pay you, of course.'

'Don't be silly,' said Jennie, who was more than happy just to have photos of work to put on her Instagram page.

'I'd insist. No further discussion allowed.'

'Then you leave me no choice,' smiled Jennie, quietly pleased that it would be another piece of work alongside Fran's wedding, hoping that perhaps the bigger dream of her own business wasn't so far out of reach, after all.

13

Jennie tried not to compare the drawing room of James and Fran's family home in Notting Hill to the small living room in her parents' 1980s Barratt home with its stone fireplace, cream MFI leather couches and faded pink carpets. Everything about James's family home had a dilapidated feel about it, which in ordinary houses would look simply tired, but in their five-storey townhouse spoke of affluence and grandeur. Everything from the eclectic vintage furniture and artwork to the threadbare rugs and electric heater shoved in the majestic fireplace screamed of old money. Even the family photographs on the mantlepiece were framed in walnut or gold, unlike the mirrored frames her mum always chose.

As she waited for Fran to return from the kitchen, she imagined her parents in their kitchen that morning, getting ready for work before the sun was up, eating their cereal together at the breakfast bar, and composing the text she was looking at now: *So proud of you, Jennie. You show 'em!* It gave her goosebumps to think of them there, and her here, a world away from home.

'Coffee?' asked Fran, returning to the living room with a coffee tray, and Jennie admired her natural beauty as she knelt down at the ottoman. Her lean physique gave her the appearance of being taller than she actually was, and her soft blond hair hung in choppy waves.

'Yes, please,' said Jennie, popping her phone away. The dog, which had followed at Fran's heel since Jennie arrived, jumped up next to Jennie on the old floral sofa, and settled down beside her.

'Push Buckley off if he's annoying you,' said Fran, removing dog-eared copies of *Tatler* and *Town & Country* to make more room for the tray, then pouring coffee.

Jennie ruffled the dog's ears and his soft curly coat, which wasn't dissimilar to Fran's own hair, just shorter, and she had a sudden pang of missing Bruno. 'He's gorgeous. What sort of breed is he?'

'A Bedlington terrier,' she replied, handing Jennie a coffee.

'Will he be at the wedding? I could do a corsage for his collar,' she suggested, remembering the collar she'd done for Bruno at Claire's wedding, which everyone had adored.

'Fran would love that,' exclaimed James, strolling into the room and sitting on the worn leather lounge chair to the left of Jennie. He looked different today, even more relaxed at home than he'd been last night in the restaurant, if that was possible. Jennie put it down to the nicely fitted faded T-shirt he was wearing, which showed off his arms: tanned arms, which looked as if they'd rowed and played rugby in days gone by. And though Jennie was still disappointed about last night, she too felt more at ease today, knowing where she stood, more comfortable in her role as florist than as dinner date.

'It's true,' she said, kissing the dog and sitting on the opposite chair. 'We've had him since I was a teenager. He's like a second brother to me.'

'Charming!' laughed James, reaching for a biscuit.

Jennie took her notepad from her woven bag, which looked shabby and out of place in the surrounds of the drawing room.

'It could be something similar to the groom's buttonhole – have you had any thoughts about colour schemes?'

'Not really,' winced Fran. 'The truth is, I'm not that interested in weddings, and I haven't given it very much thought at all.'

'Fran's always been more comfortable in wellies and a Barbour than high-heels and couture,' chuckled James, looking affectionately at his sister.

'I can't deny it,' she said, offering Jennie a biscuit.

'But that's good,' said Jennie, refusing the biscuit and jotting down wellies and Barbour. 'It gives me a clue as to what sort of flowers you might prefer, perhaps more relaxed and natural than formal and sculptural. Does that sound right?'

'Precisely,' said Fran.

'Didn't I tell you she'd be perfect for you?' said James, beaming at his sister.

'He did,' replied Fran, who Jennie noticed had the same wide infectious smile as her brother.

Jennie had a fleeting buzz of contentment – all the years spent with Dorothy had been worth it – she was living her big dream, discussing beautiful flowers for intimate occasions on her own as Jennie Treloar. It was even more thrilling than working for Sarah Cunningham. She mentally crossed her fingers that Fran would choose her designs over those of anyone else she might be talking to.

'So,' said Jennie, breaking her own reverie and clicking her pen on and off. 'When's the big day?'

'June 1st,' said Fran.

She calculated that would give her almost four weeks to the day to prepare. Given that the money from Stephen was due later today it felt like fate that this potential job had come up when it had.

'Early summer weddings are beautiful,' she said, thinking of her own. If it hadn't been for Stephen insisting on a spring wedding, she would have definitely planned hers for early summer, too. 'Everything is so lush at the start of the summer. Have you decided on a venue, and numbers?'

'We're having the ceremony at the village church next to our grandmother's home in Gloucestershire.'

'Okay.' Jennie made a note. 'And the reception?'

'A marquee in the grounds of the house. We're trying to keep it under two hundred.'

Jennie tried to imagine the size of country home capable of accommodating a marquee for two hundred in the grounds. It was a job to pitch a two-man tent in her parents' back garden.

'Fran thinks two hundred is about one hundred and ninety-six too many,' said James.

'If it weren't for Oli's family, we would definitely elope,' confessed Fran.

'I can see the appeal in that,' said Jennie, who, after her wedding disaster, could understand the desire to keep things as small as possible. 'Are you having bridesmaids?'

'Just my best friend, and Oli's little sister.'

'And ushers?'

'Two ushers on the door and a best man.'

Jennie wrote everything in her book, mentally calculating flower and labour costs as she did so. Fran wanted to keep the church flowers as pared back as possible, a pedestal at the front door and something for the altar, no flowers round the door or pew ends. And for the marquee she

147

wanted a simple centrepiece for each table. By the end of the hour, Jennie had a complete picture of what was needed and a good sense of Fran's style.

'I can put together a quote and some sketches for you within the next few days,' she said, giving Buckley a fuss before getting up to shake Fran's hand.

'Thanks, Jennie,' said Fran, warmly shaking her hand. 'I'll let James see you out.' Jennie couldn't help but notice Fran's eyes flicker brightly towards her brother.

'You put your feet up,' he laughed. 'All this wedding planning can take its toll on a girl.'

'My big brother, always the comedian,' she quipped, with a wave, calling Buckley and departing.

'She really would prefer to elope,' he confided, as they descended the wide, curved staircase, James leading the way, Jennie trying but failing to keep her eyes off his upper arms.

'Why doesn't she?'

'Oli's family doesn't believe in doing weddings by halves, they're kind of the opposite of us. Kind of showy, if you know what I mean,' he said, stretching past Jennie to open the front door. The intimacy of the moment, and the waft of his scent, like soft cotton, sent a little tingle up her spine. 'Truth be told, Oli's parents had a florist of their own in mind for the wedding, but Fran thought they were far too fancy. In the end they conceded to Fran having her choice.'

'That was big of them,' laughed Jennie, moving out onto the front step.

'Weddings, huh? They seem to bring out the worst in people.'

'Isn't that the truth?' she mused, the mess she'd made of her own forefront in her mind.

Outside they loitered a while, James gabbling on about Oli's family politics and Fran's displeasure, Jennie listening attentively to his animated chat and admiring the pastel pink, blue and yellow facades of the neighbouring homes.

'I really enjoyed spending time with you last night,' he said, after he'd finished on the subject of weddings.

'Me too,' said Jennie politely.

'Maybe we can do it again sometime?'

Jennie paused, surprised, uncertain what he was suggesting.

'Are you free on Tuesday?' he asked.

'I think so,' she faltered, knowing that this could be neither sympathy nor business, and a bubble of excitement began to grow inside her.

'I could pick you up around seven.'

And then the bubble suddenly popped and was replaced by a wave of worry about where she lived, or not where, exactly, but the *contrast* to where James lived.

'Perhaps I could meet you somewhere? I'm not sure how Kat feels about me having visitors. It's all so new,' she said, conscious of her little white lie. And her thoughts turned to Stephen and how he hated Jennie bringing anyone back to the cottage.

'I understand.' He thought for a moment. 'Meet me at Richmond station. Do you know where that is?'

'No, but I'll figure it out,' she said, tingling with delight.

'Then it's a date,' he said, placing his hand on Jennie's arm and softly kissing her cheek, making it crystal clear that this was definitely something more than friends.

'See you then,' she said, hoping he wouldn't make out the goosebumps that tickled every inch of her skin.

14

Prisha handed Jennie a freshly made cup of chai, the warming scent of which filled Jennie's nostrils. 'You must be excited about doing such an important event on your own,' she said.

'It's still to be confirmed, and at the moment I feel too daunted to be really excited,' said Jennie, who'd spent the past twenty-four hours working on ideas for Fran's wedding. She'd kept away from the obvious romantic pinks and white and chosen instead an English cottage-garden feel using blue grape hyacinths, soft cream ranunculus and lily of the valley, which, she felt, would suit Fran's tomboy personality.

'You'll get it for sure,' encouraged Prisha, sitting at her family sized kitchen table and giving Jennie's wrist a reassuring squeeze.

'I hope so,' replied Jennie, quickly checking her phone. Since emailing a quote and sketches of the flower designs to Fran yesterday evening, she'd been watching her phone like a hawk for a reply. She was also watching for Stephen to confirm that the funds had been transferred; when she'd checked yesterday evening, they hadn't come through and she'd tossed and turned all night, unable to put it out of her mind. 'More important is Aanya's corsage. We need to decide on size and shape.'

Jennie spread out the flowers Prisha had brought for her daughter's prom corsage on the table. To Jennie they were a little old-fashioned – white roses, pink spray carnations and baby's breath – and for a moment she felt she was back with Dorothy at Brompton Floristry. It was only the hypericum that offered much in the way of anything contemporary.

'What would you suggest?' asked Prisha.

'Smaller is usually more elegant. I prefer one large flower in the centre with clusters of smaller ones around it.'

Jennie took the white rose and some pieces of baby's breath, and to that she added some small pink spray carnations creating a tear-shaped arrangement.

'It's very pretty,' said Prisha.

Jennie scrunched her nose unhappily, feeling it was a bit dated, a little like Prisha's family's kitchen, which was all dark wood cabinets with tinted glass.

'It needs a little height,' she said, a lavender plant on the windowsill catching her eye. 'Can I?' she asked, pointing to the plant.

'Of course,' said Prisha, and she went to fetch it.

Amongst the spray carnations Jennie dotted three lavender heads, then held it at arm's length for perspective.

'Beautiful,' said Prisha.

'But now it needs something dainty and vibrant to lift it.' Jennie wove the bright green hypericum into the design. 'There. Better, I think.'

'It's very nice,' said Prisha, admiring Jennie's work. 'But how do we hold it all together?'

'That's the tricky part,' smiled Jennie. 'Let me show you.'

From her supply box, Jennie took a wristband and cut the stems to about an inch long. She bound each stem diagonally with florist's tape and then tied the rose and carnations together. She did the same with the baby's breath, hypericum and lavender, before placing the two bundles together and attaching them with wire to the wristband. Prisha watched every intricate step.

'You can add little trinkets if you like: pearls, crystals, anything that might bring out the detail of her dress,' said Jennie, making a bow out of pink ribbon.

'You make it look easy.'

'It's not so hard when you get the hang of it; like motherhood, it takes practice!'

And at that, a little girl, her hair dark and thick, burst into the kitchen yelling, 'Mum, Mum. Nambi stomped on dolly's head.'

153

'Nambi!' Prisha called, and almost immediately a boy, a head above his sister in height, and with deep rich eyes, came into the kitchen.

'She started it—' he began, but Prisha cut him off.

'I don't care who started it. Can't you see we have a guest?'

'Sorry,' they said in unison, their eyes cast to the floor.

'Nambi, apologise to your sister. And don't let me hear another word from either of you,' she ordered, and they left.

'They're so obedient.'

'They're so challenging!' Prisha laughed.

'Now your turn,' countered Jennie, turning her attention back to the flowers.

'I don't think I'll be any good,' she said reluctantly.

'Do you do crafts with your kids?'

'I'm the craft master!'

'Then just think of it like that – some flowers and sticky tape.' Jennie handed her the flowers and a pair of scissors. 'First choose your flowers, then trim the stems.'

'Okay,' said Prisha hesitantly, reaching for a white rose. 'I'll try, but don't think for a moment that Aanya will allow me to make the real thing for her prom night! You must promise to do it for her.'

'I promise,' said Jennie, casting her eye around the myriad of photographs all over the walls – photos of young kids holding hands, school portraits with missing teeth, and high school class photographs. And not just of

Prisha's children but, Jennie suspected, of Prisha and her siblings, too. As she drank in the photos and the trinkets that filled a corner cabinet, her phone pinged, causing her heart to skip a beat. Hoping it would be from Fran, she picked it up to discover a text from Stephen instead.

Delay in house funds. Will keep you posted.

How long? Jennie wrote, trying not to worry but failing. *I have a potential job in four weeks that I need to place an order for.*

She hit send and immediately regretted it. Mentioning the job let Stephen know that she was working for herself, not Sarah Cunningham. His reply was instantaneous.

What happened to the apprenticeship?

The last thing she wanted was for Stephen to know what she was doing; she knew the apprenticeship not working out would only make him gloat. He'd tell Jennie that he'd been right all along, that moving to London was a mistake. She didn't want to get into it all again, to have to press home the point that even with the apprenticeship over she still didn't regret not marrying him. But whether she wanted to reply or not, she needed to know how long the money would be. Without it, doing Fran's wedding, even with a deposit, would be impossible.

I decided to branch out on my own. Any idea how long the money will be?

He replied instantly, making Jennie wonder if he was home in the living room, sitting by the wood burner that he'd chosen even though Jennie had preferred another, and watching *Sherlock* on the preposterously large television he'd insisted on buying when Jennie had thought it a waste of money.

Probably another week.

She released a sigh, which sounded as if it came from the bottom of her boots. Another week meant the money arriving a week and a half before she'd have to place her order. It made things uncomfortably tight.

'Is there a problem?' asked Prisha, who was battling florist's tape, pulling and shaking and rubbing, trying anything possible to remove a piece from her fingers.

'Just my ex,' replied Jennie, sipping her tea.

'It's a long time since I had one of those.'

'How long have you been married?'

'Eighteen years.'

'That's incredible.'

'To me eighteen years is nothing, my grandparents were married for almost seventy!'

'Wow, Prisha,' she exclaimed, watching Prisha tie the baby's breath, hypericum and lavender together, and listening to all the movement in the maisonette. Through the ceiling above she could hear music, through the wall of the kitchen a television blared, and doors seemed to open and close endlessly, with footsteps thumping up and down stairs. 'How did you and your husband meet?'

'We grew up together. He lived on the ninth floor.'

'But there was someone else before him, an ex?'

'The son of a friend of my father's, who my parents were adamant I should marry. We "dated" for over a year. They had the whole thing pretty much arranged, but it wasn't what I wanted.'

'How did you get out of it?'

'It took all my courage, but in the end, I told them I would rather leave the family and marry Simon than keep my family and marry Rahul.'

'And I'm guessing Simon isn't Indian.'

'Not at all. He's Irish Catholic!'

'How did that go down?'

'My father didn't talk to me for months. Can you imagine, here in the cramped surroundings of this flat. It was horrid. But I won round my mother, and in the end, she won round my dad.'

'How?'

'She recognised that Simon and I had been friends all our lives, grown up in the same place, held the same values. It wasn't so very different from what my father had planned for me. He agreed to it so long as Simon moved in with us after we were married.'

'And Simon didn't mind?' asked Jennie, taking the two miniature bundles of flowers from Prisha and showing her how to position them together.

'I think the only thing he minded was that our bedroom was, and is, right beside my parents'!'

'No!' Jennie shuddered at the prospect of having to conduct her love life in audible distance of her mum and dad.

'But within the year I was pregnant with Aanya—'

'So it didn't interfere too much!' laughed Jennie, taking a wristband from the box and handing it to Prisha.

'One way or another we managed to have six children!'

'And you've been happy?'

'We have,' she said, as a teenage boy entered the kitchen, heading straight to a biscuit tin.

'Only one,' reprimanded Prisha.

'Yes, Mum,' he breathed, in a way that suggested he'd heard the instruction several times before.

'We share the same values, the support of two extended families, and the knowledge of where each of us has come from. These are the things that sustain marriage, for us,' said Prisha, as she fiddled awkwardly with the flowers, wire and strap.

Jennie found her mind wandering to James, and how very different their upbringings must have been. She worried it didn't bode well for any future they might have, then kicked herself for thinking long-term about a man she'd only dated once, and hadn't even been sure it was a date.

'Nowadays things are different, but me marrying Simon back then was quite the talking point,' said Prisha, focusing on tight, neat binding.

'No regrets?'

'It's not been a complete bed of roses. I've made sacrifices along the way for my family, not all of which have come easy.'

'Still, it sounds as if you have great security.'

'That I have,' agreed Prisha, holding out the completed corsage for Jennie to assess. 'Though there are days I can't help wishing for a little bit more.'

'How do you mean?' Jennie took the corsage from Prisha, and watched as her mother entered the kitchen, dressed in a red and orange sari, her hair tied at the nape of her neck. She checked one of the pots on the stove and then left without a word.

'I dream of having something in my life other than family – a career maybe, a skill.'

'Do you ever imagine living somewhere different?'

'No. I love the tower. I couldn't live anywhere else.'

'And never a different husband?'

'Never,' giggled Prisha, as if she were twenty-one again.

Just then there was a knock at the front door. Prisha went to open it and returned with Mary, wearing her nurse's tunic and trousers.

'Jennie, thank God!' she said, pulling out a chair. 'I've been looking everywhere for you.'

'What's the matter?' asked Jennie.

Mary sat down at the table with a thump and picked up both corsages. 'You can tell which was done by the professional,' she said dryly.

'Mary! Be nice! Prisha's done a great job.'

Mary cocked her head at Prisha and raised her eyebrows, and both women, close as they were, burst into laughter.

'What's going on?' asked Jennie, as Prisha poured Mary some chai.

'I've to do the flowers for church next week, and I don't know how. You have to help! I'll never live it down if I do it on my own.'

'Of course I'll help. What do you need?'

'Something for the altar, and something for the entrance. The woman who does it normally is in the hospital.'

'I'd love to help.'

'There's money for the flowers and what's left is yours.'

'Great. I'll go to the flower market next Saturday morning and buy everything we need,' said Jennie, elated to have another event to add to her website and Instagram feed.

The three women spent the afternoon putting the world to rights until late afternoon when Prisha had to start cooking and Mary needed to prepare for a shift. Jennie was about to put a ready meal in the microwave when the buzzer rang.

'Hello,' Jennie called into the plastic receiver.

'It's Lauren.'

'Oh hi,' faltered Jennie. 'Kat's not in.'

'I'll come up anyway.'

Jennie thought it a bit odd that Lauren should want to come up without Kat being there, but she buzzed her in and went to the door of the flat to wait on the lift. The tower's janitor, Omar, was up a ladder repairing a ceiling panel. On seeing Jennie, he offered a little nod of recognition and a wave, the light glinting off his gold cross at the neckline of his overalls.

'Lauren?' asked Jennie, when the lift doors opened. Lauren wasn't quite what Jennie had pictured. Rather than the large, imposing woman of her imagination, she was a rather petite, plain woman with straight brown hair and a permanent furrow between her brows. 'I'm Jennie,' she said, offering her hand.

Lauren didn't shake it, but instead tightened the belt of her fitted trench coat. 'Where's Kat?' she asked, with a hint of a Yorkshire accent.

'Not here, I'm afraid. I'm not sure when she'll be back.'

A sense of foreboding crept through Jennie, as if she'd been dropped into the bar of some old Western, where all she could hear was the swing door banging behind her and the tumbleweed rolling down the dirt road.

'Would you like to come in?' she asked cautiously, after an uncomfortable stand-off. Jennie was conscious that up until a couple of weeks ago this had been Lauren's flat, not hers. It felt awkward asking her in, as if it should be the other way around. So it took her by surprise when Lauren accepted, entering immediately, and looking around disdainfully as if her former home had suffered a termite invasion rather than the arrival of Jennie and her belongings.

'I'm not sure when Kat will be back,' Jennie repeated, going to the kitchen to put on the kettle, even though she was sort of hoping Lauren wouldn't accept the offer of a drink, not wanting to prolong their meeting any longer than necessary.

As Jennie made tea, Lauren leant against one of the white units, her arms crossed, checking out the changes that had been made since she'd left – the flower vases on the windowsill, Jennie's snowdrop oven glove on the cooker handle, her sandwich maker on the counter. 'Kat told me you're from out of town,' she offered eventually.

'Right,' said Jennie, refraining from telling her where from.

'And you're a florist?'

'I am,' she replied, busying herself with the tea, a task that felt suddenly hard with Lauren watching her. 'What is it you do?'

'I work in a call centre.'

'Oh,' replied Jennie, struggling to find any common ground the way she usually could with people. It seemed the only thing the two women had in common was Kat, and Jennie knew that topic of conversation was better left alone, despite her desire to reassure Lauren that her feelings for Kat were purely platonic.

'I might nip to the bathroom,' said Lauren, after she'd watched Jennie squeeze the teabags against the side of the cup and dump them in the food waste bin.

Breathing a sigh of relief, Jennie brought the tea to the table and sat down to check her messages. When she saw one from Fran, her heart leapt.

Hi Jennie, thanks for coming by yesterday and for getting the designs to me so quickly. I absolutely love them! Can I book you? Fran

Her hands trembled as she typed her reply:

So pleased you like them. Date in the diary. Jennie

After a couple of texts back and forth to put initial details in place, including a further meeting next week, Lauren returned.

'I'll head off,' she said, with the first flicker of lightness Jennie had seen, as if she were pleased about something, though Jennie had no idea what.

'Sure, okay. Maybe see you again,' said Jennie, out of politeness, and showing Lauren to the door, perplexed as to why she'd bothered to call round in the first place.

15

'Oh, this is gorgeous,' said Jennie, drinking in the aesthetics of the glasshouse restaurant, which James had chosen for supper.

'I thought you'd like it,' he smiled.

As they wove their way through the higgledy-piggledy antique tables and chairs, Jennie gazed at her surroundings: the charming structure of the glasshouse itself, the jasmine and bougainvillea cascading from the roof, and the fairy lights twinkling all around. It put her in mind of the feel of the walled garden back home on the Brompton Manor estate: rustic and whimsical, and bursting with life and stories.

'It's a florist's dream,' she said as he pulled out a seat for her, and she sat, unable to imagine anywhere more 'Jennie' than this, other than her beloved walled garden. She could only imagine how excited her mum would be for her if she could see this now, she'd been excited enough when Jennie had told her about the date. 'I told you!' she'd squealed, rushing to tell Tony.

'Everything is made with ingredients from the kitchen garden. It's all organic, and they minimise waste,' enthused James, reflections from the fairy lights dancing in his eyes.

'What's not to love,' she cooed, as the waiter presented her with a Bellini, impressed that James had put so much thought into where to take her. Just being in such a beautiful, atmospheric space made her feel spoiled. 'Tell me something about your day?' she said, surprised at how different she felt this evening, not just more relaxed in the environment but also more confident that this really was a date. And despite all her insecurities about being inexperienced and unworldly, and wondering how someone like James could be interested in someone like her, she couldn't help but get caught up in it all.

'I spent most of it dealing with George.'

'How come?' she asked, curious to know how someone as low-key as James could be friends with someone as high-maintenance as George.

'She's in a tizz about something, I'm not entirely sure what. I think turning thirty has sent her off the rails!'

'How do you guys know each other?'

'School. There's a group of us – me, Fran, George, my friend Henry, and then Oli, Fran's fiancé. And our parents are all friends, too. I can't remember what came first – the kids' friendships or the parents' – but either way, our lives are all intertwined, whether we like it or not.'

'Sounds intense,' said Jennie, thinking of her own parents and Stephen's, and how glad she was that they'd found their way through the mess that she and Stephen had made.

'Normally it's fine, but occasionally things blow up, usually because of George.'

'High-maintenance?'

'You could say that,' he laughed. 'But, to be fair, I think she's feeling a bit left behind. She's always been a party animal, you know? But now Fran and Oli are settling down, and Henry's engaged, too. George and I are the only ones left standing, flying the singles' banner. I don't think she knows how to be, which is hard when you make your living presenting your "perfect life" to millions of people every day.'

Jennie nodded lightly, not sure whether to tell him that she felt left behind for very different reasons. That a relationship had meant she'd lost most of her twenties and it was only now that she was able to start again. 'It's a weird job to have.'

'It's certainly not work as we know it.'

'My dad can't get his head around it, that people can make money out of breathing. He calls it "a lot of old bollocks"!'

'He's not wrong!' laughed James.

'I wouldn't have enough confidence to do something like that,' she confessed, the Bellini loosening her tongue.

'I think if George can do it, you could too.'

'Maybe,' Jennie tailed off, the warmth of the alcohol causing her thoughts to swim. 'My self-confidence is so low I wasn't even sure our first dinner was a date, until you spelt it out for me on your doorstep.'

James laughed, his smile filling his face. Jennie liked the way his shoulders and torso moved when he laughed, as though his whole body felt joy.

'You thought the supper at Lemonia was just about friendship?'

A light blush heated Jennie's cheeks and she looked down, trying to avert her attention from the open buttons of James's soft blue shirt, an exposed triangle of tanned skin and a smattering of chest hair igniting her imagination.

'I thought you felt guilty about George's behaviour and me losing my job,' she confessed, looking up to find him gazing fondly, his eyes sparkling. 'Or maybe I thought it was about the offer of work. I don't know. Romance hasn't exactly been high on my list of priorities these last few weeks, years . . .' she said, drifting off, amused at how she'd been so adamant that first evening that he wasn't interested in her.

'How are things between you and—'

'Stephen,' she prompted.

'Right. How are things?'

Jennie shrugged, sobering up at the mere mention of his name. 'He's dragging his feet over some money that he owes me . . . other than that, things are pretty much non-existent between us!'

'Sounds like a real gent,' said James, his voice laced with sarcasm.

The subject of Stephen was quickly forgotten and over dinner James told Jennie all about his loving childhood. He told her he spent it mostly between the house in Notting Hill, his grandmother's place in Gloucestershire, which he adored, 'outside all the time, climbing trees and building dens' and his secondary boarding school near Oxford. 'My choice, not theirs' he clarified, because by then his parents had decided to teach abroad and 'rarely stayed in one country for longer than a year'. Then there was his gap year in South Africa followed by medical school in London, and a series of rotations culminating in his present position of registrar.

'I have my consultant exams coming up,' he said, finishing his trout. 'So my social life is pretty much a black hole. I haven't seen my best mate, Henry, in months. And you're the only person I've seen this week other than George.'

'Seriously?' Jennie was flattered and surprised that he should choose to spend time with her over his close friends.

He nodded his reply, his eyes fixed on Jennie's mouth.

The first quiet moment of the evening fell comfortably between them and Jennie couldn't help wondering what it might feel like to kiss his firm lips, which weren't large but shone a brilliant, irresistible red.

'Forgive me,' he said, shaking his head and taking a drink of his wine. 'I've been gabbing on about me. What about you? All I know is you're a bloody good florist, your ex is Stephen, and you grew up in Brompton Marsh, which is beautiful, by the way.'

'You know it?'

'I do. Our grandmother's home is close by.'

'Oh,' said Jennie, enquiring no further. 'Well,' she played self-consciously with the napkin on her lap, far more comfortable hearing about James than talking about herself, 'there isn't too much else to tell, really.'

She told James about growing up in the village, going to the primary school there and the secondary school in the neighbouring town. At nineteen, after a tedious year studying business at college, she started working for Dorothy and met Stephen five years later, on a girls' night out. Until a couple of years ago, she'd lived at home and saved every penny in the hope of setting up her own business, until Stephen had convinced her to plough it into a house instead.

'I haven't travelled the world or saved lives, all I've ever wanted is my own flower business,' she said, hoping not to sound too provincial, conscious of the difference in their upbringings and worrying it might get in the way. 'In my dream of all dreams I run it from an old gardener's cottage on an estate close to home, growing flowers in the walled garden and the Victorian greenhouse, not dissimilar to this,' she said, glancing up.

'It's a great dream to have.'

'It's not an important one. What you do has real value.'

'What you do has real value too. Through flowers you spread love.'

'Yes,' said Jennie humbly, quietly delighted that James recognised something in her work that Stephen had failed to see in the five years they were together.

'The truth is, if I weren't a doctor – and let's face it, I'm only a doctor because my grandmother spent a lot of money on my education and I felt she should get some return at the end of it – I'd be a landscape gardener.'

'You're kidding,' said Jennie, taken aback by this revelation.

'I'm not,' smiled James, his eyes alight. 'I always liked the idea of my own pickup truck, wearing robust work clothes instead of scrubs, and getting my hands dirty with soil instead of blood.'

'Why don't you?'

'Two reasons: first, I do love the difference I make being a doctor, and second, once I'm a consultant, I'll have more time to help out at my grandmother's garden.'

'It's a large garden?'

'Large enough to warrant a full-time gardener.'

'Right,' said Jennie, curious to know what size of garden required a full-time member of staff but deciding not to pry.

*

'May I?' James asked, reaching out to take Jennie's hand as they strolled away from the restaurant, alongside the river.

'Of course,' she said, reaching out her hand and interlocking her fingers with his. Her first thought, which made her feel guilty, was of Stephen, and of how different James's hand felt to his. She remembered how Stephen would clasp her hand in a tight, proprietary fashion. It was only then, in that moment, that she realised she'd felt all those years as if she was being led rather than held, and inwardly she delighted in being free of him.

'Your hand feels wonderfully warm. My ex's hand was always so cold.'

Jennie smiled, glad that James had had a similar thought.

'Oh God,' he blurted. 'Sorry, that's such an inappropriate thing to say. Talk of exes isn't really second-date material.'

'Don't be silly,' said Jennie, squeezing her fingers more tightly and swinging his arm lightly, and only feeling a smidge guilty for not mentioning that she'd been thinking of her ex, too.

172

'Shall we sit for a while?' he asked, when they happened upon a bench, a soft meadow behind, the river in front.

'I'd like that.'

They sat watching the water, the dusky pink light colouring its surface. James placed his arm unselfconsciously behind Jennie.

'It's beautiful,' he said.

'It really is.' Jennie shifted her bum a little closer towards him, watching the ducks settle in for the night on the bank.

They sat quietly, their bodies closer than they'd been before. Jennie thought how unexpected it all was, and how surprisingly uncomplicated it felt.

'What are you thinking?' James asked, after watching the swans gliding towards the banks to roost alongside the ducks for some minutes.

'That I wasn't expecting this when I left Brompton Marsh.'

'"This" being?'

Jennie pulled away to gauge his expression, worrying she'd spoken too soon. She was so inexperienced that she didn't know the etiquette of dating. She thought quickly about the best course of action – retract the comment, or speak honestly? Scanning his eyes in the dim light she thought she saw a hint of concern, similar to her own.

'The beginning of something?' she gambled, trusting in honesty.

Jennie knew immediately from the look of relief that shone from James's eyes that she'd chosen correctly. He wasn't trying to catch her out; he had been looking for reassurance that he wasn't alone in his feelings. He breathed a long, contented sigh, clutched Jennie's shoulder and pulled her close.

'I hope so,' he said, kissing her lightly on her lips, unaware of the fireworks exploding inside her, and slowly, hungrily, drawing her in.

16

'Hiya, love. Can you hear me?'

A drunk woman belting out 'I Will Survive' in the background told Jennie immediately that her mother was at the monthly karaoke event which took place at the Fox and Hounds.

'Just about,' called Jennie, who was taking advantage of Kat being out for the evening by having a 'self-care' night. It wasn't yet eight o' clock and she was already tucked up in bed in her blue flannel pyjamas, moisturising her hands.

'How about now?'

'Better,' she answered.

The voice of two passers-by and the soft thud of the pub door helped Jennie to visualise her mother standing out front in the car park. A little pool of homesickness welled in her stomach as she thought of the pub she'd known all her life, its owners, Bob and Lisa, as good as family. She smiled at the memory of Sunday afternoons spent with Claire, running through the beer garden with bubble wands, winding their way between picnic benches while their parents chatted the hours away over slow drinks with friends.

'How have the last couple of days been?' Her mother's voice sounded tight and shivery.

'Mum, go inside and keep warm. I'll call you later.'

'I'm fine, love, I was too hot anyway, and you know I hate to miss your calls. What's been going on?'

'Fran confirmed she wants me to do her flowers, and Prisha and Mary have asked me to help with flowers for two separate events.'

'That's great, love. I'm really pleased. It sounds as if they're becoming good friends, no?'

'I think so.'

Jennie thought about the two women, their backgrounds and situations so different from her own. Back home they'd have been the most unlikely of acquaintances, but here, in the 'big city', their friendships seemed entirely natural.

'And what about Kat?'

'I've barely seen her all week,' said Jennie, thinking of how she hadn't even had a chance to talk to Kat about Lauren's visit. 'Her ex popped round. Other than that there's not much to tell. How are you?'

'Same as always.'

'Have you seen the consultant yet?'

'Still waiting. They're busy, love. And if it was really important, I'd have been seen by now. Stop worrying. We're not.'

'And Bruno?' she asked, wishing her mother would chase the hospital appointment but knowing better than to interfere.

'He's had us up at night with a bad stomach. Every time he wants to go out, he cries like a baby.'

'Poor thing.'

'Your dad thinks he must have eaten something up at the estate. He's threatening him with a kennel,' laughed Irene, through chattering teeth.

'Never.'

'It won't happen; it's just Dad being Dad.'

In the background, the pub door squeaked open and a few bars of 'Summer Nights' drifted into the car park.

'Who are you out with?'

'The usual suspects – Tina, Beth, and Tracy's here too.'

An image of Stephen nursing a pint sprung into Jennie's mind. The Fox and Hounds was the one place they used to go together on a semi-regular basis, particularly on karaoke night. Stephen was never comfortable with Jennie getting up to sing, even though Tracy usually dragged her up and he had no choice but to sit and watch the two of them belting out 'Enough is Enough'. 'How is she?'

'Hammered!'

Jennie laughed. Tracy was known for two things: being a strict mother, and being able to drink anyone under the table. It wasn't a good karaoke night if Tracy didn't end up staggering home, belting out a Whitney anthem at the top of her lungs.

'Actually, I meant to say, love, I let slip last week about you setting up business on your own. I hope you don't mind. I said it as a positive thing, not that you'd lost the apprenticeship.'

'Right,' said Jennie, slowly beginning to join dots in her mind. 'I don't suppose—'

'What, love?'

'No, it's nothing.' She shook away the thought.

'What?'

Jennie scrutinised her fingernails, the cuticles always tinged with green regardless of how often she scrubbed them or soaked them in nail polish remover. 'I had a message from Stephen today saying that the funds from the house have been delayed. You don't think—'

'What?'

The night before the wedding came flooding back, and Jennie heard Stephen telling her, 'I'll make sure you never make a success of yourself'.

'You don't think Tracy told him and he's held back the money knowing I'm more in need of it now than ever?'

she asked, remembering a time when she'd lent him some money for new clothes when his card was declined, and he'd never repaid, even when she'd asked. In the end he kept the money so long that Jennie let it go, embarrassed to keep asking. She wouldn't put it past him to be doing the same thing now. Not that she'd let him get away with it this time.

'I doubt it, love. I know things didn't work out between you, but he's not a bad lad, not really.'

'No, I'm sure you're right,' said Jennie. She thought about what her mother would say if she knew of how he'd threatened her, and how hurt she'd be that Jennie had kept it from her. She hated not to tell her everything, but she still worried her friendship with Tracy would suffer because of it, despite how well they'd been getting along.

'Are you okay for money?'

'Absolutely,' lied Jennie, who had no desire to burden her mother with her financial problems. The money her parents earned between them was hardly enough to cover their own costs, let alone hers, and she knew they'd only try to help if they found out she was struggling.

'Because if you're not, you know, your dad and I—'

'Mum, I'm fine, I promise.'

'Alright, love. I just couldn't bear to think of you struggling.'

'I know,' she said, torn between fibbing to her mum and protecting her from the truth.

'Have you heard from James since that kiss?' she asked. Jennie had messaged her after they'd said goodnight to tell her what had happened.

'We've messaged back and forth,' said Jennie, playing it coy, though her cheeks flushed pink at the thought of him. 'More importantly, I'm seeing his sister tomorrow to discuss the flowers again; that's what I'm in the city for, work, remember, not men.'

'That's true, love,' said Irene, her teeth now chattering uncontrollably. 'But remember to make a little room for romance, it makes life all the sweeter.'

'Mum, go inside, before you freeze to death,' ordered Jennie, knowing but not wanting to admit that her mother was right.

Jennie heard the creak of the pub door and the rush of noise as Irene entered. 'Alright, love, if you're sure. Good luck tomorrow!'

*

'James says he's really sorry not to be here, he was called in on an emergency,' said Fran, showing Jennie through to the huge kitchen on the ground floor at the back of the townhouse. Buckley followed at her heels, his claws clicking on the flagstone floor.

180

'Sure,' said Jennie, too distracted by the scale of the kitchen, which spanned the width of the property, to worry about her disappointment at James not being there.

'Grab a seat.'

Fran indicated to a chair at a battered farmhouse table in the centre of the room. It was positioned opposite French doors, which opened onto the garden, beautifully landscaped in shades of purple, white and grey, with alliums, lily of the valley and sage. On the other side of the table was a black Aga surrounded by a stone mantle, with tired, painted wooden units on either side.

'Lime and mint cordial, tea, coffee or water?' Fran asked, opening an old-style refrigerator, big enough to hold the contents of an entire deli counter.

'Cordial, please,' replied Jennie, who took a seat on one of the pine and wicker chairs.

Fran made the drinks and joined her at the table with tall glasses, rattling with ice. Buckley settled into his scruffy dog bed by the Aga. 'Thanks so much for coming.'

'That's okay,' said Jennie, sampling the beverage. 'I'm glad you liked the sketches.'

'I did. But unfortunately, Oli's family have decided the scale of things needs to be bigger – more bridesmaids, groomsmen, church decoration. The reception will be bigger too, so we'll need extra table pieces, decoration for the marquee – you name it, it's bigger.'

Jennie took out her notebook and pushed away the thought of the cost involved, not only of flowers but also of the manpower she'd need to assist her, and how on earth she was going to find helpers in the space of three weeks.

'Does that make it difficult for you?' asked Fran, her pale blue eyes, the same almond shape as her brother's, pleading with Jennie to say no. 'I know you've only recently set up on your own and I don't want to overwhelm you but—'

Jennie sipped her drink in the hope of swallowing back her growing anxiety about whether the house funds would come through in time. The money was meant to have been transferred by now but, so far, nothing, despite numerous messages and a call to Stephen that morning.

'It'll be fine,' she said, refusing to let Stephen get to her, and assuring herself that he'd do the right thing in the end. 'I'll have to ask for a deposit for the flower order but other than that, I'll manage.'

'Oh, thank goodness,' said Fran, relaxing into her chair.

'Do you want the designs to reflect the increased scale – something more formal or bolder in colour, so they stand out more in the venue?'

'No!' exclaimed Fran, putting her foot onto the chair beside her. 'I love the designs, they're exactly what

I would have chosen if I'd bothered to look at any magazines.'

'Great,' said Jennie, scribbling some notes in her pad. 'Let me write down the new numbers and we can take things from there.'

The two women discussed the arrangements for a half hour or so. Oli's family were now insisting on a minimum of three bridesmaids, including George, and two flower girls, plus the groomsmen had doubled to accommodate the number of guests, which had also doubled; the number stood at almost four hundred. His mother wanted pew ends and decorations around not only the church door but also the gate mantle; there was also the matter of a larger altar piece with another smaller arrangement on either side, and something for the vestry. The cars, four in total, were to be adorned, and the venue, now twice the size, was to be festooned liberally – even the Portaloos were to have flowers on the vanity units. Jennie didn't like to say that she'd never been in a Portaloo with a vanity unit. She knew from that one sentence alone that this was a wedding in a different league from anything she'd worked on before.

'Are you certain it isn't too much?' asked Fran, after they'd chatted through all the details.

'Certain.'

'Because we could always hire a bigger firm, use your designs and pay you a consultant's fee.'

'Really, it's fine,' said Jennie, brimming with delight that Fran thought her good enough to be a flower consultant rather than just a simple florist.

'Good, well, if you're sure, can you put another quote together?'

'Of course, I'll do it tonight.'

After Fran saw her out, Buckley by her side, waving as heartily as her brother did, Jennie walked down the colourful street towards the bus stop, thinking how odd it was that such a joyous, unaffected person should be so bound by her fiancé's parents' desire for a big wedding. She found herself wishing that Fran would run away and be married in a field in her wellies, even if it did mean Jennie losing out on the gig.

At the bus stop she wrote a to-do list:

- draft a quote
- advertise for assistants
- contact Van Beek's to set up an account
- chase Stephen

Then she pulled up Henrik's details to send him a message:

Hi Henrik, can I take you up on that offer of help?
Jennie (previously Sarah Cunningham Flowers).

Almost immediately a reply came through:

Of course. Name the time and place.

Jennie, uncertain where to suggest, opened her internet banking to check if the house funds had come through. Her heart sank when she saw that they hadn't. She was in the middle of phoning Stephen, the call ringing out twice, when another message pinged through:

Loved seeing you on Tuesday. Can I take you to Kew on Sunday afternoon? James x

Jennie boarded the bus with the biggest smile on her face, even though she was aware that people were looking at her as if she were crazy. She replied uninhibitedly:

Sounds perfect

And took a seat on the bus wishing she didn't have to wait forty-eight hours to see him.

17

It took Jennie a few failed attempts to locate the stallholder at the flower market that she was looking for, but when she did at last find it, she knew she'd made the right choice. The flowers in front of her were bold, statement pieces – anthuriums, birds of paradise, and large headed roses – exactly what she had in mind for Mary to bring a taste of Nigeria to her church.

'Can I help?' asked the stallholder, busy tidying the buckets of blooms.

'I'm looking for flowers that will create a flavour of Nigeria. They're for a large church, so the bigger the better.'

The woman showed Jennie what she had, and Jennie was transfixed by the drama of the birds of paradise, and the extraordinary sheen of the anthuriums, which almost looked as if they weren't real.

It took her a while to make a decision, everything calling strongly to her, but in the end she selected birds of paradise, white and pink anthuriums, a selection of roses, chrysanthemums, alstroemeria, banana leaf and baby's breath.

'What a stunning collection,' said a voice behind her when she was settling up with the stallholder.

Jennie glanced over her shoulder to find Louise from Sarah Cunningham's, happed up against the early morning cold.

'Louise!' she called, giving her a big hug. 'What a coincidence!'

'How are you?' she asked, helping Jennie to gather up the wraps of flowers and place them on a trolley.

'Fancy a cup of tea and a bacon roll? I can tell you all about it.'

The small cafc in the corner of the market, with its white plastic table and chairs, may not have looked much, but the bacon butty and brew they served was the best Jennie had tasted in a very long time.

'Nothing like an early morning to make things taste great,' said Louise.

'Can't beat it,' replied Jennie, through a mouthful of buttery roll, enjoying the salty goodness.

'I heard you got the Cavendish wedding.'

Jennie cast Louise a quizzical look, finishing her mouthful and wiping her lips of flour with a non-absorbent napkin. 'How do you know that?'

'George Arbuthnott was in. She mentioned it.'

'Makes sense,' said Jennie, knowing it wasn't beyond the realms of possibility that James or Fran would have told her.

'How did that come about?'

Sheepishly, Jennie told Louise about her dates with James.

'Go Jennie!' she said, raising her polystyrene cup in a congratulatory gesture.

'It's early days.'

'I'm pleased for you, for getting the wedding, I mean. Sarah is too. How many guests?'

'Four hundred.'

'Ooh-eee, that's a lot! Have you got some helpers?'

'I need to advertise, but I'm not sure where.'

'Try Gumtree. You can always pick up ad hoc workers there.'

Jennie made a mental note to follow up on the suggestion. 'I also need to meet Henrik. Do you think Sarah would mind if I arranged to meet him when he's next at the shop?'

'Of course not! Come by on Friday. And you're sure you're covered financially? It's a big ask to put an event together for four hundred.'

'The money from the house with Stephen is due, and once I've got that, I'm sorted,' said Jennie, though she wasn't as certain as she sounded. She knew, after the money hadn't arrived yesterday, the earliest it could get to her was Monday. If it wasn't in by then, she was going to have to threaten Stephen with legal action, something she really didn't want to have to do.

'I wish I could offer to help but—'

'You're busy enough, Louise. No, this is my gig. I'll manage.'

'Like before though, if there's anything I can do to help, *anything*, be sure to give me a call.'

*

'Look at this!' said Mary, her hands spread wide at the sight of all the flowers in the dining area of the flat. With Kat heading out for the afternoon, Jennie didn't feel too bad that the place was a complete pigsty of flowers already.

'Pretty good, huh?' said Jennie, running her fingers over the tops of the blooms.

Mary whistled, impressed at the display. 'You got all this on the church budget?'

'With money to spare!'

'They're just like the flowers we have back home.'

'I thought so,' smiled Jennie, tinkled pink that Mary was happy with her choices. 'Shall we start with the piece for the altar? I think we've enough flowers for one large and two small arrangements.'

'Girl, we've enough to deck out all of heaven,' laughed Mary, sitting down at the dining room table where Jennie had placed a green plastic tray filled with oasis that had been soaking overnight.

'I thought it might be nice to create a star shape; they fill up large spaces really well.'

Jennie picked up handfuls of foliage to cover the oasis and create the basic shape of the arrangement. It wasn't something she'd usually do, she shied away from geometric shapes, preferring instead to create more natural arrangements but, from the images she'd found online, she thought it might be something that Mary would be familiar with and appreciate.

Mary rolled up the sleeves of her patterned sweater. 'How do we do it?'

Spreading the foliage out on the table Jennie began selecting the larger pieces.

'Start with these bigger leaves and position them in the oasis in a basic five-point star shape.' She demonstrated by doing three of the points and then had Mary copy what she'd done with the other two.

'You just shove it in?'

'Sure, they're just leaves in oasis; we're not operating on anyone.'

Mary took a stem and stabbed it into the arrangement.

'That's it,' said Jennie encouragingly. 'Maybe not quite so hard, we don't want to break the oasis.'

Mary inserted another leaf a little less aggressively.

'Better,' said Jennie, and went on to show Mary how to build up the design until all the oasis was covered and they had a solid star shape made out of greenery.

Jennie stepped back to view what they'd done so far. 'It's good,' she said, pleased with the shape. 'Now we need to put the flowers in, let's start with the biggest.'

'Jennie?' said Kat, coming into the dining area where she started lifting items and putting them back down again. 'Have you seen my compact mirror?'

'Your grandmother's?'

'Yes, the black one with the rose inlay.' Kat lifted flower buckets and oasis bases searchingly.

'Can't say I have,' she replied, clocking the fact that Kat's jaw was locked tight. 'The table was clear before I brought the flowers in, so I don't think it's in here.'

'Right,' said Kat, distracted by her ringing phone, and doing one final rummage of the table before answering.

With Kat on the phone, Jennie and Mary positioned the pink roses and red anthuriums, with their huge white stamens. They started in the middle and worked out, the flowers decreasing in size towards the points of the star.

'Maybe this is what I should be doing after my retirement,' laughed Mary, when Jennie complimented her on the work she'd done.

'Is it coming soon?'

Mary made a light clicking sound with her tongue and shook her head. 'This summer will be my last at the hospital.'

'How long have you been a nurse?' asked Jennie, taking chrysanthemums and smaller rose heads from the buckets to fill in the gaps in the display.

'Since before I married.'

Jennie cut the stems to size. 'It never occurred to me that you're married, even with your boys.'

'*Was*. That ship sailed a long time ago,' said Mary, watching what Jennie was doing. Somehow it didn't surprise Jennie that Mary was divorced; she had an air of independence about her that suggested she wasn't someone who needed a man in her life.

'I'm sorry to hear that.'

'I wasn't!' Mary laughed, taking the cut flowers and positioning them where Jennie indicated. 'Faithful wasn't a concept my husband was familiar with.'

'Ah,' replied Jennie, watching Mary's face for any signs of bitterness but there weren't any.

'Faithful wasn't a concept he was familiar with several times over.'

'Jeez,' said Jennie, repositioning stray leaves. 'How long were you married?'

Mary stepped away from the arrangement, allowing Jennie to do the final tweaks. 'Long enough to have two boys, and for my husband to know better.'

'He left you with two young kids?'

'*I* left *him* and took the boys with me to England. I wanted a fresh start; I knew if I worked here as a nurse, we could have a good life.'

'Did you move into the tower straight away?'

'Nuh-uh. The first year we lived with an auntie, all three of us in one small bedroom. I never forget the day we moved into the tower, or the look on my boys' faces when they saw their rooms for the first time. They thought all their Christmases had come at once,' she smiled widely at the memory. 'That was over thirty years ago.'

It occurred to Jennie that Mary had more of an insight into Zaynab's situation than she'd realised. 'It must have been hard, moving to a new country, and working and looking after the kids on your own.'

'It was easier than if my husband had been with us. When he was with me, it was like having another four kids!'

'And now they're grown?'

'Mmm-hmm. With kids of their own.'

Jennie stretched out her back, which was beginning to pinch. 'Do they live nearby?'

'David's back in Lagos with his three children, but Izaiah is here.'

'Do you seem him often?'

'Not often enough.' Mary watched Jennie spray the foliage with leaf shine. 'The grandbabies are thirteen and eleven; they have lives of their own. If I'm lucky I see them once a month at church, and on holidays.'

'But work keeps you busy?'

'And church. But I can't lie, I don't like the idea of retirement.'

'Well, maybe you have a second career in floristry ahead of you,' said Jennie, picking up the arrangement and standing back for Mary to admire it. 'Looks pretty great, no?'

'It sure does,' said Mary, nodding contentedly and smiling broadly. 'It's a little piece of Nigeria, right here in London.'

As the two women admired their work, Kat came back from her phone call, wearing an even tenser expression.

'What's up?' asked Jennie.

'That was Lauren. She said she thinks she saw it on the kitchen table when she was round.'

Jennie sensed from Kat's tone that she was unimpressed that this was the first she'd heard of Lauren's visit almost a week ago.

'I can't believe I forgot to tell you she came by.'

'Nor can I,' muttered Kat in the kitchen, where she was searching every inch of the surfaces.

'It'll turn up,' said Mary, trying to ease the tension. 'These things always do.'

'But not when you need them, given that I need it now,' she said, and left the room, moments later slamming the front door behind her.

'What was that about?' asked Mary.

'I'm not sure,' said Jennie, trying not to dwell on the matter but failing. She hated upsetting anyone, but particularly someone who'd been so generous towards her. 'Why don't you try replicating what we've done with the big piece on the smaller ones?'

'Are you serious!' said Mary, her hands on her hips.

'Sure!' laughed Jennie. 'They're only flowers. If you mess up, we can redo it; nobody dies.'

'If you say so,' chuckled Mary, reaching into a bucket of water for another piece of oasis. 'Have you any more dates planned with that doctor?'

An involuntary smile spread across Jennie's face. 'We're going out tomorrow.'

'Looks like someone's pretty happy about that.'

'I'm sure it will come to nothing.' Jennie didn't want to get Mary's, or her own hopes up. 'But it is good to have something fun to look forward to. He's a really nice guy.'

'And wealthy!'

'Which may be a problem,' said Jennie, who still worried that their backgrounds might be too different to make a go of things, even if they were getting along great.

Mary raised her eyebrows at Jennie as if she were talking nonsense.

'Prisha told me a couple of days ago that the bedrock of her marriage is their common background, their understanding of where each other came from. James and I would never have that, our backgrounds are completely different.' Jennie felt ridiculous mentioning it when they'd only been out on a couple of dates. She knew she was jumping the gun, but there was something about him that had really got under her skin, and she found it impossible not to think about him.

'My husband and I grew up in the same neighbourhood, went to the same school – look how that turned out.'

'Still,' said Jennie, taking some comfort from Mary. 'Having similar roots probably does help.'

'What helps is having the desire to make it work, to enjoy the same things; without those, you have nothing.'

'Don't you ever wish you had someone in your life?' asked Jennie, hoping she wasn't being too personal.

'I'm too old for a man,' she dismissed, checking a message on her phone, which she read with a suck of her teeth.

'What's going on?'

'It's a message from Prisha,' said Mary seriously.

'What's wrong?' Jennie immediately thought of baby Mohammed.

Mary looked up from her phone, a look of disbelief on her face. 'It's just been confirmed that Zaynab's husband is dead.'

*

Prisha had been at Zaynab's when the news came through, and was now pacing the living room with Mohammed on her shoulder, circling his back with her hand, trying to wind him. Seeing him there, so helpless, Jennie was hit hard by the cruelty of how he would never know his father.

'Where's Zaynab?' she asked quietly.

'In the bedroom.'

'Should we go to her?'

Prisha shrugged gently, her brow etched with worry.

'I'll go,' said Mary.

A wave of gratitude passed over Jennie that Mary had offered. She knew she couldn't really understand what Zaynab was going through: neither the loss of a husband nor what it was to be without language or possessions in a strange country. Only Mary had any sense of how it felt to be alone in a new country with a child, and how to comfort the bereaved.

From the bedroom came the sound of Mary greeting Zaynab, a scant few words in an uncharacteristically muted voice. And after that there was little sound at all. Jennie only heard the gentle rubbing of Prisha's hand on Mohammed's back, and distant sirens from the city below. She wished that Zaynab would wail as loud as her lungs would allow, louder than little Mohammed searching for milk in the dead of night, anything other than the present, numb silence that filled the flat.

'Do you know where Kat is?' asked Prisha. 'We need her here to communicate with Zaynab.'

'She's still out; her phone's probably off,' said Jennie, feeling utterly helpless. 'I've sent a message and left a voicemail; she'll come as soon as she can.'

It was less than an hour before Kat arrived, her cheeks flushed from running between the tube and home. On her arrival she, Prisha and Jennie all went into Zaynab's room.

'Zaynab,' Kat said, crouching down beside her bed, where Zaynab lay in a foetal position. Kat laid a hand on hers.

'Zaynab,' said Kat, again, her voice low. 'Mohammed?'

Zaynab's eyes, hollow and afraid, met Kat's. She shook her head and slowly let out a sound, ancient and low. Her head slumped to her chest. Kat waved the others away, clutched Zaynab's hands, and waited.

Prisha walked the hall with Mohammed; Mary made tea in the kitchen; Jennie stared out of the window, uncertain what to do.

By the time Zaynab was calm, the tea had turned cold and Mohammed was asleep; outside the sun was lower. She and Kat entered the living room, where all four women gathered around her on the sofa.

Taking out her phone, Kat showed Zaynab a map, she pointed to England and then to Syria. 'You go?'

Zaynab shook her head. 'No safe.'

This time Kat pointed to Syria and then to England. 'Mohammed here?' she said, suggesting Mohammed's body be brought here.

Again, Zaynab shook her head. 'No money.'

Kat looked to Jennie who was sitting on the arm of the sofa and said, 'If nothing else, we should do a service for him here.'

'I agree,' said Mary, bringing everyone a fresh cup of tea.

'Me too,' said Prisha.

Zaynab looked to Kat for translation.

'We,' said Kat, indicating to everyone then pausing, searching for the right words from the smattering of Arabic she'd picked up from her travels and pupils over the years. '*Janazat* for Mohammed. Here. *Janazat* – a funeral.'

'*Janazat? Huna?*' Zaynab asked weakly.

'Yes. *Janazat huna.*'

The faintest smile formed on Zaynab's lips, enough for Jennie to know that even in the depth of her despair she was still able to see a ray of light.

'Thank you,' she said, gripping both Kat's hands and managing to acknowledge Mary, Prisha and Jennie too.

'It will be our privilege,' said Prisha, placing her arm around Zaynab. 'I'll do the catering.'

Kat indicated to Zaynab that Prisha would prepare food.

'And I'll conduct the service,' said Mary. 'If you'd like.'

Kat pointed at Mary and said, 'Imam?'

The relief from everyone in the room when Zaynab managed a laugh at the suggestion was palpable.

'Yes,' she said, wiping away a tear. 'Thank you.'

'And I'll do the flowers,' said Jennie, pointing to a small arrangement on the windowsill.

'Thank you,' Zaynab said, again.

'You're welcome,' said Jennie, placing her hand on Prisha's shoulder, completing the circle of women.

18

'It puts my worries into perspective,' said James, after Jennie had relayed yesterday's events to him.

'It's unimaginable,' she said, the contrast between her situation and Zaynab's especially sharp as she strolled lazily down a gravel path topped with crushed shells in the small kitchen garden at Kew. Jennie thought it sweet that James was quietly showing her the beautiful green spaces of London, even though she'd never once mentioned her desire to see them, and this one was particularly delightful. 'It makes me appreciate just how important my own family and friendships are.'

James ran his hand over beans tangled around canes in one of the four ordered growing beds. 'I could learn from that.'

'How do you mean?'

'George is driving me mad,' he sighed. 'It's not her fault; she isn't coping, and needs someone to lean on, but I haven't been as patient with her as I could have.

'Sorry to hear that,' said Jennie, even though she felt a small surge of jealousy that George should be commanding so much of James' attention, even it was only platonically.

'I should have seen it coming. She comes across as uber-confident but she's really the exact opposite. Fran getting married, and her turning thirty, it's really knocked her off course.'

'She'll get through it, with a little help from her friends.'

'I hope so,' said James, locking eyes with Jennie, whose cheeks reddened at the intensity of his gaze. Despite their first kiss, there was still a part of her that felt entirely naked every time he looked at her.

'Still, it sounds really stressful, bearing the brunt of it, especially with your exams coming up,' she said.

'Tell me about it. Until they're over, I can think of little else,' he said, but a longing glance told Jennie that she was occupying his mind too. 'But enough about me, what about you?'

Jennie wanted to tell James everything about Stephen and her very real worry that he was deliberately withholding the money but, not wanting to give him reason to worry about his sister's wedding, she held back. She thought also about telling him about the tension with Kat but, unsure what was going on, she left that too. 'I picked up a few extra flower gigs. With a bit of luck, it won't be too long until the business is really up and running.'

'That's great news,' beamed James.

'Thank you,' she said, loving his enthusiasm. He had a childlike quality, a real lack of inhibition, finding joy in the smallest things, that amused and delighted her. She couldn't get enough of how his eyes shone with happiness, and she found herself wondering how they might look next to her pillow at night.

'I really admire you following your dreams. Working with flowers must bring you so much pleasure.'

'It's not a bad way to earn a living,' she said, thinking about just how many people's lives she'd brought a little bit of joy to since she began over ten years ago.

James paused to admire the full layout of the garden, from the rhubarb, and strawberry sets, to the potato patch, and the brilliant pink of the chard. 'One day, I'd love to create something like this at my grandmother's home. I love the sense of history and continuity in kitchen gardens, it's so easy to imagine someone a hundred years ago doing exactly the same thing as we do today – planting the seed, tending to the seedling, watching it grow and ultimately being rewarded by its yield.'

'I know what you mean,' she said, sitting on a little bench amongst the apple trees growing against the wall. She was touched by his words, wondering how she managed to spend so many years with a man who didn't share or even understand her passion. 'I wish I had the opportunity to do something similar, but our flat is one of the few without a balcony.'

'You could get an allotment.'

'I guess I could,' she said, giving the idea some thought. 'But the thing I love most is roses. I'm a sucker for a rose garden. The walled garden on the estate back home is bursting with rambling roses, they're overgrown and in urgent need of some TLC but still, it's beyond perfect. The scent in the summer is thrilling beyond words.'

'Not as thrilling I bet as picking out grubs from cabbage plants!'

'I can see the thrill in that too!' she laughed.

They sat quietly together, gazing out over the ordered little garden with the cabbage butterflies flitting this way and that, and a pair of fat wood pigeons perched on the roof of the old potting shed. James reached out and held Jennie's hand, his fingers curled softly over hers. She imagined his fingers amongst the soil, carefully tending to his plants, and then she found her mind drifting into imagining them unbuttoning her blouse, then slipping beneath the fabric.

When she woke from her daydream, she found James's eyes locked on her, soft and clearly wanting. He moved towards her and, slowly but urgently, pressed his lips to hers.

'I've got the place to myself,' said James, shutting the heavy front door in a way that suggested to Jennie that he had no intention of opening it to the world again anytime soon. 'With the exception of Buckley, that is.' Buckley jumped up to greet James, who tussled him behind the ears and gave his sides a good rub.

'Where is everyone?' she asked, following James to the kitchen.

'My folks work abroad, and Fran's on her hen weekend.'

'Where did she go?'

'Some farm retreat, I think. She's probably talking to cows as we speak,' said James, his head in the fridge.

'That's so Fran,' laughed Jennie. Her own experience of hen dos, pre-Stephen, was more a night out in Birmingham city centre or day trip to Cardiff, resulting in someone wearing a tutu on their head and vomiting on a station platform.

'Fancy a beer? Or I could make some Pimm's.'

'Pimm's would be great,' she said, sitting at the table and enjoying seeing James move easily around the kitchen, filling the jug with ice, grabbing Pimm's from the old larder, and topping it with lemonade. His muscles flexed as he chopped the fruit and squeezed an orange to finish.

'*Pour toi, ma chérie*,' he said, pouring her a glass and garnishing the drink with a straw and a sprig of mint.

'Delicious,' she said, as she sipped the drink, and thought of something else in the room that was delicious.

'Let's take it outside to the garden.'

As he took her hand, a rush of endorphins shot round Jennie's body, and her skin shivered in delight, his touch still new and invigorating.

'This is beautiful,' she said, grey grasses tickling her feet and the scent of lavender filling her senses. Buckley followed at James's heel.

'I had fun designing it.'

'*You* did this?' she asked, stopping in her tracks.

'Sure.'

'It's stunning,' she said, imagining him with his hands in the dirt potting grasses and flowers for his family and friends to enjoy.

In the far corner of the garden, hidden under leafy sycamores, James showed Jennie to a circular, canopied rattan daybed. She climbed on, James holding her drink as she did so.

'It's enormous!'

'Pretty great, huh?' he said, handing her the drinks and clambering on beside her. He wrapped his arm around her shoulder and pulled her close, Buckley nuzzling in next to them.

'I can't believe you have a bed in the garden,' she said, trying to imagine something similar back home in her parents' tiny garden. The most they could manage was a small swing seat.

James smiled mischievously, leaving Jennie under no misapprehension as to what was on his mind.

Sipping more of her cocktail for courage, Jennie placed a leg just above James's knees. Reaching down, he pulled it a little higher and rubbed her thigh as he drank his beer. She liked the way his lips caressed the bottle, and the way his Adam's apple was accentuated when he tilted his head back to drink. His cool lips moved from the bottle to Jennie's mouth, and she savoured the taste of beer and lime, almost spilling her drink as the intensity of his kiss rose.

'Let me take your drink,' he said, placing both glasses on the ground before crawling back towards her. He began exploring her neck and collarbones – an erogenous zone Stephen had failed to find in all their dutiful exploits – kissing, nibbling and tasting every inch of her. Jennie bit her lip, and looked up into the early summer sky, a brilliant blue with only the slightest wisps of white cloud.

As he undid the buttons of her blouse, she thanked her lucky stars that she'd chosen a pretty pink bra that morning with, luckily, a front clip. James placed a finger beneath it, released it, admired her small breasts and slowly, teasingly placed his mouth around a nipple.

Kneeling back, he moved slowly down from Jennie's chest onto her stomach, undoing her skirt and slipping it off.

'Don't tease,' she whispered, as he ran a finger round the top of her underwear.

Just as she thought he was about to remove her knickers, James held up a finger to pause proceedings. Jennie watched, wondering what he was going to do. First, he dismissed Buckley, the dog's pitiful expression causing Jennie to giggle, and second, he turned away, his V-shaped back to Jennie, and drew the curtains of the daybed, making it into a private Bedouin tent.

'Do you want to go further?' he whispered, his hands on the top button of his trousers.

Jennie nodded, biting her bottom lip, now certain in the knowledge that instinctive, animal magnetism really did exist after all.

19

Zaynab's kitchen was rich in the aroma of slow-cooked lamb, and rose-infused rice pudding, as the women prepared for Mohammed's service. Jennie was soaking oasis in buckets, and Prisha was busy sealing Tupperware boxes of falafel and humous.

'How was your date?' whispered Mary, stirring rice on the stove.

'We slept together!' Jennie replied excitedly, who still hadn't come down from Sunday. For the last forty-eight hours they'd been locked in a series of romantic text messages, which Jennie couldn't help reading over and over again. And they'd already arranged to meet on Friday at his grandmother's place – where he was keen to show Jennie the garden.

'Who slept together?' asked Kat, popping in for some kitchen roll.

'I did, with James,' she whispered, knowing it wasn't exactly appropriate to be discussing it on the morning of Zaynab's husband's funeral ceremony, but unable to resist.

'Oh,' said Kat, her disinterest written all over her face.

'What's with her?' asked Mary, after Kat had gone back to the lounge.

Jennie had been wondering the same thing. Since the incident with the missing compact, which still hadn't turned up, it had been like living with a bear with a sore head.

'She's focused on Zaynab,' said Jennie, not absolutely convinced it was the reason for Kat's surliness. She worried increasingly it had something to do with her, that perhaps Kat was regretting offering her a home and workplace, or wishing she hadn't been so relaxed about the rent.

'We should be focusing on Zaynab too,' said Prisha, standing back to admire her mountain of Tupperware – enough to feed a small nation.

Pushing aside her worries, Jennie took the base of the wreath to the lounge and laid it on the floor next to the bundles of jasmine, orchids and cabbage flowers she'd bought from the market that morning. The day before, Jennie, Kat and Zaynab had talked about the flowers of Syria. From the limited vocabulary Zaynab had, Jennie understood that scent was as important as colour, and she hoped the flowers she'd chosen might evoke memories of Mohammed, and of Syria itself.

'Beautiful,' said Zaynab, with a light smile, sitting next to Jennie on the floor. 'I,' she said, tapping her breastbone, 'help?'

'Of course,' said Jennie, full of enthusiasm. When Zaynab looked confused Jennie simplified it to a vehement, 'Yes!' and reached for the dark-leaved ruscus.

'Strip the bottom leaves like this,' she said, demonstrating how to remove the leaves with her hand. 'Then cut to size.'

Between them Zaynab and Jennie covered the wreath in greenery in no time. As they worked, Prisha attended to baby Mohammed, Mary to elements of her service, and Kat helped Jennie interpret when necessary.

'How did you meet Mohammed?' Jennie asked Zaynab, with Kat's help.

'My mother and father.' Zaynab spoke slowly and clearly.

'They introduced you?'

'Yes.'

Kat explained that it had been an arranged marriage, only two years ago, and that Zaynab fled Syria eighteen months later when she and Mohammed discovered she was pregnant. Mohammed was meant to follow soon after but never did, the conflict preventing him from doing so, and in the end was killed, his exact cause of death unknown.

Eventually, Zaynab was housed in the tower by the local authority, after being granted leave to remain.

'How old are you?' asked Jennie, cutting the thick stems of the cabbage flowers and showing Zaynab where best to place them in the wreath.

'Twenty-one.' She looked to Kat to confirm she had the correct number.

'That's young,' said Jennie, realising that she must have married at nineteen.

'And you?'

'Thirty.'

'Old!' said Zaynab with a light giggle, which she quickly swallowed back.

Jennie nodded; twenty-one felt like an eternity ago. When she was that age, she was single, living at home, and working for Dorothy.

'You marry?'

'No!' laughed Jennie.

'Why?'

Zaynab's ability to ask such a direct question with only the simplest of language caught Jennie off guard.

'It's a long story,' said Jennie humbly, acutely aware of how privileged she was to be able to leave a man at the altar because he didn't support her career.

'You have love soon,' said Zaynab, a spark of pride in her eyes at her four-word sentence.

'I hope so,' said Jennie, glancing at Prisha, holding Mohammed. Babies hadn't made it on to Jennie's list of 'life goals', but even she could see the precious bond between Zaynab and her baby. It was as if, through baby Mohammed, the man Zaynab loved was still alive.

Continuing quietly, Jennie showed Zaynab how to cut the orchid stems in such a way that three smaller stems could be created from one longer piece.

'Position them around the cabbage flowers and then use the smaller jasmine to fill in the gaps,' she explained.

Quietly the two women worked together, methodically creating a beautiful, scented tribute to Mohammed. When they had finished and were satisfied with their work, Prisha came in from the kitchen where somehow, whilst tending to the baby, she'd also managed to bake some orange blossom and honey biscuits.

'Who wants cookies?' she asked.

'Yes, please,' said Zaynab, taking one from the plate. 'Home,' she said, inhaling the familiar scent, her eyes welling with tears.

*

'I know having a water fountain made for a funeral is tradition in Syria, but it was a bit beyond my means,' said Mary, standing next to the Boy and Frog statue

213

in the Begonia Garden in Regent's Park. 'I hope the setting is appropriate – I thought it would be a nice place for Zaynab and baby Mohammed to visit as he grows.'

Jennie liked the formal layout of the garden, which felt respectful, but which was also complimented by cheerful planting; the playful statue made it an ideal spot for both reflection and fun.

'Mohammed like,' said Zaynab approvingly, clothed in Syria's customary black.

'It's a good choice,' said Kat, drinking in the calm beauty of the place.

'Shall we gather round the fountain?' asked Jennie.

With everyone assembled and Mohammed asleep in his buggy, Mary began.

'To open the service, I ask Kat to come forward and read the first verse of the Koran.'

Kat stood in front of the statue and, Mary having prepared her, read aloud in Arabic the first verse of the Koran. Jennie didn't understand the words, but she did understand the power they had over Zaynab, whose frame weakened and strength dissolved. She began to sob uncontrollably, releasing cries of anguish far stronger than anything Jennie had heard from her so far. Prisha and Jennie supported her by the elbows as her grief flowed.

'And so we pray for Mohammed's soul to rest in peace,' said Mary, taking the framed picture of Mohammed from her bag and placing it by the statue. Zaynab wailed disconsolately. 'We see in Mohammed's child something of who Mohammed was. We will remember him through his son. And together we vow to support Zaynab and her baby, as Mohammed would have done.'

'Yes,' said Prisha solemnly.

'Jennie, would you come forward with Zaynab and lay the wreath?'

Jennie took Zaynab's hand and led her towards the statue. Together they bent down and placed the wreath next to Mohammed's photograph. Zaynab placed her hands on the ground and her face against the photo as if it might pull her in and take her back to her husband and home.

Stepping back, Jennie linked arms with Kat and Prisha, allowing Zaynab a moment of solitude. It was only when baby Mohammed cried himself awake that Zaynab returned to the group, her son the only thing that could tear her away from that final moment with her husband. She scooped him up and held him tight against her chest. Jennie could almost see the bond of love flow between mother and child.

'I have myrtle,' said Jennie softly, breaking the silence and handing it to Zaynab, knowing myrtle symbolised love and courage.

'It is love.'

Zaynab laid it by Mohammed's picture, kissed two fingers and pressed them against the photo. As her hand lingered in those final moments, baby Mohammed began attempting to suckle at her chest. With a long accepting sigh, Zaynab nodded pragmatically, removed her hand from her husband's image and smiled at her son. In that gesture, Jennie saw the vacuum of loss being filled by love. Baby Mohammed was her flicker of light at the end of a very dark tunnel.

With the short service over, the five women and baby Mohammed sat in the gardens and picnicked on the food Prisha had prepared. Via Kat's phone they played traditional Arada music – joyous, clamorous hand drums and chimes – that reverberated round the enclosed space. After a while Zaynab smiled tentatively, taking in the surroundings, her child, the food, her friends and the music. With a little thought she reached out her hands, taking hold of Kat and Prisha's arms, and looking at Jennie and Mary said slowly, importantly,

'Thank you, my friends.'

*

'I think I'll go to bed,' said Kat, after she and Jennie had returned from Zaynab's, where all five women had spent time after the service. It had turned into a beautifully warm, late spring afternoon, and they'd lingered in the park far longer than planned. By the time they arrived back at the tower it was almost six o'clock. Prisha warmed up leftovers whilst Mary bathed Mohammed; Kat and Zaynab watched *The Simpsons* as Jennie washed up. By the time Mohammed was settled and they'd eaten and cleared dinner it was getting late, and whilst everyone was tired nobody wanted to leave Zaynab. In the end, Mary and Prisha left together, ambling up the stairs. Kat and Jennie stayed only a little longer, and left after seeing Zaynab to bed.

'Sleep well,' said Jennie to Kat, aware that the emotions of the last four days had weighed most heavily on Kat, but sensing something else was troubling her, too. It didn't surprise Jennie at all that Kat was irritable and tense. On top of her break-up with Lauren, and work, she was now spending most of her free time with Zaynab, getting home late and climbing straight into bed. By the time Jennie woke, Kat was inevitably at Zaynab's again, trying to support her in her grief with little common language between them. Even with all Kat's help, and the women rallying round as best they could, it was clear Zaynab needed more emotional and practical support.

With the flat quiet, Jennie made herself some warm milk with cardamom and snuggled into the corner of the sofa with her phone. The past few days had been so overwhelming that Jennie had neglected the admin of her life.

Opening her inbox, she found several replies to the Gumtree advert she'd placed on Saturday lunchtime looking for a florist's assistant. There were a couple of responses from people with no experience – to those Jennie replied with a generic email saying that they 'lack the necessary experience but thank you for the interest'. There were however three emails that were promising: one from a girl named Nell, who'd just arrived from Australia and was looking for cash-in-hand work – she'd worked for a season in a florist in Adelaide before setting off on her gap year; and another from someone called Andy, who didn't have any formal experience, but he'd sent photos of the arrangements he'd learnt to do via online tutorials, which looked technically strong. The last email was from Linda, an older woman who'd worked as a florist years ago and was looking to build up her experience again before applying for full-time jobs. Jennie sent all three the details of the wedding, what they'd be required to do, and how much she could pay them. She pressed send and crossed her fingers, hoping that at least two of them would get back to her.

That done Jennie scrolled through her messages, indulging in rereading the texts she and James had exchanged over the past few days. As she was reading them a text pinged in from Henrik.

Are we still on for Friday?

After bumping into Louise at the flower market, Jennie had messaged Henrik to arrange their meeting outside Sarah Cunningham's. They'd already confirmed the appointment for Friday morning. It struck Jennie as strange that he should be reconfirming.

She momentarily left Henrik's text and focused on James's instead. After a day of witnessing just how short life can be and how happiness should be seized, she quickly wrote him another.

Hope your day's been good. Really looking forward to seeing you. J xxxxx

Then she turned her attention back to Henrik, writing simply:

See you Friday!

Jennie's heart skipped a beat when her phoned pinged almost immediately with a reply from James, but it soon plummeted when she discovered the contents of the message.

Really sorry, going to have to cancel. Will get back to you ASAP.

Totally understand, she replied, though she wasn't sure she did, and the disappointment of not having the opportunity to see his grandmother's garden stung. She guessed he had to work or study, but it was unlike him not to explain, or to be so unemotional in response to a warm text. After the passion of Sunday, it cut deep, and she prayed she hadn't misread his signals. *Speak soon. J xx*

When her phone beeped again, she felt the dull ache of disappointment when she discovered the text was from Henrik not James.

Look forward to seeing you. X

Jennie reread the text, surprised by the kiss but too gutted at her date with James being cancelled to give it much thought.

20

Kat stood in the doorway of the bathroom, where Jennie was brushing her teeth before bed. 'Could you show me how to make a posy?' she asked.

'Sure. When?' asked Jennie, through a mouth of foamy toothpaste.

'Now?'

Jennie spat into the sink and wiped her mouth with her flannel.

'Like now, now?'

'If you don't mind.'

In truth Jennie had been looking forward to going to bed early before a busy day tomorrow when she had to meet Henrik and hold interviews for the assistant position. But, not wanting to disappoint or upset Kat, and, given they'd hardly spent any time together recently, she agreed.

'I don't have much to demonstrate with,' she said, plodding about the dining area in her Garfield and Odie slippers. She gathered some flowers from the bucket of leftovers from Mary and Zaynab's posies.

Kat took a seat at the table.

'Why the sudden interest in flower arranging?' asked Jennie, joining her.

'I thought it would be nice to make one for my mum's birthday tomorrow. Is it hard to do?'

'Not at all,' said Jennie, thinking it sweet that Kat should want to make something handmade for her mum. 'Choose your main flower for the centre of the posy, something reasonably large.'

Kat selected a cabbage flower.

'Then you need to frame that with foliage.'

Jennie demonstrated how to place the stems at angles to the centre flower, and how to turn the flowers before adding another.

'It's tricky,' laughed Kat.

'You'll soon get the knack,' she said, watching as Kat struggled with the grip and intricacy of adding flowers.

'How's that?'

'It's nice, but the height's a bit uneven. Pull on the bottom of the stems to help reposition the heads.'

By pulling gently at the base of the posy, Jennie quickly turned Kat's unpolished arrangement into something much more professional.

'What do I do next?'

'Just keep adding flower, foliage, flower until you've reached the size you want.'

Jennie continued to watch Kat as she tried to manage the flowers, but her hands wouldn't coordinate easily, and her elbows seemed always to be pointing at uncomfortable angles.

'You're getting the hang of it,' she encouraged, trying not to think of bed and the details of Fran's wedding order. She'd made list after list of the types and quantities of flowers she would need but still she was worried that she'd forgotten something, or that she wouldn't get the order in on time. And the worry of when the funds would arrive hung over her; Stephen still hadn't stumped up the cash.

'It's much harder than it looks.'

'I'd forgotten,' said Jennie, trying to remember how long it had taken her to get the hang of hand-ties and posies. She recalled Dorothy loitering over her for months before she was entrusted to create a hand-tie without supervision, and it must have been over a year before she was allowed to make wreaths on her own.

'I certainly won't be swapping TEFL for floristry.'

'I wouldn't have the patience for teaching English. I've seen how patient you are with Zaynab. At least I can throw flowers in the bin when they don't do what I want them to do.'

'I've definitely had students I'd like to throw away; it's like bashing your head against a brick wall some days.'

'I can imagine,' said Jennie as her phone beeped. She checked it immediately, hoping it might be from James, but it was only from her mum.

'Are you waiting for something important?'

'Not really,' said Jennie, which wasn't quite the truth. Since texting James two days ago she'd been like a cat on a hot tin roof every time her phone had pinged, waiting to hear when she could see him again. And then there was the hope that Stephen would message to say he'd transferred the money.

Kat cocked her head at Jennie with raised eyebrows. 'Are you sure?'

'James had to cancel our date. I was kind of hoping that might be him, wanting to fix up another,' she said, embarrassed that she sounded like an anxious teenager, not wanting to admit that she'd been in knots about whether to call him or not, worried that she might appear too keen. And she hated that she'd slept with him when she had an inkling that there was someone else, somewhere in the background.

'I'm sure he's super busy.'

'Right. I'm probably just being paranoid,' said Jennie, knowing how time consuming his exam preparation must be, wondering if actually her imagination was just getting the better of her.

'Maybe a bit,' said Kat, gripping the flowers so tightly that her knuckles were white. 'I'm sure there's a perfectly good reason why he hasn't been in touch.'

'Absolutely,' agreed Jennie, aware that Kat's patience was waning, and her mood slipping. 'I was thinking, there's a loan that Zaynab could apply for that would enable her to pay for English classes, take some of the strain off you. I could give you the forms.'

'Sure, why not?' she said unreceptively, which wasn't like her at all. If there was one thing Jennie knew about Kat it was that she was always open to pragmatic suggestions.

'Is everything okay?'

Kat paused, her eyes fixed on the flowers. 'Not exactly . . .'

Jennie gave her time, watching the thought process pass over Kat's face, an internal debate as to whether to say something or not.

'I just can't help feeling that if . . .'

'What?' asked Jennie tentatively, not really wanting to hear the answer, feeling instinctively that it was something she had done.

Kat concentrated on the flowers, not looking at Jennie. 'If the flat weren't such a mess with flower stuff, I might not have lost my compact.'

Jennie looked around the kitchen; there were buckets and floristry paraphernalia littered everywhere.

'I'm sorry,' she said guiltily. 'I know it's a mess. I'll have a really big tidy up as soon as I'm back tomorrow, I promise!'

Kat inhaled and exhaled, slowly putting the posy on the table. The flowers collapsed. 'Thank you,' she said, making fleeting eye-contact with Jennie, who couldn't help but feel there was something else Kat wasn't saying.

'And just as soon as Stephen pulls his thumb out and sends me the money, I promise I'll pay you some rent, I know I promised you it two weeks ago now, it's just been out of my control.' The shameful situation that Stephen had created for Jennie made her furious. It was one thing for him to mess with her life, but another thing entirely when it interfered with those of her friends. She vowed to have it out with him as soon as she could.

'Honestly, it's not the rent,' said Kat in a way that suggested there *was* something else the matter, but for the life of her, Jennie had no idea what it could be.

*

Outside the tower, Jennie sat on a slab step staring up at the stars, listening to the sound of her mum's dial tone. As she waited, Omar left the tower for the night.

'Night, Omar,' she said.

'Goodnight,' he replied gently, clutching tightly to his rucksack. She watched him walk up the path, get on to his bike and cycle away, wondering where home was for him and who with.

'It's late, love,' her mum answered, sounding tired.

'It's not that late, not in the big city,' Jennie heard her dad say. She could tell by the soft acoustics that they were in bed.

'Is everything alright?' Irene asked.

'I've upset Kat.'

'How, love?'

'By not keeping the place tidy enough. She still can't find the compact that went missing recently. I feel dreadful.'

'I'm sure after a bit of a tidy-up she'll be fine.'

'I guess, but I'm worried there might be something more to it.'

'Like what?'

'I'm not sure,' said Jennie, picking blades of grass to the side of the slab step where she sat. 'Maybe it's just because she's tired, what with helping out Zaynab and dealing with Lauren but . . . I don't know.'

'Is Lauren still jealous of you being there?'

'I think so.'

'So that's probably it, love. She'll be pointing out all your bad points to turn her against you.'

'You think? I'm not certain.'

'That's because you're kind and not cynical.'

'Unlike your mum!' chirped her dad, which cheered Jennie for a moment.

'And you know in some ways, love, Kat may be feeling a bit jealous, too.'

'Of what?' asked Jennie.

'Of you running your own business, your talent.'

'Mum, my business is in its infancy, it's barely embryonic. And Kat's an experienced teacher, I doubt very much she's jealous of my floristry skills.'

'Plus, you've been dating a nice young doctor,' Irene went on, as if she hadn't heard Jennie, 'when Kat's stuck at home dealing with a paranoid ex-girlfriend.'

Jennie thought for a moment, gazing up at the stars, for once not comforted or reassured by her mother's take on things at all. 'I'm sure it's something I've done.'

'If you have then she has to be the one to say it. You can't force it out of her.'

'I guess,' she said, knowing her mother was right, but still finding it hard to let go. 'Have you had your appointment yet?'

'The letter from the hospital arrived yesterday. It's another six weeks before they can see me.'

Jennie heard her dad mutter, 'Bloody farce'.

'Now, tell me, when is that next date?' Irene continued, never one to focus on the negatives in life.

'I don't know,' she said, throwing the blades of grass into the night.

'He must be busy, love.'

'That's what Kat said. But I've been worrying our backgrounds are too different, maybe he's thinking that too,' she said, pushing aside the other thought that had been bothering her, that she'd disappointed him in bed, or that sex was all he'd really wanted in the first place and now that he'd got it, he wasn't interested.

'You and Stephen came from the same background – look how that turned out.'

'With me out of pocket,' chuckled Tony.

Jennie heard her dad groan, a sure sign her mum had just elbowed him to be quiet.

'Sorry, Dad.' Jennie still felt guilty about all the wedding deposits her dad had lost, and she wished again that she'd made the decision to call off the wedding sooner. And for all she planned to pay him back when Stephen had coughed up the money, she knew he wouldn't accept.

'It's alright, I'd rather be skint with you happy than have money to burn and you be miserable.'

'Give James time, love,' soothed her mum. 'You'll see. It'll all work out in the end.'

Jennie wasn't so sure. If her luck was anything to go by, it would be over before it had really begun.

21

Jennie waited for Kat to leave the flat before getting out of bed. She thought it might be easier for both of them if the next time they spoke Jennie had given the place a good spruce-up. Only when the front door banged closed and the flat was quiet did she venture out of her room.

Over breakfast she checked her bank account to see if the house funds had arrived. Panic set in when she saw she was overdrawn by ten pounds. She picked up her phone and called and called Stephen, her hands shaking, trying to steady her erratic breathing, but regardless of how many times she tried, he didn't pick up.

Just after ten, still no word from Stephen, but having tackled the buckets and binned the wilting flowers, Jennie left for a coffee shop in Baker Street where she'd agreed to meet Nell, Andy and Linda, individually, to discuss Fran's wedding. Jennie, never having interviewed anyone before, was nervous, probably more so than her candidates, particularly Nell, who arrived with the no-nonsense confidence that Jennie thought was innate in most twenty-something Aussies.

'Have you had experience of creating the pieces I outlined in the email?' she asked over coffee.

'I can do anything, just show me once and I'll be fine, mate,' said Nell. She said it with such conviction that Jennie didn't feel able to push the question of whether she'd *actually* had experience of making the arrangements or not.

Andy was quieter in his approach, apologising for his lack of experience but emphasising that this really was his passion, and he was desperate to get his first step on the ladder.

'Why are you so keen to work for me?' Jennie asked.

His answer was almost reverential, 'You worked for Sarah Cunningham!' Jennie could have hugged him.

Linda was much more solid. She had several years' experience, though it was some time ago, and was able to speak competently on everything Jennie asked her about. Linda, for Jennie, was a dead cert: someone she knew she could depend on to deliver anything she asked; she offered her the job then and there.

That left Andy and Nell for Jennie to choose between and, seeing something of herself in Andy, she opted for him. She was thankful that, when she called to tell Nell that she wouldn't be offering her the job, it went straight to answerphone.

After her interviews, Jennie walked through Regent's Park, past the lake, football pitches and zoo, and across the road to Primrose Hill where she'd arranged to meet Henrik in the flower truck outside Sarah Cunningham's.

'Jennie,' he said, standing at the top of the steps to the van, which gave him the appearance of a real-life giant. 'It's good to see you.'

'And you,' replied Jennie, ascending the stairs. It felt comforting to be back on the truck, amongst the endless wraps of fresh, vibrant flowers.

'So,' said Henrik in his thick Dutch accent, even more relaxed and open than usual. 'You have a big event of your own?'

'I do. A wedding.'

The sound of footsteps caused Jennie to turn, and she was surprised to find Fiona, Sarah's weekend help, joining them on the truck.

'Hi Jennie,' she beamed, her hair pushed back off her face with a fabric headband. 'Nice to see you.'

'And you,' replied Jennie, kissing her on both cheeks. 'Have you taken on extra hours?'

'Just some cover,' she said, in a way that they both knew meant 'filling in for you' although Fiona was kind enough not to say it. 'Whose wedding is it?'

'Fran Cavendish.'

'Oh, that's right, I remember hearing about that. Congratulations.'

'Thanks, Fiona, but I only really got the gig through knowing her brother.'

'You mean James?'

'Exactly.'

'My brother, Henry, knows James well. Heard he's dating Camilla Forsythe, you know her?'

Jennie felt her eyes prick with heat, and she stared hard at some early sweetpeas to prevent tears from forming. Swallowing, she cleared her throat and, knowing Fiona had made the comment innocently, said, 'I don't. I really don't know him all that well, he's more of an acquaintance,' she said, her words feeling closer to the truth than she wanted to accept.

She was pleased when Henrik took that moment to steer the conversation in another direction.

'What can I get for Sarah today?' he asked Fiona, putting his hands in the pockets of his short money apron.

Fiona presented her list to Henrik and as they gathered the stock, Jennie tried to compute the information Fiona had just given her, which apparently had come from James's best mate. *Was Camilla the girl James had said had 'caught my eye'?* she wondered. *Is it possible that since we slept together, less than a week ago, he's started seeing her, or that he was seeing Camilla even then? Was she the reason he cancelled our date?* Jennie felt her head might burst.

'That's everything,' said Henrik, placing a final wrap in the crate, before generating an invoice and helping Fiona off the truck with the flowers.

'Are you okay?' he asked, once they were alone.

'Absolutely,' said Jennie stoically, not wanting to appear unprofessional.

'You like this James?'

'No,' she scoffed, as if Henrik had said something plainly ridiculous.

'Good,' he replied, a slight glint in his eye, which Jennie thought strange in the circumstances. 'So, how can I help?'

'I need to set up an account,' she said, putting the oddly personal exchange down to a language or cultural barrier. 'Is that possible without a VAT number?'

'For you I can do anything!'

Flattered, Jennie talked through Fran's requirements, the dates involved, and the fact that Henrik would need to deliver to her home. And all the while, she prayed Stephen would send the money in time to settle up.

'Just make sure the online order is confirmed *one full week* before you need the flowers, if it isn't then we might not be able to provide what you need.'

'I understand, Henrik. Thank you. I owe you,' she said, scribbling 'one full week' in her notepad and underlining it several times.

'Not at all,' he said, sitting at his computer and processing the relevant paperwork.

'If there's anything I can do in return—'

Henrik paused and thought for a moment, then asked, 'Would you go out with me?'

Jennie, caught on the back foot, found herself blurting, 'Uh, sure!' Her mind immediately occupied with thoughts of James, and how prior to seeing Fiona she might have felt some loyalty towards him, but now she knew that he wasn't being exclusive, she figured she was free to date whomever she liked, too.

'I have an overnight stay in London a week on Tuesday. I could take you out for dinner, if you like.'

'Why not,' said Jennie, keen to show willing after Henrik had helped her so much, even if she wasn't interested in him in that way. 'Send me the details.'

'Great,' said Henrik, looking just like the cat who'd got the cream.

*

'Only me,' said Jennie, returning home after a couple of hours in the park where she'd created a schedule of work for the days leading up to Fran's wedding, and tried hard not to fret about Camilla.

She wasn't certain what sort of welcome to expect from Kat, if any, so what she found in the dining area took her completely by surprise. On the table was a lunch set for two, with a pink peony posy at the centre, a posy that had clearly, from its haphazard appearance, been created by Kat.

'I didn't realise you were having company,' she said, when Kat appeared in the kitchen doorway looking less overtly gothic than usual, having swapped her dark make-up for something more natural.

'It's just Lauren,' said Kat.

'Oh,' replied Jennie, surprised by this turn of events, and wondering why Kat had said the posy was for her mum. 'Are things back on with you guys?'

Kat shoved her hands in the pockets of her black skinny jeans and raised her shoulders uncertainly. 'I guess.'

'What do you guess, sweetie?' asked Lauren, appearing in the doorway and putting her hands on Kat's shoulders.

'That things are back on with us.'

'You could say that, though I'm not sure we were really off in the first place,' she said, running her hand over Kat's back.

Jennie thought that a strange thing to say given that the two of them had broken up and Lauren had moved out, but Kat didn't dispute it. Her body language was different around Lauren, more demure than Jennie was accustomed to, and she found herself thinking of how she'd been around Stephen. More constrained. Smaller.

Going to the kitchen, Kat fetched a bottle of prosecco. 'Thanks for doing a tidy-up.'

'No problem. I feel bad I let the place get a little out of hand.'

'A little?' said Lauren scathingly, as Kat attempted to open the wine.

'It's no problem,' Kat reassured Jennie.

'Sweetie,' said Lauren patronisingly, taking the bottle from Kat and opening it for her. 'It's okay to be upset with Jennie.'

'But I'm not upset,' replied Kat, her brow furrowing.

One of Lauren's eyebrows raised up as she cocked her head at Kat.

'Well maybe I was, a little,' said Kat, glancing apologetically at Jennie. 'But it's all sorted now.'

Lauren cleared her throat. 'Even though the compact is still missing?'

There was something in Lauren's tone that Jennie found troubling, and she realised then that Lauren suspected Jennie of having taken it. And that Lauren must have put the thought into Kat's mind, which explained the heavy atmosphere between them.

'You don't think I took it, do you?' asked Jennie.

'Of course not,' said Kat quickly.

'Kat,' said Lauren reproachfully.

Kat inhaled slowly as if harnessing courage. 'I thought in all the mess it might be possible that it had been swept into a bucket, that's all.'

Jennie worried that Kat was glossing over the truth, that she actually believed Jennie had stolen it. Her heart sank that Kat, at best, thought Jennie could be so careless as to throw out something that was clearly precious to her, and at worst, had been manipulated into believing Jennie was a liar and a thief.

'I saw it only recently, when Lauren was last here,' she said, wondering how she could ever persuade Kat to believe her.

'But Kat hasn't seen it since,' piped up Lauren.

'Right,' said Jennie. Anger at Lauren's influence over Kat bubbled inside her. 'But that doesn't mean it's been thrown out *or* that I've taken it.'

'Perhaps if you'd taken better care of the flat, the space you're paying no rent for and running your business from, it wouldn't have gone missing.'

Jennie stood dumbstruck, amazed by Lauren's cattiness, but more than that, astonished that Kat would have fallen for someone so acerbic in the first place.

'I really don't think—' began Kat, attempting to stand up for her friend, but Lauren spoke over her.

'Sweetie, that's your problem – you only think kindly of everyone, hence why you've been taken advantage of.'

'No, but I—'

But before Kat had the chance to defend Jennie any further, Jennie decided to leave. 'I think it's best I go,' she said, sensing that if she stuck around, she would say something she regretted to Lauren.

'No—' said Kat, looking to Lauren to encourage Jennie to stay, but Lauren didn't. Jennie gathered up her things.

'Have you seen my phone?'

'It's here,' sneered Lauren, looking at it for a moment longer than was necessary. 'You've got a message.'

Jennie held out her hand. 'Thanks,' she said, snatching the phone from Lauren and heading out the door.

Jennie, waiting for the lift, couldn't believe what she was reading on her phone. There, like a further dagger to her heart, was a message from Stephen. It read:

Further delay in funds. Could be another month, at least.

'Shit,' she said, knowing in her gut that there was no delay, that this was his way of screwing with her; his way of getting revenge for her ditching him at the altar.

She threw her phone into her bag and pressed the lift button several times. Given she had nowhere to crash in the city, she figured she may as well take a train home, and have it out with him for good.

22

As Jennie walked up the slab path of her old home, she noticed that the rose she'd planted round the front door was in bud, but the soil was bone dry. Her skin prickled that Stephen hadn't noticed, and that such a beautiful plant might die from his neglect.

She banged the knocker on the black door and pressed her finger hard on the doorbell, hearing it ring inside, but Stephen didn't answer. Knowing it was unlike him to be out on a Friday night, she cupped her hands on the living room window and peered in, her heart quickening at the thought of confronting him. Seeing the dark grey corner sofa in exactly the same place that she'd left it unsettled her; she felt as if she might see herself stroll into the room at any moment, sit down next to the stove, and turn on the telly.

In the end there was no sign of Stephen, other than his car magazines on the glass coffee table and the odd mug of tea he hadn't washed up. And there was no answer on his mobile either. Jennie tore a sheet of paper from the notebook in her bag, and scribbled a hurried note:

Call me. We _need_ to talk! Jennie

Having shoved the note through the chrome letterbox, she turned and hurried down the garden path towards her mother's home, on the other side of town. As she walked her phone rang.

'Jennie?'

'Yes,' she replied, walking quickly through the high street, attempting to make out whom the voice on the phone belonged to.

'It's Fran Cavendish, sorry to call in the evening.'

'It's no problem,' she said, trying to temper the edge to her voice, her anger at Stephen still forefront in her mind. 'How can I help?'

'There have been some discussions,' Fran's voice was bright, yet Jennie could hear a hint of trouble. 'The outcome of which are . . .'

'Go ahead,' said Jennie, thoughts rushing through her mind. _Has she found another florist, whose work she prefers? Does she want a complete change of look and feel at the last minute? Does she need more of something that I can't manage?_

'Oli's family feel the wedding *still* isn't big enough. We need to do more of everything—' Fran broke her sentence with an emphatic pause that made it clear this was not what she wanted. 'I'm really sorry.'

There was a moment of quiet between the two women while Jennie gathered her thoughts, something she found hard enough in a good frame of mind but particularly difficult when she was spitting nails about her ex. As things stood, she couldn't afford to pay for the flowers or the helpers, let alone increase the flower order and employ more staff, which she'd undoubtedly need.

'Are you still there?' Fran asked.

'Sorry, yes,' she replied, shaking herself out of her stupor.

'Do you think you can do it?'

On a deep inhale, working purely on instinct, Jennie said, 'I'm sorry, Fran, I don't think I can.'

Fran didn't respond.

'I just can't manage that sort of scale on my own,' said Jennie, realising that for a bride to lose her florist two weeks before the wedding was a fairly major setback, so a little more sensitivity on Jennie's part wouldn't have gone amiss. She wanted to say that if Fran was prepared to pay for everything up front, including increased labour, she could do it in a heartbeat, but pride got in her way. Her parents hadn't raised her to accept favours. They'd always said, 'If you can't pay for it yourself, you go without.' 'Why don't you try Sarah Cunningham's? I'm sure they'll be able to accommodate your needs, even at such short notice.'

'I'd much prefer to have you. Perhaps we could use the consultancy idea we discussed – Sarah's team creates the pieces from your designs?'

'It's a nice thought,' said Jennie, wishing it could happen. 'But I know Sarah won't be able to do that.'

'Why not? We'd pay her exactly the same as if we were using her designs, and your fee would be paid directly by me.'

'I understand. It's not to do with the money . . . it's pressure from outside the company.'

'You mean because of George not wanting you working with Sarah?'

Jennie hesitated, not wanting to blur professional lines with personal, knowing that whatever she said to Fran would inevitably get back to George, and Sarah.

'Let me talk to Sarah,' pressed Fran.

'I'd prefer you didn't, if you don't mind. I don't want to make things awkward for her.'

Jennie wasn't entirely sure why she was so keen to protect Sarah but, as someone who'd been a mentor to her, given her an opportunity, she felt it the right thing to do. The last thing she wanted was the Arbuthnotts telling their circle of friends not to use Sarah Cunningham Flowers anymore and jeopardising Sarah's business.

'Bloody George. I don't know why she has to make everything into such a drama. If she'd think more about people's feelings rather than her followers, she might be in a happier place.'

'I just don't see any other way,' said Jennie, knowing Fran must be super disappointed to be speaking badly of George.

After saying their goodbyes Jennie slumped down on the nearest street bench, exhausted with the day's event, and stared to cry.

'A failed engagement, apprenticeship, romance, and now, to cap it all, a failed flower gig. Classic, Jennie. Go you!'

She was contemplating her life back in Brompton and a lifetime of Interflora orders, when she became aware of someone standing a little distance away peering at her.

'Jennie?' the voice asked.

With her eyes full of tears, it took her moment to see who it was.

'Tracy!' she exclaimed, when she made out her familiar curls and petite frame hidden beneath a padded green jacket.

'What are you doing here?' asked Tracy, taking a step closer, her motherly eyes full of concern. 'Aren't you meant to be in London?'

'I had some business to take care of,' said Jennie hurriedly, wiping her eyes with the heel of her hand, and gesturing in the direction of her old home.

'With Stephen?'

Not wanting to get into the details, she simply nodded.

'Why don't we take a walk,' suggested Tracy. 'Have a catch-up, like old times.'

'Sounds good,' said Jennie, following Tracy down a little path that led towards the estate. 'It's been a long time since I walked this way in the evening,' she said, imagining the last time must have been when she was trying to escape Stephen for an hour or two and would lose herself in her fantasy of growing flowers in the walled garden to make into fresh, wild bouquets. And it stung, that she was still trying to escape him here, even after breaking up.

'Whatever time of day or year, it's always invigorating. Clears the mind, cleanses the soul.'

'I couldn't agree more,' said Jennie, admiring the flashy red poppies skirting the young rowan trees, the scent of their white blossom high on the evening air.

'How have you been?' asked Tracy, her voice full of warmth and concern, as the path opened out into the woods that formed the boundary of the estate.

'The last eight weeks have been a whirlwind. Mostly good, sometimes challenging. In the most part, I'm happy,' said Jennie, pushing away a thought of James, the sting of Fran's wedding and her anger at Stephen. She was acutely aware that she and Tracy hadn't spoken since before the day of the wedding, and of how much had been left unsaid.

'I'm glad, Jennie.'

'How about you?'

'We're just the same really. Alan's busy at the garage, I'm still plastering make-up on women at the counter.'

'And Stephen?' she asked uncomfortably, loath to mention him but feeling it would be remiss not to.

'He's the usual self-centred Stephen.'

Tracy's comment caught Jennie on the back foot, and she stopped where she stood on the path. She'd been expecting Tracy to defend her son, not attack him.

'I feel terrible that I didn't come and see you after what happened,' said Jennie, holding Tracy's gaze, keen to seize the moment. 'I wanted to, very much, but I could never find quite the right time and then, I don't know, it felt as if too much time had passed.'

'I feel the same, Jennie. I lost count of how many times I put on my coat to come see you, then took it off again, not certain how to open the conversation. All I had was Stephen's version of events to go on, and I knew they were likely skewed.'

'It must have been difficult to be objective in that situation,' said Jennie, wondering what Stephen had said but not feeling she had the right to ask. They continued on up the path towards the walled garden.

'He told me you chose your career over him. That he didn't see it coming. But I found that hard to believe.'

'In some ways he's right, I did choose my career over him, but only because he said he wouldn't support it.'

'How do you mean?'

Entering the walled garden, they took a seat on a rickety bench next to the old cold frames. As Jennie absorbed the view of the brick-lined raised beds across the garden, and drank in the scent of the early roses, she explained how Stephen told her he wouldn't marry her and would ensure she never became successful if she took the apprenticeship. 'I knew I couldn't live my life with someone who didn't support my passion, and who found it so easy to threaten me. So I left him. It was the hardest, and easiest, thing I've ever had to do.'

'I knew he wasn't telling me the whole truth. As a mother, it hurts. To think that I raised someone who thinks it's okay to act like that. I trust he's left you alone since?'

'In the sense that he hasn't hassled me. But he owes me money from the house, and he's been keeping that from me. I think intentionally.'

'The little bas—' exclaimed Tracy, only just stopping herself, her neck muscles tight with tension. 'Is that the reason you're in town?'

Jennie nodded, and a thought to why he was doing it, what she'd ever done to him, snuck up on her. If she wasn't so mad, she would have cried at the deep sadness she felt at it all turning out the way it had. 'I had an event I was meant to be doing, a wedding. Without the money, I've had to let it go. I guess he really meant what he said. He found a way to prevent me making anything of myself after all,' she said, regret at not having left him years ago to follow her passion coursing through her.

'Do your mum and dad know?'

'I didn't want for any of you to know. I didn't want it to mess up your friendship.'

'We're made from steelier stuff that that, Jennie. Tell them. They deserve to know. And as for Stephen – he's always been a controlling little tyke, ever since he was small – let me take care of him.'

'Thanks, Tracy,' said Jennie, her attention caught by a familiar figure, hands clasped behind her back, walking down the little gravel path towards them.

'Lovely evening,' the old woman said to them with a brief nod, as her ageing dog hobbled past.

'Isn't it?' said Tracy, and the woman stopped a short distance away from them.

'The scent is heavenly,' said Jennie, drinking in the light aroma of the early roses, blended with a hint of lavender and sage.

'There isn't a finer scent in all the world,' said the woman, her cloudy eyes coming to life.

'No cut rose ever smells as rich,' said Jennie.

'The scent begins to fade as soon as they're cut,' the woman told her.

'It's beautiful while it lasts.'

'With enough care and effort they'll bloom throughout the summer.'

'Someone's got serious commitment, that's for sure,' said Tracy, casting her eyes around the garden.

'Time and hard work,' said the woman.

'And a little bit of luck,' sang Jennie, remembering what the old woman had told her last time, realising now, after these last few months, what an important role in life luck played.

'Yes,' said the woman, and she smiled as she had last time, distantly, wistfully, conveying something Jennie couldn't quite put her finger on. 'Well, good evening.'

'Good evening,' replied Jennie, watching the old woman walk away, her clothes grubby, her body stooped to one side. 'I've seen her here before,' Jennie told Tracy, when the old woman was far enough away. 'Do you know who she is?'

'No idea,' said Tracy, getting up with a stretch and a yawn. 'Just some old dear and her dog.'

*

Jennie's parents' cul-de-sac, after the scale of London and the tower, felt toy-like in comparison, with its neat little lawns, hedges and formulaic layout. She walked up the garden path, cheered by her mother's garden gnome and planted miniature wheelbarrow by the front step. As she placed her key in the lock, she heard Bruno bark, then saw the shape of him bounding to the door through the frosted glass.

'Hello!' she called, opening the front door and stopping him from jumping up to greet her, his tail thumping excitedly. 'Anybody home?'

'Jennie?' she heard her mother call from upstairs.

'Surprise!' she said, though her tone was still a little flat.

Irene appeared at the top of the narrow staircase in her favourite capri pants and tunic top. 'What are you doing here, love?'

Putting down her bag, Jennie watched her mum walk down the stairs, a slight awkwardness to her gait.

'I thought I'd surprise you,' she said, squeezing her Mum, who felt a smidge thinner than normal. 'Is it okay?'

'Of course,' she laughed, hugging Jennie tightly. 'We've missed you.'

Jennie, her mum and Bruno all went through to the kitchen, with its window at the sink overlooking the garden.

'You've cut back the buddleja,' said Jennie, standing at the window and studying the neat little garden. The small patch of lawn was illuminated by the late evening sun, the flowers in the borders held their heads high, and the whirligig spun gently in the breeze.

'You don't miss a thing!' laughed Irene, as she prepared tea. Jennie turned to notice that there was something about her that was different, but she couldn't quite put her finger on what it was.

'Are you okay, Mum?'

'Sure,' she said, putting on the kettle.

'You look a little pale.'

It was then that Jennie realised her mother didn't have any make-up on, and her hair had lost its usual razor-sharp edge.

'I'm still not sleeping well.'

'Why?'

'It's just my age, love. You know, perimenopause, women's stuff. I don't want to bother you with it.'

'Mum, I want to be bothered. What's going on?'

Irene drummed a teaspoon on her hand. 'Mostly it's the usual things that women my age get – hot flushes, tiredness, brain fog – you know.'

'And?' asked Jennie, sensing her mother wasn't telling her everything.

'I'm also anaemic, and breathless, and having headaches.'

'Anything else?'

'Where do I stop, love? It's everything – sleep, cramps, bladder infections, sore joints, heavy periods. It's not easy, but I'm managing. And it's nothing more than the "change of life".'

'How did the G.P. suggest you manage it?' asked Jennie, in awe of her mother for putting on such a brave face.

'She said I should eat plenty of iron and calcium, exercise more, drink more water and less alcohol.'

'Sounds like a hoot!' joked Jennie, her heart going out to her mum. 'Does Dad know?'

'He probably knows more than he's comfortable with. But never mind that,' she said, shooing away Jennie's concern and getting the milk from the fridge.

'Why didn't you tell me before?' asked Jennie, refusing to allow Irene to sweep it under the carpet.

'You've been busy, love. I knew if you knew you'd worry and come home, and you need to be in London, that's where your life is now. This is your time, not mine.'

'Mum, my life will always be here, too, with you and Dad.'

'I know that, love. But I'm not your responsibility. You're mine, but I'm not yours. Never have been. Never will be.'

Jennie rolled her eyes, knowing whatever she said her mum wouldn't back down on that one.

'Tell me what you're doing here?' she asked, handing Jennie her tea.

Jennie groaned and sat at the breakfast bar before telling her mother all that she'd just told Tracy.

'Your dad and I always knew there was something you weren't telling,' she said, stroking her daughter's hair at the breakfast bar. Whenever she sat there, she always thought of eating sausages and beans with Claire before going to Brownies on a Tuesday night. And tonight, more than ever, she felt just like that little girl all those years ago.

'I should have said something sooner,' she said, feeling already as if a heavy weight had been lifted.

'Why didn't you, love?'

'Probably for the same reasons you didn't tell me about your health. I didn't want it to get in the way of your life, of your friendship with Tracy and Alan.'

'Tracy will be furious with him. I can guarantee it,' she said.

'She did give that impression,' said Jennie, thankful that if she couldn't give Stephen a mouthful face to face, then hopefully Tracy would.

'Your dad and I always thought he was a bit controlling of you, but we didn't like to interfere. I thought to say something so many times. It was the biggest relief of my life when you told us you'd called the wedding off.'

'Tracy said something similar,' said Jennie, relieved to hear her mother was glad that she'd called off the wedding. 'Do you think he really was controlling, I mean intentionally so?'

'I don't know, love. But whenever I'd question something, you'd always say, "because Stephen likes . . ." "Because Stephen likes minimalist furniture." "Because Stephen likes me home with him." "Because Stephen likes me slim." You always put his needs ahead of your own. After a while I began to wonder if it was Stephen putting his needs ahead of yours.'

'My personality was always less dominant than his,' said Jennie, conscious that it sounded as if she was defending Stephen, which she wasn't – more herself, for going along with that power dynamic. 'Over the years, things became routine, habit, I suppose. It didn't feel controlling, exactly . . .' she mused, wondering if at times it had.

'Because he was smart, love. I reckon he saw from the start that your self-confidence was low, that you were flattered by his interest. He saw an opportunity.'

'I hope it wasn't that cynical. What would that say about my judgement?' she asked, wondering again if she really had almost married a man who didn't love her, *and,* more concerningly, if she was now reading the relationship with James all wrong, too.

'I think it says less about you and more about him. *And* that it's not worth losing a wink of sleep over,' said Irene, taking an iced lemon cake out of a box and cutting two large slices.

'I've plenty more to worry about anyway,' said Jennie, suppressing her annoyance that Stephen's actions still had a grip, all those doubts eating away at her. 'Because of Stephen withholding the money, I've lost the wedding I was meant to be doing. It's just not viable without the house funds in place.'

'I wish your Dad and I could help—'

'Fran still has time to use Sarah Cunningham's, it'll all work out in the end.'

'Is that what you suggested she do?'

'What else could I do?' she asked, accepting a slice of cake. 'Stephen's not going to stump up the cash in time, and money's not a big deal to Fran or her fiancé's family. They can throw their money at the situation, and Sarah will be delighted to have the business.' Even though there was a solution, it still made Jennie's blood boil that Stephen was going to win.

'But why not ask the bride to pay for the flowers and staff now? It sounds as if they can afford it.'

Jennie shook her head, swallowing down a mouthful of cake, despite her flagging spirits. 'It's not the way things are done.'

'Says who?' asked Irene.

'Says everyone. It's just not the way flower businesses operate,' she explained. She had a reputation to build, a name to make for herself, the last thing she wanted was to go begging for favours from a client, even if it was good-natured Fran.

'Are you sure? It strikes me Fran wouldn't mind paying up front. Like you said, they have money to throw around.'

'I couldn't,' she said, even though she knew Fran wouldn't mind.

Irene drew up a stool. 'And you're certain this isn't about a young doctor, who just happens to be the bride's brother?'

'James has nothing to do with this,' dismissed Jennie, injured pride welling inside of her. She pushed pieces of cake around her plate.

'Oh really,' Irene chuckled knowingly. 'If he hadn't cancelled your date, don't you think you'd be working a little harder to make the wedding happen?'

'No!' said Jennie, offended by the remark, but only because she recognised a hint of truth in it – she probably was trying to distance herself from the situation. 'I think I misread the situation.'

'What happened to make you say that, love?'

The moment on the flower truck when she'd learnt about Camilla sprang into her mind. She tried pushing it away, not wanting to dwell on it, but it remained obstinately, clear. 'He's seeing someone else.'

'Really?' asked Irene, ducking a little so her eyeline might meet Jennie's.

'I think so,' said Jennie, the sting of it really hitting home.

'Maybe keep the door open, just a bit?'

Jennie shook her head. 'I'm sure it wouldn't have worked out anyway, not with our backgrounds being so different.'

'Sounds to me as though you've created a storm in that head of yours.'

'I don't think so,' said Jennie, mulishly. 'He told me early on that there was someone else who'd caught his eye. I'm sure this Camilla is her.'

'I think it might be a case of crossed wires, love.'

Jennie, keen to move on from the subject of James, quickly steered the conversation in another direction. 'Talking of crossed wires . . . can you believe Kat's back with her ex-girlfriend?'

'I didn't see that coming.'

'And you were right, Lauren has been planting seeds of doubt about me in Kat's head. She pretty much accused me of stealing Kat's compact. Any advice?'

'Talk to her, love. It sounds as if she's in need of a friend right now.'

'What would I say?'

'Tell her about Stephen's behaviour, and how you don't want her to end up in a similar situation.'

'I don't know, Mum. I don't want to interfere; I think they still love each other.'

'But sometimes people act in ways they're not fully in control of, and Lauren may well love Kat, but that doesn't give her the right to manipulate her.'

'You mean the way Stephen did to me?'

'Exactly.'

'Mum?' said Jennie, feeling a surge of readiness to confront the question that had been troubling her.

'Do you think Stephen loved me? I mean, really loved me?'

'I think you're looking at it all wrong, love. The question isn't whether he loved you, the question is, did you really love him?'

Jennie allowed Irene's question to sit for a moment.

'Eleven or twelve weeks ago I was convinced that I did, but now, now that I've got friends around me, and a life of my own . . .' she paused, the magnitude of what she was about to say taking the wind out of her sails, 'I think I almost married a man I didn't love.'

'Through no fault of your own, love,' said Irene, wrapping an arm tightly around her. 'The bastard had a grip on you.'

'Just as Lauren does on Kat. Why do you think she's doing it?'

'The same reason Stephen did it to you, to make himself feel important. People who bully and coerce, love – they're insecure, they need something to make them feel powerful. And Lauren's insecure about you. She knows if she can get you out, there's room for her to get back in, to feel important again. It's hardly a coincidence that the compact went missing around the time Lauren visited the flat.'

'You think she took it?'

'I'd bet my last penny on it.'

'But how can I prove that to Kat?'

'That I don't know, but if I were you, love, I'd try to figure it out sooner rather than later. She's been a good friend to you, you wouldn't want to lose her, and there's a very real chance you could.'

23

After a good night's sleep in her old bed, Jennie woke with a clear head, ready to return to the city and tackle life and all its problems head on. From the train, she called Andy and Linda, explaining to Linda's answerphone that the job had fallen through and therefore the work had, too. Andy replied sympathetically via text, saying he understood and was disappointed not to have the chance to work with her. They messaged back and forth several times so when her phone pinged, she fully expected it to be him. Jennie's stomach flipped when the text turned out not to be from Andy, but from James.

> *Hi Jennie, sorry I've been out of touch. Don't suppose you're free to meet today?*

Jennie read the message several times, her hands trembling, trying to decipher whatever subtext might lie beneath it.

On the surface it seemed surprisingly chatty, as if nothing were amiss at all.

When and where?

She replied, wanting to see him one last time to give him the opportunity to tell her about Camilla and reassuring herself that even if he was seeing someone else, if he was man enough to confess, she hadn't fallen for another total arsehole. After confessing about Stephen's ultimatum the previous evening, she had a newfound determination to live her own life, not someone else's.

Can do 2.30 at entrance to Primrose Hill?

He replied.

Sure. See you there.

She wrote, figuring she'd head straight there.

Rereading their exchange, a bland interaction devoid of any spark, she ran through their dates until the day they'd slept together, wondering again how she'd misinterpreted things so badly. *How can it be*, she wondered, *that only one week on, we're meeting at two-thirty in the afternoon, with him seeing someone else, and me feeling like an utter fool.*

*

James greeted Jennie with a kiss on the cheek, where he lingered longer than she expected. His familiar scent of clean cotton caused a rush of memories to flood over her and, despite herself, she felt the hairs on the back on her neck stand on end.

'Are you alright?' he asked as they began their walk into the park, the sun bright in the afternoon sky.

'I'm fine,' she said curtly, not wanting to allow him to wangle his way back into her affections.

'How's your week been?'

'Okay,' she replied, keeping her chin down, her eyes on the path that wound its way slowly up the hill.

'Only okay?' he asked, swooping in to catch her eye, and flashing one of his show-stopping smiles.

'It's been a difficult week,' she said, supressing a smile, annoyed that his charm was already working. She reminded herself that, regardless of how charismatic or handsome he might be, he was still fundamentally a player.

'Fran told me you've had to pull out of the wedding,' he said, stepping aside to allow a guy in rollerblades past.

'Right, I don't feel good about that,' she said, her gut twisting at the mere mention of it.

'You know she's still desperate for you to do it. She even spoke to George, and insisted she contact Sarah to take you back.'

'That's sweet of her,' said Jennie, genuinely touched, despite asking Fran not to bother Sarah.

'Tell me to butt out if I'm crossing a line here, but is the reason you had to pull out down to money? You know Fran could pay you up front, for everything, materials *and* labour?'

'I don't want to talk about that,' dismissed Jennie as they climbed higher, the sweeping outlook over the city coming into view in the distance. She hated allowing pride to stand in her way, but she didn't know how else to be.

A heavy silence fell between them.

'Well,' said Jennie sharply, stopping in her tracks, angry that James was showing no sign of talking to her about Camilla, and fed up with men playing her. 'If that's all you wanted to discuss, I should go.'

'Am I missing something here?' asked James, scratching the back of his head.

'I can't do Fran's wedding, so, if there's nothing else you want to tell me—'

She allowed a pregnant pause to give James the chance to explain about Camilla.

'I . . . I have a feeling there's something you want me to say, but,' he eyed Jennie for a clue that might be written on her face, his brow furrowed, 'I'm really not sure what it is.'

Jennie felt her heart rate quicken, and her throat felt as if it might burst as the words of confrontation welled inside her. 'I'm not a plaything, James. I'm not a toy you can pick up and have fun with until something more "suitable" comes along.' She did little finger quote marks around the word suitable, her hands shaking at the vertiginous sensation of finally standing up for herself.

The furrow in James's brow deepened.

'I know you're seeing that girl you mentioned,' she went on hurriedly, shoving her handbag furiously up her shoulder and clutching tightly to the strap.

'Which girl?'

'The girl you said you had your eye on – Camilla!'

'Who told you that?' he asked incredulously, following Jennie as she continued up the hill at a pace.

'Fiona, the assistant at Sarah Cunningham's, Henry's sister,' she said.

James raised an eyebrow, a little glint that said 'really?' in his eyes.

'What?' she asked, too proud to admit she might have got it wrong, and that it might have been better to run it past James first. 'You're seeing her, right? That's why you cancelled our date.'

At the top of the hill, James sat on a bench and stretched his arms across its length. Jennie stood, clutching her bag to her shoulder.

'First of all, you're getting your information from someone third hand at the flower shop instead of asking me?'

She drummed her fingers on the leather strap, fully aware that he had a point but still not prepared to back down.

'And second of all, I explained why I cancelled.'

'No, you didn't.' She took out her phone and scrolled through her messages. 'You just sent me that really cold message after I'd sent you . . . Oh God!'

'What?'

Jennie stared at her phone, her mind cartwheeling over her mistake.

'What is it?'

She looked at James, mortified, and blurted out a laugh. 'That it explains it.'

'Explains what?'

'Why Henrik, the flower truck guy, was so flirtatious with me.'

James looked blank.

'Look,' said Jennie, sitting down beside him and showing him her phone. 'I sent him a message that was meant for you!'

James read the text aloud. '*Hope your day's been good. Really looking forward to seeing you. J xxxxx.* You sent this to one of your suppliers?'

She nodded, cringing as she did.

'And at the same time you messaged me with . . .' Jennie flicked to the messages from James. '*Really sorry, Jen, going to have to cancel. Will get back to you ASAP.*'

'That did sound a bit clinical . . . but I thought the next one was good.'

'There is no next one, just the one you sent today.'

'No, I—' James looked at Jennie's screen. 'That's weird.' Taking out his own phone he showed Jennie his message log. There, under the text cancelling their date, was another.

I really am sorry. I was so looking forward to more kisses. But this exam prep is killing me . . . just a few more weeks, I promise, and then . . .

And beside it a telling red exclamation mark.

They both laughed, embarrassed at the misunderstanding, and relieved that it was sorted.

'And I sent another yesterday to chase you up.'

'You did?' Jennie scrolled through her phone again. 'I don't see that either.'

'That one I definitely sent,' he said, checking his phone. 'Look again.'

'Nothing,' confirmed Jennie, having scrolled through her inbox several times. 'Let me see it.'

She read the message on James's phone that he'd sent the previous afternoon.

Desperate to see you. Don't suppose you're free for a drink now?

She couldn't help but slightly enjoy the fact he'd been 'desperate' to see her but one way or another had been left to agonise about how she felt about him. It felt nice, after all these years, to have a little control.

'It must have been deleted,' she said.

'Maybe subconsciously you had no desire to see me!'

Jennie laughed. 'Hardly.'

'Then how?'

A thought came to her. 'I suspect I know exactly how . . .'

James cast her a quizzical look.

'It's not important,' she said, pushing the thought away. 'We're here now, that's all that matters.'

'Exactly, and I promise you, I'm really not seeing anyone else. Camilla is the girl I broke up with when you came along. Fiona probably hadn't heard, I haven't seen Henry in ages to tell him.'

'Ah,' said Jennie, wishing she hadn't jumped to conclusions, or doubted his intentions, furious that Stephen had brought her to this – to doubt everyone, even someone who'd done nothing to deserve it.

'I was racking my brains last night trying to figure out what I'd done for you not to reply. Would you have met me if you'd got the message?'

'Of course. Except for the fact I was busy having a very awkward conversation with my flatmate and her ex,' said Jennie, not mentioning the mad dash home in a desperate bid to get the money she needed to pull off his sister's wedding.

'Kat?'

'Yup.'

'What happened?'

'Long story—'

'I've plenty of time?'

A gentle shake of her head told James it wasn't fair to go into it, not until she and Kat had had the chance to talk things through. 'Suffice to say, I don't feel particularly welcome at the flat right now . . .'

'In that case, do you want to come back to mine for the rest of the afternoon? Fran's gone to our grandmother's, and I make a mean steak fajita.'

'Sounds perfect,' she said, relieved to have a reason to be out of the flat and to spend more time with James. 'But let's sit a while together and enjoy the view.' Her eye scanned over all the people on the hill below her, clustered in groups, lazing in the first really warm Saturday of May. And beyond the hill, the trees of Regent's Park – strong and secure like James – that led to the city, sprawling beyond.

Sitting there, in the warmth of the spring, the city spread out before her, Jennie reflected on the last couple of months, all that had happened and how far she'd come. Within two months she'd found a place to live, a brand new set of friends, had the beginnings of a business, and had freed herself of Stephen. If it weren't for the money he owed her, and the issue with Lauren and Kat, she would have felt as if life was very much on track.

'What's that noise?' she asked, as she watched two guys, topless and in long shorts, throw a frisbee.

'Oh bollocks,' James started, delving into his pocket.

'What is it?'

'My pager,' he said, looking at the little screen then calling the number shown from his mobile. 'Dr Cavendish,' he said, all trace of daydream gone from his voice. He listened attentively before saying, 'I'd better come in. I'll be there as soon as possible.' He turned to Jennie with an apologetic shrug.

'You have to go?' she asked, her face crumpling in disappointment.

'Forgive me,' he said, moving towards her and kissing her as tenderly as time would allow. 'Sit a while. Drink it all in. And let me make you dinner when I'm done!'

'Sure,' said Jennie, as he ran down the hill, her heart and head quiet at last.

24

'So, when are you going to talk to her?' asked Mary, in her colourful sitting room, artwork and cushions scattered everywhere, after Jennie had explained what had happened with Kat and Lauren on Friday afternoon.

'Just as soon as I see her,' she answered, a tray of flowers for Aanya's prom on her lap. 'She hasn't been home all weekend.'

Since Jennie arrived back at the tower on Saturday evening, she hadn't seen hide nor hair of Kat. It had been almost seventy-two hours since the encounter with Lauren, and Jennie was increasingly anxious about what Kat was thinking. She'd spent Sunday scouring the flat and searching for Kat's beloved compact, but she still hadn't found it, and she wondered if she'd thrown it out with a bunch of foliage after all, unwilling to believe her mother's theory that Lauren took it. By the end of the day, she'd worked herself into a knot so tight she couldn't eat. She worried that Kat might believe she'd lied about the compact, she worried about the future of their friendship, worried how to talk to Kat about Lauren's behaviour and, less important but still a concern, where she'd live and work if Kat and Lauren really were back together and Lauren were to move back in. The whole situation ate away at her, and she wished more than anything that the compact would turn up, and all the trouble would wash away.

'It's all a big misunderstanding,' said Prisha gently, getting up from the bright yellow sofa to pour tea from Mary's earthenware teapot, which took pride of place on her teak coffee table.

'I don't know. Maybe I did take advantage of her kindness. I could have been tidier, kept on top of things more. Maybe I did accidentally throw out her compact.'

'Kat knew what she was getting into when she asked you to stay, and you're forgetting how much she loves flowers. Having all those flowers around the flat is a dream come true for her,' reassured Mary, offering round a plate of pound cake before returning to her orange mid-century armchair.

'She couldn't have known fully. Until you've worked in a flower shop you can't possibly know how much kit and mess comes with the work,' said Jennie, who wished every job she did was as simple and tidy as Aanya's prom flowers.

'Give her time, Jennie. She's had a lot on her plate.'

'You're right,' said Jennie, a message from her mum distracting her.

Check your bank account. Mum x

Odd, thought Jennie, punching her passcodes into her online banking app.

When her account summaries appeared, she saw instantly that there had been a significant deposit. A 'Jennie's share of the house'-sized deposit. Her heart leapt, and she excused herself to call home from Mary's balcony.

'Mum?' she said, when Irene answered, gazing out over the never-ending stretch of city in front of her, Mary's tomato plants brushing her legs. 'What's going on? How come the money's suddenly in my account?' she asked, wondering what could possibly have happened to make Stephen cough up.

'Let's just say, Stephen experienced the wrath of Tracy, and there's nothing like motherly wrath to make you do the right thing.'

'What happened?'

'She called round this morning to tell me she'd sat on Stephen's doorstep until he came home last night, then wouldn't budge until he promised to send you your money. I think she may also have administered a threat of her own.'

'Really?' probed Jennie.

'Pay Jennie what's rightly hers, or risk losing what's rightly yours – his inheritance.'

'Oh my god!' chuckled Jennie. She'd always admired Tracy's ballsy approach to motherhood, but this was in a whole other league. 'Will you thank her from me?'

'Of course, I will, love.'

'In fact don't, I'll call her myself. God love that woman,' she laughed, tickled pink that Stephen had at last got his comeuppance.

'You look pleased,' said Prisha when Jennie slid the balcony door closed behind her.

'Stephen has at last stumped up the money he owes me,' she told them, sitting back down on the sofa and picking up her work, but a wave of relief washed over her that was so strong she had to put down the flowers and gather herself.

'Now you can really move on,' said Mary, holding up her slice of cake by way of celebration.

'Yes,' said Jennie, overcome with emotion. A small tear escaped from the side of her eye and trickled down her cheek. Realising she hadn't truly loved him, realising he'd had a control over her she hadn't fully understood, those things were important, but they were abstract. The money, however, was tangible; it felt as if the final tie he'd had with her had suddenly been cut, and she could set sail to wherever she chose, whenever she wanted.

'Did you sort things out with James?' asked Prisha. Jennie was grateful for the segue.

A smile spread across Jennie's face so widely that her cheeks ached, and the thought of him felt immeasurably greater now that Stephen was completely out of her life.

'That smile says it all,' laughed Mary. 'Things are back on track?'

'Appear to be,' blushed Jennie, busying herself with binding flower stems with tape. The emergency he'd been called to on Saturday had proved more complicated than expected so they'd decided it was best that they didn't meet that night, and agreed to see each other again on Wednesday, after James's long shifts came to an end. Jennie could barely wait. 'You know, Mary, you're a romantic. How come you don't have someone of your own?'

Prisha's brow raised in anticipation.

'What I want a man for?' rebuked Mary, clicking her tongue against the roof of her mouth.

'Oh, I don't know,' laughed Jennie. 'Companionship. Fun. A little romance. Someone to share your retirement with.'

'Girl, I said it before – I'm too old for all that nonsense.'

'Hardly, and I know you're independent and capable and all that, but you're always the first one to ask me about my dates with James. Don't pretend you're not a romantic at heart.'

'I have plenty enough in my life without wanting no man.'

'But everything you have is about others – church, your family, work – it wouldn't hurt to have something, *someone*, just for you.'

'And where you think you're going to conjure this person up, huh?'

'As it happens, I have someone in mind,' said Jennie, and she paused for theatrical effect, taking her time to cluster the flowers of Aanya's wrist corsage together.

'Who?' Mary laughed, though it wasn't her usual hearty laugh, it was laced with apprehension.

'Omar.'

A little moment hung in the air before Mary said, 'Omar? As in the tower janitor?'

'Exactly. He's about your age. Christian, I think. And I've never noticed a wedding band.'

Mary shook her head, but Jennie noticed a little look from Prisha, directed at her old friend, which said, 'It's not such a crazy idea.'

And though Mary said nothing in reply, and Jennie busied herself in her work, she had a feeling she might just be on to something.

*

'Kat?' Jennie asked, knocking quietly on Kat's door, once she'd finished the prom flowers.

'Come in,' she called.

'It's me, Jennie,' she said, peeping round the door to find Kat sitting up in bed removing her make-up.

'Who else would it be?' she laughed. "I wasn't expecting Cara Delevingne."

'Right.' Jennie laughed too, and felt her shoulders drop. 'Can I sit down?'

Kat patted the floral bedspread by her feet. 'What's up?'

'I'm sorry about the other night—' Jennie faltered, casting her eye round Kat's zen room with its dark green walls, wicker furniture and pot plants.

'You're sorry about Lauren saying you were an ungrateful, thieving oik?'

Jennie bit her lip and traced a flower on Kat's bedspread with her finger. 'Not for Lauren saying it, but for behaving in a way that meant something had to be said in the first place.'

'You don't have to apologise, Jennie. If anyone should apologise it's me – for not telling the truth about who the posy was for, and for allowing Lauren to speak to you in that way.'

'But some of what she said was true, I had made a mess.'

'Right, but it's not as if I didn't know that was going to happen when you moved in. Mess doesn't usually bother me. But one way or another, Lauren mentioned it often enough that it built up in my mind.'

'Stephen used to do the same with me, in different ways, all those little insidious comments I told you about,' she said carefully. 'I had a good chat with his mum and mine, and they pointed out that he was controlling in a way I hadn't really registered, or I'd been in denial about, at least.'

Kat brushed her nails across her bare lips. 'Do you think Lauren's been a bit controlling of me?'

'I might have seen something in the influence she has over you that put me in mind of Stephen. And I'd hate for anyone else to have to live with that for longer than necessary,' said Jennie, hoping she was saying the right thing.

'Listening to you talk about him over the past few months, seeing him withholding the money from you, it made me think about how Lauren is with me. We had a long conversation about it over the weekend.'

'You did?'

'That's where I've been these last few days, with Lauren, thrashing everything out; I don't think we left a word unsaid, even down to the fact that she confessed to deleting a text of yours from James.'

Jennie laughed wryly, holding Kat's eye. 'I had a feeling that might have been down to her.'

'I guess she figured if her love life was up the creek, she wanted someone else's to be, too. I'm sorry if it caused trouble between you guys,' said Kat, tucking the longer side of her hair behind her ear.

'That's okay, trust me, after what I went through with Stephen, I get it. Are you and Lauren giving things another try?'

'No. We came close but . . . for all I still love her, I see now she's not good for me: the jealousy, the control, the deceit. I couldn't go back. What about you and James?'

Not wanting to rub Kat's face in her joy, Jennie underplayed her reply, 'We're back on track.'

'I'm glad, Jennie. You deserve a little happiness.'

'As do you.'

'I'll get there,' she said.

'So, you don't want me to move out, even though the compact is still missing?'

'No, I really don't,' she said, reaching out her hand to Jennie. 'Life wouldn't be the same around here without you. And the compact will show up, I know you didn't take it.'

Jennie believed Kat, but until it turned up, she couldn't fully feel that the issue was resolved. She reached over and gave her friend a squeeze, 'Thanks, Kat. You're the greatest!'

'I'll take that,' she said, letting Jennie go. 'By the way, Zaynab's applied for that loan, and signed up for English lessons. Prisha's agreed to babysit.'

'That's so cool,' smiled Jennie, loving that between them they were making a small difference for Zaynab.

'How are Fran's wedding plans coming along?'

Jennie filled Kat in on the last increase in numbers, Jennie having to pull out, and now, after all that, receiving the money. 'It royally pisses me off that Stephen's still won. Even though I've got the money, I haven't got the gig. If only he'd sent it before the weekend, things would have been very different.'

'It might not be too late, you know. Give Fran a call, tell her you can do the wedding after all.'

'I can't. I already cancelled my assistants, and it's too late to advertise and interview for new ones.'

'Far be it from me to tell you how to run your business, Jennie, but haven't you got ready-made helpers in the form of Prisha, Mary, Zaynab and me?'

Jennie's brow crinkled, her mind beginning to whirr.

'Prisha knows how to make corsages, Mary's done church flowers, Zaynab did the wreath and I've made posies. Doesn't that cover all bases?'

'I can't believe I didn't figure that out for myself!'

'Nor can I!' exclaimed Kat, giving her a playful push. 'So, isn't it time you called Fran and got this wedding back on the road?'

25

The last thing Jennie wanted on Tuesday evening was to meet Henrik for a drink, but they'd made the arrangement and she felt it unfair to break it, even if it was only to explain she was no longer single, and had unintentionally led him on with her text message. She entered the pub to find him sitting waiting for her with a wrap of red roses.

'Not the most original of gifts from a flower seller to a florist,' he remarked, standing to greet her.

'But very sweet,' she said kindly.

'May I get you a drink?' His voice, naturally staccato, sounded even stiffer today, and Jennie could tell he was nervous, which made her feel even worse about having to let him down.

'That would be nice. A gin and tonic, please.'

With Henrik at the bar, Jennie took off her crochet peach cardigan, sat on the pew facing the bar and door, and flicked through her messages. She reread the texts

James had sent during his breaks at work, after getting home late the last few days, and even in the middle of the night. Some of them made her cheeks flush with heat.

'Sorry,' said Jennie, when Henrik returned from the bar. She stuffed the phone in her handbag, hoping that Henrik hadn't seen what she was looking at.

'Phones!' he laughed. 'What did we do without them?'

'Right,' said Jennie, taking a slug of gin – she had the feeling she was going to need it.

Henrik sat down beside Jennie on the pew, rather than opposite her, which felt uncomfortably close, and not a bit as she'd felt sitting next to James. 'How have you been?'

'It's been quite the week,' she said, edging away and twisting her body discreetly in a way that allowed her to face him, rather than sitting shoulder to shoulder.

She told him the broad strokes of the past seven days: the money being held up, her pulling out of Fran's wedding, Tracy sorting out the mess with Stephen and the wedding now back on again. Fran had been beside herself with delight when Emma had called, and all the ladies had said they'd help, just as Kat suggested they would.

'I'm seeing the bride tomorrow to discuss some last-minute changes, and then I'll get the order to you,' she said, feeling terrible that she was keeping conversation to the safe territory of work, but also hoping that if she stuck to boring chat, he might lose interest, negating the need for her to tell him that she wasn't available.

'I'll be waiting,' he said, sounding a lot like Arnold Schwarzenegger, and Jennie giggled. 'Did I say something funny?'

'Sorry,' she said, with another pang of guilt. 'I was thinking about something else. Tell me a little about yourself.'

Henrik began to tell Jennie about growing up in Holland with his parents and three sisters, and how, since he was four years old, he'd always wanted to be a truck driver. She listened as attentively as her busy mind would let her.

'It must be a lonely life,' she commented.

'Not so much. I meet people all the time, and I have very nice customers, like you.'

'You don't miss your family?' she asked, deflecting the comment.

'I see them every weekend. It works very well. And I have all the friends I grew up with to share a beer with.'

As Henrik chatted on about his life back home, Jennie found herself drifting into a daydream of James, imagining their next date and the fun they might have. These last few days she'd found herself fantasising about him in a way she'd never done about Stephen. She thought about James in the shower, and in bed, and while making dinner, imagining all the things they might do together, things she'd never once done with Stephen in all their five years together.

'Jennie?' Henrik's voice pierced her dreaming. 'Are you okay?'

'Pardon.'

'Are you okay? You seem, how do they say, "away with the fairies"?'

Jennie snapped out of her dream, back to the reality of the pub and of Henrik, and took another gulp of her drink.

Turning squarely to him she said, much to her surprise, 'The truth is, Henrik, I'm not available.'

Henrik looked at her blankly.

'I'm seeing someone else,' she explained. 'I really shouldn't even be here, but you've been so nice to me, so considerate, that I hated to let you down.'

Henrik's brow crumpled in confusion. 'I thought from your text that you were interested. I thought the other guy was seeing someone else.'

'Fiona got her wires crossed.' Jennie paused, not wanting to trample too heavily on Henrik's feelings, choosing not to tell him her affectionate message hadn't been intended for him. She figured one blow was enough.

'He's someone important?'

'No,' said Jennie, with a light laugh. 'Or yes, in the sense that he's a doctor, which makes his job important, I suppose. And he's important to me.'

'And he's rich?' Henrik said it in a way that suggested this was one thing he could not compete with.

'I guess, for all that matters,' said Jennie, wishing she felt the conviction with which she said it. The truth was that it still bothered her that she and James had such different upbringings.

'And you like him?'

'Very much,' said Jennie.

'Then you must be with him. And I must move on.'

'I really am sorry, Henrik; I didn't mean to give you false hope.'

'I believe that, Jennie. I know you have a good heart; it's what drew me to you in the first place.'

Jennie liked that he'd said that; liked his kindness. She knew that at any other time she'd be lucky to have Henrik interested in her. 'Thank you.'

'May I ask one thing of you?'

'Of course.'

'May I steal one kiss?'

'Yes,' said Jennie, thinking it was the least she could do. She leaned in and placed a delicate kiss on his dry, pale lips, feeling absolutely nothing other than skin touching skin. It was as near to an opposite sensation as she could get from the one she'd experienced when she first kissed James. As Jennie pulled away, Henrik moved closer, and as he did she saw from the corner of her eye the door of the pub open and, glancing over, the now familiar figure of James, his silhouette clear in the doorframe. In turn, he saw her, her lips on Henrik's, and quickly retreated.

'Oh God!' she said hurriedly, pulling away.

'What?' asked Henrik, his eyes springing open.

'James, that's what!'

Jennie grabbed her bag, abandoned Henrik and ran to the door, which she flew out of searching for James. She saw him in the distance, heading quickly down Regent's Park Road.

'James,' she yelled, running after him, reaching down to take off her heels.

He picked up his pace, not looking back.

'James,' she yelled again, slowing to a stop, her lungs already beginning to burn, realising there was no way on earth she was going to catch him.

26

Buckley jumped up to greet Jennie as soon as Fran opened the door.

'He's as happy to see you as I am,' said Fran, her arms wide.

'You're kind,' said Jennie, hugging her. 'I really wouldn't have blamed you if you hadn't picked up my call. I'm sorry for the chaos I've caused.'

'It's not your fault, we're the ones who keep changing the parameters,' said Fran, showing Jennie into the kitchen. The memory of James preparing drinks and leading her out to the garden came flooding back to her. And then the night before, of running after him until her lungs burned, and calling him more times than she cared to remember, leaving message after message to explain. She was amazed he hadn't called Fran and told her not to give Jennie the privilege of creating her wedding flowers.

Fran carried on, oblivious to Jennie's turmoil. 'Don't be silly, I was beside myself when you called. I hadn't realised how important the flowers were to setting the tone of the day, until I saw Sarah Cunningham's take on an English cottage garden.'

'Not to your liking?' asked Jennie, feeling a guilty frisson of pleasure that Fran preferred her designs to Sarah's.

'Compared to your design it felt formal and stiff. It put a real downer on things, when I was already down enough about the number increase.' Fran took two coffee cups out of a cupboard.

'Where do the numbers stand now?' asked Jennie, taking a seat at the familiar table.

'I've put my foot down and said five hundred is the limit,' she said, slotting capsules into the coffee machine, Buckley settling into his bed by the range.

Jennie let out a whistle.

'It's big, right? Are you sure you can do it?'

'Absolutely,' said Jennie confidently, even though she had no idea if her friends were up to the task.

'You're amazing, Jennie. Thank you!'

Taking out her notepad Jennie opened it at a new page and began afresh. 'So,' she said, once Fran had delivered her coffee and some florentines, and sat down opposite her. 'Let's start with bridesmaids.'

Fran groaned and rolled her eyes. 'There's four of them, plus three flower girls *and* three page-boys.' Jennie raised an eyebrow. 'Don't ask!'

The two of them sat for the best part of an hour discussing the new requirements. The church decoration was to be elaborate, with flowers over the gate and door, a pedestal in the vestibule, pew ends, altar and vestry flowers, and also arrangements for the cars. The marquee, three times the original size, needed decorating: fifty table pieces, five hundred napkin rings and chair backs, plus vases for the toilets and vanity units.

'It's big,' said Jennie, looking at her notes, trying to decide which tasks she could allocate to whom and how long it might take them. She quickly realised that if she were to be successful, she would need to get the flower order in today, as they'd need to arrive three days before the wedding to have everything ready in time.

'But not impossibly big?'

'No, not impossibly big.'

'Even at such short notice?'

'I'll have my work cut out,' she said, determined to make it work, still riding her wave of newfound independence. 'But I have four assistants and between us we can do it. I'll need the address of the church closer to the day, and where you want bouquets and corsages delivered.'

'Of course. I thank my lucky stars for the day James met you.'

Jennie felt her face fall at the mention of James.

'Is something the matter between you guys?'

Jennie nodded, fighting back tears. Exhaling slowly, she said, 'I messed up.'

'How? Last time I saw James he regaled me with just how incredible you are. If I'm completely honest, I tuned out after a while, my head was still a bit woozy after my hen weekend.'

'Things were fine. Last night, however . . .' her heart sank at the memory.

'What happened?'

'Nothing, precisely, he got the wrong end of the stick. He thinks I was on a date, which technically I suppose I was, but it was a favour date, you know? It was set up when I thought James was seeing someone else. I spent the evening telling the guy that nothing could happen because I've fallen for someone else. When I apologised, the guy leaned in to give me a "no worries" kiss, and that's when James walked in.'

'And let me guess, he didn't stick around for an explanation?'

'Who can blame him?'

Fran reached for a Florentine, snapping it in half. 'If I were you, I wouldn't worry about it; he's under a lot of pressure at work at the moment with exams. Let me talk to him.'

'Thanks, Fran. I'd appreciate it if you would. All my messages have gone unanswered.'

'That doesn't surprise me. Let me tell you something about my brother so you don't waste time and energy figuring it out for yourself: he's incredible. Everybody loves him. He'll do anything for anyone. But he has one major Achilles heel and that is, he can't multitask. I mean seriously, if he has something on his mind, he will neglect everything else, not maliciously, not purposefully, and he'll do so until he's finished whatever it is he has to do. It will take a very special sort of person to tolerate it. Camilla definitely wasn't that person, but I think you might be the one who can.'

'Thank you,' said Jennie, blinking back tears, praying she hadn't blown it.

'James thinks the world of you,' reassured Fran, reaching out to squeeze Jennie's hand. 'Give him time; I promise, it *will* be worth it in the end.'

*

'Do you really think we can do this?' Prisha asked Jennie at the kitchen table where all five women were assembled.

'Yes,' said Jennie confidently, knowing that if she didn't exude confidence the whole thing could fail. She neglected to mention that she hadn't been able to get hold of Henrik or his office, who she'd been trying to reach all day, and

291

that if she didn't confirm the online order that evening there would be no flowers to work with at all.

'How long have we got?' asked Kat.

'A little over a week.'

'Aye, aye, aye,' breathed Mary, clearly not sharing Jennie's confidence.

'It is difficult, no?' asked Zaynab, Mohammed asleep in her arms.

'No, it's easy,' replied Jennie, ignoring the sceptical looks being exchanged across the table. To put their minds at ease she took out a colour-coded chart, which she'd drafted to make things clearer, and placed it in the centre of the table for everyone to see.

'Zaynab, your tasks are in red.' She pointed to Zaynab's name in red and the picture of the table centrepieces, of which she had to make fifty.

'Fifty?' asked Zaynab, knowing that she couldn't have made a translation error given that 'fifty' was written in numerical form.

'Yes, fifty,' stated Jennie matter-of-factly, hoping that her doubts regarding the scale of the task to be completed by her novice helpers weren't betrayed by her tone.

Zaynab nodded with quiet determination.

'Mary, you're in charge of the church flowers and helping with the napkin rings, of which we need five hundred.'

Jennie coughed in the hope that nobody would hear or read this ludicrously large number.

'Did you say five hundred?' asked Kat.

Jennie pushed on, hoping to avoid a mutiny. 'Prisha, you're on corsages and buttonholes, only fifteen in total so you'll also be on napkin-ring duty. And Kat, you're on bouquets, car flowers and vases for the toilets. My jobs are outside the church, inside the marquee, and helping with table pieces and napkin rings.'

'It reminds me of my own wedding,' said Prisha. 'We had close to a thousand people downstairs in the community room.'

'You're kidding?' said Jennie, who couldn't imagine the ground floor of the tower ever being a presentable entrance, let alone a venue for a wedding.

'Not at all. The hall is vast. We got everyone in easily. There's even a kitchen, so my mother roped in all the aunties to cook, and I got ready upstairs. It was quite the event; my father even decorated the lift for the occasion.'

'Wow!' cried Jennie, wishing there was some way of opening up the space again for events, and extending their little community of five to more of the tower's inhabitants.

'When do we start?' asked Mary.

'I figure that between us we can do it all in two and a half days. We have Saturday morning for doing pieces in situ and positioning, so if we start on Thursday morning, we should get this done, whilst still keeping the flowers beautiful and fresh.'

'Have you factored in how slow we're likely to be?' Prisha asked, her mouth twisted with concern.

'I have. Once you've learnt to do one, the rest is simple repetition, so we'll do a run-through of each piece over the next week and iron out any problems then.'

'Is everybody still on board?' asked Kat.

'Absolutely,' said Prisha, rallying the troops.

'I'm excited,' said Mary.

'If Mohammed sleep,' said Zaynab.

'We're all behind you, Jennie,' smiled Kat.

'Thank you, you all amaze me,' said Jennie, thankful for the reassurance, and for having these wonderful new friends in her life.

*

'Pick up, pick up, pick up,' chanted Jennie as Henrik's phone rang and rang. It had to be the twentieth time she'd called, and she'd left as many messages. She wondered if he was ignoring her, if his pride had been injured and he was purposefully punishing her by refusing to answer her calls.

'Don't worry so much,' said Kat, when she found Jennie fretting in the dark of the living room long after her usual bedtime. Jennie was scouring the internet for other suppliers who might have a shorter lead time, but by eleven at night she still hadn't found one.

'The order had to be confirmed today for delivery next Thursday. Even if I reach him tomorrow, there's no way we can manage to get everything done in the space of a day and a half.' Jennie threw herself back on the sofa, running her hands through her hair. 'I have absolutely no idea what to do.'

'Can you call Sarah Cunningham's to ask for an alternative?'

'Their supplier is Van Beek's too, that's why I'm using them. I'm totally up shit creek.'

'Aren't there other options, like the flower market? We could all go down there early on Wednesday, I'm sure the others wouldn't mind.'

Jennie smiled at Kat's naïve pragmatism. 'I couldn't take the risk. If they didn't have what we needed we'd have to do last-minute substitutions and risk ruining the entire feel of the wedding.'

'So, what will you do?'

'All I can do is wait until morning and hope someone at Van Beek's picks up then.'

Jennie barely slept, tossing and turning all night, dreaming up all the possible outcomes of not being able to confirm the order in time. She imagined the flowers arriving a day late and only being able to do half of what

Fran had asked for. She imagined the flowers not turning up at all and having to create Fran's beautiful English cottage garden out of coarse flowers of entirely the wrong colour palette. And the very worst dream she had was no flowers and no substitutes, just Fran in a bare church without a bouquet and with the congregation all staring at Jennie, the shamed florist, instead of the beautiful bride.

It felt like an eternity before the sun rose and Jennie was able to call the office at 7 a.m., when she explained her situation to a barely awake Dutchman.

'I'll have Henrik call you,' he reassured her, sounding thankful that he was able to pass the stressed-out customer onto a colleague rather than deal with her himself.

While waiting for his call, Jennie paced the kitchen with a bowl of cereal, which she didn't eat but stirred until it turned into something resembling wallpaper paste. When her phone eventually rang, she all but spilt the slop on the lino.

'Jennie, it's my fault,' said Henrik, before she had time to ramble on about having tried endlessly to make contact with him. 'My charger broke. I only picked up your messages this morning.'

'But Henrik, I need the flowers by Thursday. I can't do this wedding properly without them here by then.'

'Don't worry,' he said, his calm, friendly voice beginning to steady Jennie's nerves. 'I've spoken to the guys in the office. They received the order. You'll definitely have it by Thursday.'

'Oh Henrik, thank you!' she said, collapsing in a heap at the table, and almost crying in relief. She wanted to say she could kiss him but, given the circumstances, she thought it best not.

'You're welcome, Jennie,' he said, without any resentment or malice. 'I hope it's a big success.'

'Me too,' she said, her body limp from relief, hoping this would be the one and only near disaster.

27

Once the order had been confirmed and the adrenalin rush of the immediate wedding preparations had worn off, Jennie found herself at a loose end. With still no word from James, no plans for the weekend, and wanting to check on her mum, she decided to head home.

As the train pulled out of Paddington, Jennie gazed out of the window, watching London sweep past, and then the suburbs blend into the countryside, her mind inevitably drifting to James. She flicked through the messages she'd sent him.

Tuesday 21st
Please pick up my calls, I need to explain, it wasn't what it looked like.

Wednesday 22nd
I understand if you're angry with me, but you have to know, what you saw was purely platonic. Please call.

If you won't talk to me then at least talk to Fran,
she knows what happened.

Thursday 23rd
I guess since you aren't answering my calls or reply-
ing to my messages that you've decided things are
over between us. Please allow me to explain but not
via text.

She decided to swallow her pride and try one last time.

Friday 24th
Heading home for the weekend but please call. I
need to talk to you, even if things are over between
us, I still need for you to know what really happened.

Jennie reminded herself of what Fran had said – 'he thinks
the world of you' – and that she shouldn't worry too much,
but one way or another, as the train pulled into Brompton
Marsh, Jennie couldn't shake the dread in the pit of her
belly that James wasn't going to forgive her.

Exiting the station, Jennie walked along the high street
towards home, stopping outside Brompton Floristry to
look at the window display, which was exactly as it had
been on her last day – a blue baby bouquet and balloon,

a thirty-pound Interflora arrangement in pink and white, and a tired – looking display of lilies. Three arrangements to cover Dorothy's bread and butter – hatch, match and dispatch. In the reflection of the glass, she saw the new Jennie – standing taller, more poised, with a style of her own. Beyond the glass she saw Dorothy serving a customer. Dorothy, catching sight of Jennie, smiled and waved fondly. Jennie thought to go in, to say hello, but her three months away suddenly felt like three years, and uncertain what to say she continued on her way.

At home, Jennie and her mum curled up on the sofa and talked about James until her dad came home. Then they ordered a takeaway and ate it in front of the telly, just like old times.

'I think I'd better go up,' her mum said, just a little before ten.

'It's early, love,' said Tony.

'Maybe we should *all* have an early night,' suggested Jennie, sensing her mother could do with one. She'd been taking ibuprofen most of the day, and had dozed off on the couch after dinner, a hot-water bottle clutched to her stomach. 'We can get up in the morning, take Bruno for a walk at the manor, burn off some of this curry.'

Her mum got up slowly, reaching out to steady herself on Tony. 'Sounds like a plan, love.'

'Good,' said Jennie, clearing plates and foil trays from the coffee table, and watching her mother head gingerly upstairs to bed.

*

Jennie woke to sounds of moaning and muffled voices. At first, in her half-asleep state, she wondered if it was her parents having sex in their room, but when she heard a knock at her door, she realised that couldn't be the case.

'Jennie?' her dad called. 'Are you awake?'

Turning on the bedside light, Jennie got up and went onto the landing. 'What's going on?'

'It's your mum, love. I don't know what to do.'

In her parents' room her mother was writhing in pain on their queen-size bed, the delicate floral bed linen scrunched around her.

'Mum? What is it?' she asked, terrified that it was something really serious.

Her mother was bent double clutching her abdomen; it was only when Jennie pulled back the duvet and discovered blood soaked into her mum's nightie that she realised the enormity of the problem.

'Has this happened before?' she asked her dad, covering Irene up to keep her warm.

'It's been going on for months, but this is the worst I've seen it.'

'Does she have any pain medication?'

'Just the ibuprofen, but it doesn't help.'

'Call NHS 24, see what they suggest.'

While her dad was downstairs, Jennie sat next to her mum trying to reassure her that they'd get hold of stronger medicine soon, even if that did mean a trip to the local hospital in the middle of the night.

'They said paracetamol and ibuprofen, and to sit it out until morning,' said Tony on his return.

'That's bollocks,' said Jennie, going to grab her phone from her room.

'What you doing, love?' Tony asked on the landing.

'Contacting James. He works in obs & gynae, he'll know what to do.'

Jennie composed a text to James without a care as to how it might be received. Right now, she was more concerned about her mother's wellbeing than any petty misunderstanding between the two of them.

I'm with my mum, she's peri menopausal, bleeding heavily and in pain. Any suggestions what to do?

James replied within seconds.

Where are you?

Brompton Marsh

I'm nearby. Can come immediately. Address?

Jennie typed in the address and hit send.

'He's on his way,' she said, trying not to show just how surprised she was at how responsive he'd been after so many days of nothing.

'That's good of him, love,' Irene managed to mumble when Jennie told her. 'He must think the world of you.'

'I'm sure he feels it's part of his job,' replied Jennie, not wanting her mum to get her hopes up.

When the doorbell rang, Jennie's heart leapt.

'Hi,' she said, opening the door, suddenly self-conscious about the ancient Bart Simpson pyjamas she was wearing, which she'd found in her bedroom drawers when she realised she hadn't packed her nightwear. 'Thanks for coming.'

'Where is she?' James asked, stepping into the hall.

Jennie tucked her bed hair behind her ears and indicated to the stairs behind her. 'Upstairs, third door.'

James bounded up, carrying a bag, and disappeared. When Jennie climbed the stairs to join them, she found her dad on the landing, and the bedroom door closed.

'He wanted to examine her,' he explained, his back against the wall.

'Cup of tea?' she asked, rubbing his arm.

It was over twenty minutes before James joined the two of them in the living room, Jennie and her dad in their pyjamas and bathrobes on the sofa, Bruno sniffing James, wondering who he was and what brought him into the house in the dead of night.

'She's comfortable,' he said, reaching down to ruffle Bruno's head.

Jennie wanted desperately to hug him, to wrap her arms around his waist and feel her cheek against the old cricket sweater he was wearing.

'Thank you,' she said inadequately, getting up from the sofa, her dad joining her. 'Is it something to be worried about?'

'It's menorrhagia, or heavy menstrual bleeding, which isn't unusual in women her age. I've given her stronger medication for the cramping to see her through the night. In the morning I'll contact the hospital and make sure she's seen straight away by a consultant.'

'Is there anything that can be done?' asked Jennie.

'The hospital will run some tests and consider the best course of treatment after that. It's likely it will just require a course of hormone therapy, but there are other treatments available if that's not sufficient. Don't worry, it's a common problem. She'll be fine.'

'Thank you, doctor.' Tony extended his hand to James. It felt peculiar to Jennie to see the two men she was most crazy about in the world standing in the sitting room of her family home, formally shaking hands as if there was no connection between them at all. As if her dad hadn't enjoyed endless jokes at her expense about 'that posh bloke' and James hadn't talked keenly about meeting her dad one day. 'It was good of you to come in the night.'

'My pleasure, it wasn't far.'

'If you'll excuse me, I'll go be with Irene,' said Tony.

Her dad's exit left the two of them alone, and Jennie felt suddenly wooden. James turned to leave.

'Everyone's beyond grateful, I can't tell you how much,' she blurted, hoping to stall his exit.

James turned back, shoving his hands in his trouser pockets. 'It's not a problem. It's my job.'

'Right, but my mother isn't one of your patients,' pressed Jennie. 'We all appreciate you going out of your way, especially me.'

'I was just round the corner.'

'Where?' she asked, suddenly curious as to why James had been so close at hand.

'At my grandmother's house. It's on the edge of the village. Brompton Manor, it's the—'

'I . . . I know exactly where it is,' faltered Jennie, trying to join the dots – "the village church next to our grandmother's home in Gloucestershire", "a marquee in the grounds of the house", "Brompton Marsh . . . our grandmother's home

305

is close by" – and suddenly it all seemed so obvious. *Was James the man I saw working in the walled garden the day after the wedding? Were we meant to meet then?* she thought, wondering how many times they might have walked past each other, maybe even passed the time of day, over the years. 'We walk Bruno there all the time. The walled garden I love so much, the one I was telling you about, is the one on the estate,' she said, now not only self-conscious about her pyjamas but also her family home.

'It's my grandmother's favourite spot. She was a keen amateur florist when she was younger. She tended each rose plant individually, nurtured every bloom, then made them into beautiful bouquets.' Jennie noticed a small smile form on James's lips, then it disappeared. 'Not that any of that matters now.'

'But it does, it matters very much, to me, at least,' she pleaded, not even thinking about her fantasy of the walled garden, her only concern being to hold on to James and all that was important to him. 'Don't you want to hear my side of the story?'

'I can't think of any reason that would explain why you were kissing another man.'

'Will you sit for a moment and allow me to explain?'

To her surprise James took a seat, his country check shirt and burgundy chinos looking incongruous on her mother's cream MFI sofa.

'Henrik, the guy in the pub, drives the flower truck. Do you remember, the guy I accidently sent that text to?' James looked up to where she stood on the fake sheepskin rug by the fireplace, her hands all a fumble, and gave a nod of acknowledgement. 'When I "found out" you were dating Camilla, he asked me out and I, not enthusiastically, said yes. The date was all arranged, and I thought it kinder to go and let him down in person rather than to do it via text.'

'And you thought kissing him was the way to make it clear you weren't interested.'

'No,' she said, frustration welling inside her. 'When I explained the situation, he asked if he could kiss me, platonically, and I, naively, said I didn't mind. It was at that moment you arrived.' She paused, suddenly wondering what he'd been doing there. 'How did you even know I was there?'

'Kat.'

'Kat? How did you get hold of Kat?' she asked, knowing she hadn't given James Kat's number, or the number of their flat.

'I remembered Mary from the night of Zaynab giving birth. We worked together during one of my junior rotations. It didn't take me long to track her down in the hospital. When I told her who I was, she was more than happy to give me your address.'

Jennie laughed. She'd forgotten Mary and James worked at the same hospital. With all that had been happening it must have slipped Kat's mind to mention that he'd come to the door.

'When I rang on the door after my shift on Tuesday, desperate to see you from where we left off on Saturday, she told me you'd gone to the pub. I'm guessing she didn't realise you were there with another guy.'

'No, she wouldn't have,' said Jennie, who knew she hadn't mentioned the date with Henrik to Kat.

'Well,' said James. 'Do you feel better now you've had a chance to explain?'

'A bit,' she said, thrown by how dismissive he sounded. 'I think it helps for both of us to know each side of the story, don't you?'

He shrugged and got to his feet. 'I hope your mother feels better. Let me know if you need any further help, but you shouldn't, she should be comfortable now.'

'Is that it?' said Jennie, her gratitude lost in all the hurt.

'Yes,' he said, going out to the hall, picking up his bag and opening the door. 'Goodnight, Jennie,' he said, stepping into the mild night. 'See you around.'

'See you,' she said, lingering by the half-open door and wondering if this was how it felt to watch your dream literally walk down the garden path, and out of your life for ever.

28

Despite Jennie's heavy heart, the practice sessions at the beginning of the week had gone better than expected. She'd started by showing everyone how to do the napkin rings, a circle of willow with soft cream ranunculus and grape hyacinth, which was simple and quick and which everyone learnt to do within minutes. From there she showed Prisha the flower combination for the buttonholes and corsages, also ranunculus, grape hyacinth and a scattering of forget-me-nots. Zaynab, after little instruction, mastered the centrepieces, and Mary completed a scaled-down version of the altar pieces, which were soft with wild rose and heavily scented with mint. Jennie left Kat to experiment with designs for the small vases for the toilets, and taught her how to make the bridesmaids' bouquets, whilst she worked on a piece for the marquee. By the end of Wednesday, everyone was feeling confident in their ability to create the pieces, if not quite so confident in the time they had to produce them.

On Thursday morning Henrik arrived, parking his truck at the foot of the tower, and invited all the ladies to come on board to take a look.

'It's a big order, no?' he said to Jennie, as her friends ooh-ed and ah-ed in the background.

'Really big,' she said, grateful that, after their date, he wasn't awkward around her or resentful in any way. It made her wonder, for a moment, if she'd backed the wrong man.

It was only as she surveyed the order laid out on the floor of the truck that she recognised how much space was required to store the flowers, let alone how much space would be needed for the arrangements once they'd been made.

With the order paid for and Henrik departed, the women, all laden with flowers, walked like ants carrying outsized burdens back to the tower. Omar emerged from the lift as it opened.

'My goodness,' he whistled at the sight of the flowers in their arms and on the floor. 'Let me help you,' he said, going straight to Mary and relieving her of the wraps that looked as if they might fall at any moment.

'Is she flustered?' Jennie whispered to Prisha, as Omar and Mary went into the lift.

'She's always had a soft spot for him,' Prisha whispered back. 'Ever since he started working here, over a decade ago.'

*

'I made cake,' sang Prisha, putting on the kettle on Friday morning and removing a large strawberry cream cake from a tin. She placed it on the only section of work surface that wasn't piled high with floristry paraphernalia, taking Jennie right back to the chaos of Sarah Cunningham's, and she had a little flutter of happiness at how far she'd come. If someone had told her, the day George had her fired, that two months later she'd be working as Jennie Treloar on the biggest wedding of her career, she'd have laughed. But here she was, and it was the best feeling in the world.

'Hallelujah!' cried Mary from where she was already working at the kitchen table. 'It's gonna take a truck load of cake to get me through this day.'

'It's not that bad,' called Kat, who was stationed in the living room, making a start on the bridesmaids' bouquets. The previous day she had made the pieces for the cars, toilets and vanity units and now they lined the hall, alongside the buttonholes and corsages that Prisha had completed. The flowers led into Kat and Jennie's bedrooms, which were full of the table centrepieces. Zaynab had worked methodically with Mohammed strapped to her chest all of Thursday, and continued to do so at the dining table.

'A slice of cake keeps the blues away,' said Prisha, handing out slices before going to the bathroom, the only available space left for creating the napkin rings.

Everyone was absorbed in their work with the radio playing in the background when Prisha called through, 'Look at this!'

'What is it?' asked Jennie, wandering through, assuming Prisha needed something checked.

'Isn't it beautiful?'

Jennie instantly recognised what Prisha was holding in her hand. Kat's compact.

'Kat!' she called ecstatically.

'What's going on?'

'Prisha found your compact!'

'No way!' said Kat, rushing through and scrutinising its every detail to make sure it was undamaged. 'Where was it?'

'Behind the cistern,' said Prisha. Both Kat and Jennie's brows furrowed, curious but too polite to ask why Prisha had been looking behind the toilet. 'I dropped some wires and had to get them out – that's when I saw this.'

'Oh—' said Kat, realisation dawning in her eyes.

'What?' asked Jennie.

'Lauren – she used to hide envelopes of money there. It was her hiding place.'

It didn't take Jennie long to work out what had happened.

'She must have put it there,' Kat realised.

'The day she came round to the flat when you weren't here – I remember, she went to the bathroom.'

'But why?' asked Prisha.

'Game playing,' said Kat.

'She figured if Kat thought I'd been stealing then I'd have to move out and she could move back in,' said Jennie, thinking of how her mum had been right all along.

'That's terrible,' said Prisha.

'That's love, or obsession, at any rate,' said Jennie, happy to be free of Stephen more than ever.

'I'd take friendship any day of the week,' said Kat, giving Jennie a reassuring hug, one that told her everything had been forgiven.

Relieved, Jennie went back to where she was working, half hidden in the living room by the pedestal pieces she was creating for the marquee, which cascaded with wild rose and lily of the valley.

'We're going to lose you amongst those,' laughed Mary.

'I think you're right!'

Jennie stood back to view her work from a distance. But with the room so full, she wasn't able to gain the perspective she needed. Walking through the flat, which had taken on the appearance and aroma of an English cottage garden, she realised she needed more space.

'Prisha, do you think there's any chance we could use the community hall downstairs?'

'I don't see why not. Let me call Omar.'

It didn't take long for Omar to answer his phone and unlock the hall. And within half an hour they'd managed to move everything – centrepieces, pedestals, corsages and vases – from the flat, to the lift, to the hall.

'It looks like Kensington Palace when Diana died,' said Mary, Omar at her shoulder, taking in the scale of it all. The space, which looked like a huge 1960s school hall, built from concrete blocks, with high slit windows, was cold and grey but brought alive with the colour and scent of the flowers.

'It's impressive,' said Jennie, surprised at just how many flowers were left in wraps. She tweaked a few flowers on the centrepieces, which stood out just a little too far. Zaynab's work was good enough for the untrained eye but to Jennie there were bits and pieces to attend to that her meticulous eye couldn't let slip.

'I haven't had a chance to ask you about James,' said Mary, after Omar had helped her set up a new work station in the enormous, industrial kitchen, then left them to it.

No,' said Jennie, rather thankful that was the case. 'And I haven't had a chance to ask you about Omar . . .'

Mary deflected her attention with a bat of her hand. 'Any news from the doctor?'

With so much to do, Jennie didn't much feel like getting into the details of their encounter at the weekend, and her heartache at feeling she'd more than likely lost James for ever.

'Not really,' she said, figuring she'd explain about him being the estate owner's grandson when they put the flowers in situ tomorrow. For now, it didn't matter.

'His loss,' Mary said warmly.

'Whose loss?' asked Kat, joining them.

'James's,' said Mary.

'What *are* we going to do about that?' she inquired mischievously.

'What are we going to do about what?' queried Prisha.

'James,' said Kat.

'James?' asked Zaynab.

'I'm not sure *we* are going to do anything,' said Jennie, secretly pleased that everyone was showing such an interest, even if it wasn't meant to be; two months ago she couldn't have imagined having the camaraderie of four close female friends.

'He's going to be at the wedding, right?' asked Mary.

'I suspect even he will remember his own sister's wedding.'

'Then I think a plan of action is needed,' said Kat, with a twinkle.

'No,' said Jennie defiantly, not wanting to think about tomorrow and the looming inevitability of another painful encounter with James. As an usher, he would be at the church where she would be attending to the last-minute floral details before the guests' and bridal party's arrival. Every time she thought about it, she felt sick with worry,

315

wondering how she could ever convince him to give them another go. 'We've got so much to do, we can't possibly be thinking about men,' she continued, scoring items off her checklist and trying desperately to push the distraction of James out of her mind.

*

It was just after five o'clock. Kat had ordered pizza for supper, Prisha had returned from nipping upstairs to check on the family, and Mary was sitting at a fold-out community table with Zaynab, who was feeding Mohammed, and eating the last piece of cake.

'We're almost there,' said Jennie, rallying her troops. 'I've another five marquee pieces, nine centrepieces and a hundred napkin rings, but we should have those done after supper. And I've the church flowers to do in the morning. Talking of which,' Jennie paused and looked around the hall at the buckets and crates full of flowers, and boxes and plastic bags full of sundries. 'Has anyone seen the door and gate garlands?'

'What do they look like?' asked Prisha.

'Like a green string of sausages.'

When Jennie was answered with a chorus of 'no's and 'don't think so's she began rifling through all the oasis items.

'Where are they?' she asked, panic rising in her chest.

'I'm sure they're here somewhere,' said Prisha calmly, joining Jennie in looking through the bags.

'They're not! I've been through all of these boxes and bags and I know I haven't seen them.'

Jennie thought about what to do. She could go to the market in the morning when it first opened but that would be cutting it too fine. She knew her only option was to call Henrik and ask for another favour, which made her heart sink, but with no other choice she made the call.

'It's my fault,' said Henrik, after Jennie had explained the situation. 'I see them lying here on the floor of the truck. Did you say the wedding's in Gloucestershire? I'm out that way tomorrow, so I can drop it at the church first thing, in a yellow bag. Send me the postcode.'

'It is, and I will. Thanks, Henrik, you're a lifesaver.'

'All sorted?' asked Kat.

'Yes, sorry for the momentary panic, I think the pressure might be getting to me!'

'What's the plan for tomorrow?' asked Prisha.

'I need to be at the church by eight in the morning, which means leaving here at six. Is everyone still okay to start loading the vans at five?' Jennie hated having to depend on others to help out at such an ungodly hour, but there was no way that she could physically move all of the arrangements on her own in the time she had.

317

'Izaiah is staying overnight so I can kick him out of bed first thing,' said Mary, who'd nominated her son to help. 'And Omar said he can help, too.'

'Oh really?' sang Jennie, but Mary wasn't forthcoming with more.

'And my two eldest know there'll be no pocket money for a week if they don't help, so they're guaranteed,' said Prisha, keeping a watchful eye on her old friend, causing Jennie to wonder if Prisha knew something about Mary and Omar that Jennie didn't.

'You guys are the best,' said Jennie, holding a much-needed cup of tea. 'I can never thank you enough.'

'We owe you the thanks,' said Prisha. 'We all have new skills. Zaynab starts her English lessons soon, once that's improved she could help you when you need extra hands; I've been looking for something of my own now all the kids are in school – who knows, maybe I'll end up helping you too – and Mary's able to help out at church in a way she never imagined.'

'It's only me that hasn't done it for personal gain!' laughed Kat.

'Well, whatever your motivation, whatever your reward, there's no way I could have done it without you. We're a real team.'

'Team Jennie, long may that continue,' sang Prisha, giving Jennie a hug, joined by Kat.

'Eh,' they heard Zaynab say, who was still feeding Mohammed but also pointing at the schedule on the wall. 'Where this?'

Zaynab was pointing at a sketch Jennie had drawn of two chairs.

Jennie broke away from the huddle to see what Zaynab was looking at, her face draining of colour when she realised her mistake.

'Jennie?' asked Prisha, coming up behind her.

'Get her a seat,' said Mary urgently.

Jennie dropped onto the chair, staring at the chart. 'What am I going to do? How could I have missed something so major?'

'What's wrong,' asked Kat.

'I forgot to allocate the chair backs and pew ends to someone. They haven't been done.'

'How many pieces are we talking about?' asked Mary.

'Twenty-five pew ends and five hundred chair backs.'

Mary whistled.

'Do we have the flowers to make them?' asked Kat.

'That's the reason I can't believe my mistake. I knew we had far more flowers left than we needed, I thought I'd overestimated. Now I realise we have excess because I've forgotten to include these items.'

'How long will they take to make?' asked Kat, ever the pragmatist.

'Eight hours for the pew ends. Twenty-five hours for the chair backs,' Jennie estimated.

'And the time is now just after five,' said Prisha.

'Giving us twelve hours,' said Mary optimistically, suggesting it was possible.

'But everyone needs at least six hours' sleep,' said Jennie, unprepared to allow anyone to pull an all-nighter.

'So, we've six hours, and five sets of hands, which makes thirty hours,' said Mary.

'Which still leaves us short,' Jennie worried.

'Between us we must know someone who can help,' said Mary.

'What about the woman from your church who does the flowers?' Kat asked.

'She's on holiday.'

'Anyone else got any ideas? I don't think I know anyone.'

Prisha shook her head, and Jennie was aware that everyone Zaynab knew in the city was standing in the room.

'Unless,' said Jennie, a thought forming, taking out her phone and scrolling through her contacts to Louise.

'Louise at Sarah Cunningham's is my only hope,' said Jennie, crossing her fingers and pressing 'call'.

*

Louise arrived only half an hour after Jennie's call. 'I can't tell you how happy I am to have a chance to make up for the mistake with George,' she said, surveying all that the five women had created.

'Thank you. You can't know how grateful I am,' said Jennie, giving her a huge squeeze, almost every ounce of worry draining out of her.

'This work is incredible, Jennie! Really.'

'It's all down to these four ladies.' Jennie introduced Louise to the girls.

'We're glad to see you,' said Mary, whose fingers were sore and working far more slowly than they had done earlier in the day.

'It's lucky Sarah doesn't have an event tomorrow, my husband is home to babysit, and Fiona said she'd cover my shift in the shop. The stars aligned.'

'Thank God for that,' said Jennie, never happier to see someone in her life, and praying there would be no more hiccups before the wedding.

29

It was midnight by the time the last chair arrangement was complete, a cluster of wild roses and grape hyacinths tied with hessian, which would attach to the back of the wedding chairs in the marquee.

'We did it!' said Jennie, thinking back to her first day at Sarah Cunningham's. She found it hard to believe just how much her life had flipped upside down, turned inside out and ultimately changed for the best since then: the realisation of her dream business, new friendships and growing independence. If it weren't for the small matter of James, she thought, she'd be perfectly content.

'*You* did it,' said Kat, all six women, their feet and backs sore, their fingers swollen, standing arm in arm admiring their completed work in the hall.

'It's a big achievement, Jennie,' said Louise, who knew exactly how much preparation went into such a huge event.

'I need to sleep,' Jennie yawned, though she had a feeling that even though she should fall fast asleep as soon as her head hit the pillow, the likelihood was that she'd be awake for hours going over every tiny detail of the wedding.

In the end she fell asleep around two in the morning and woke two and a half hours later with her alarm. Adrenalin alone pulled her out of bed and into the shower.

After a quick breakfast, into which she felt she could fall face first, she stumbled downstairs, where she found Prisha and her family, and Mary, Izaiah and Omar, already filling the lobby with the arrangements.

By six o'clock the vans that Omar had organised were loaded and ready to go.

'You guys are extraordinary,' said Jennie, who, though half asleep, was still in awe of everyone's generosity. She hugged Izaiah and Prisha's kids, and then Omar too. 'Thank you.'

'Yes, thank you,' said Mary, hugging Izaiah and then Omar.

The temptation to whoop almost broke Jennie, but there was something so tender in the way they hugged, the way Omar looked at her as if she were a real-life goddess, that in the end Jennie found herself wiping away a tear, and squeezing Prisha's hand instead.

'They've been on a couple of dates,' Prisha confided, and Jennie beamed. 'She doesn't say much, but I think it's going well.'

Having said their goodbyes, the six women buckled up and set off on the two-hour drive to the church. Mary drove Kat and Zaynab in the first van and Jennie took Louise and Prisha in the second, the three of them singing, laughing and chatting excitedly about the morning ahead.

'What a beautiful church,' said Louise, as they pulled up alongside its ancient wall and the little graveyard that skirted around the main building.

'It'll look even prettier when we've put the arches round the gate and door,' said Louise, opening the passenger door and sliding down to stretch her legs.

'Should we start unloading?' called Mary, stretching her arms above her head beside the van she'd been driving.

'Yes, please,' said Jennie.

Mary, Kat and Zaynab, Mohammed strapped to her chest, began unloading the contents of Jennie's van, which held everything for the church, and in relay carried it all up the path, which wound through the graveyard. Jennie followed behind to collect the garlands that Henrik had promised to leave by the church door. But after several minutes of looking for them, at the side of the vestibule, in the vestibule, inside the church, back down at the gate,

Jennie couldn't find them. Trying to suppress another rising sense of panic, she called Henrik.

'Did you get the garlands?' Henrik asked when he picked up.

'No, that's why I'm calling. Where did you leave them?'

'Outside, to the right of the porch, they're in a bright yellow bag.'

'Are you sure?' said Jennie, walking back up the path to take another look, hoping that she'd missed something blindingly obvious. But she still saw nothing. 'The bag's not there, and I have a bride arriving in three hours.'

At that moment, Jennie saw James pull up outside the church in his car. She swallowed hard, and felt her stomach twist. Now, not only did she have a flower crisis on her hands, but she also had to confront her broken heart.

'Henrik, where are you?' she asked, a plan suddenly forming in her mind.

'About a half hour away from you. Junction eighteen of the motorway.'

'Do you have any other garlands on the truck?'

'Sure.'

'Can you pull over for a while?'

Jennie walked towards James, who looked beyond handsome in a morning suit and gold cravat. His usually casual hair had been styled and his face was smoothly shaven. Jennie, even in the middle of the current disaster, couldn't ignore the butterflies inside of her.

'Hi,' he said, his eyes serious. 'Fran sent me to check everything's going okay.'

'We have a crisis,' she blurted, almost glad to have the flower problem, anything to take the spotlight off their personal troubles.

'What's wrong?' he asked, reassuringly calm.

'How fast does your car go?'

'Fast.'

'Can you nip along the M4 to junction eighteen and pick up two oasis garlands from the flower truck?'

'If that's what you need.'

'It is,' she said, returning to Henrik on the phone. 'Henrik, I'm sending the bride's brother to meet you. He'll be with you in—' Jennie looked to James for the answer.

'Twenty,' he suggested.

'Fifteen minutes,' she said. 'Because that's all the time we've got.'

*

'James has gone to find Henrik,' Jennie told Louise, thankful, more than ever, that she was there to help. Without her, there was no way Jennie could get all the

326

work done. 'He'll be back in half an hour. When he arrives, I'll need you to do the gate, and I'll do the door. The others don't have any experience of that, so I'll send them on to the marquee.'

'Of course,' said Louise cheerfully. 'For now, let's go inside and get everything in place. By the time that's done, James will be back, and we can crack on.'

Jennie was placing the last piece in the vestry when she heard a knock on the church door and a voice call, 'Hello?'

'In the vestry,' she called, thinking it might be a guest who'd arrived early and was looking for instructions to the nearest coffee shop or pub, a request she'd dealt with numerous times when doing weddings with Dorothy.

It took Jennie a few seconds to place the woman who appeared in the arched doorway, and when she did, she couldn't quite understand why she was there.

'Sarah!'

'Jennie,' replied Sarah, who was dressed in wedding attire rather than her usual jeans and Sarah Cunningham apron. 'The church looks sensational.'

'Thank you,' said Jennie, thrilled by praise from Sarah, but also recognising herself that the designs were a success. 'What brings you here?'

'Fate, I think.'

Jennie waited for Sarah to elaborate, but when she didn't, Jennie said, 'I don't understand.'

'No. there's no reason why you should,' said Sarah, finding a little wooden seat to sit on. Jennie sat next to her, glad of a moment's break.

A moment of what felt to Jennie like confessional silence passed between the two, Sarah thinking, Jennie waiting. Eventually Sarah spoke.

'Fiona sent me a text last night to say she'd be covering Louise's shift in the shop this morning.'

Jennie said nothing. The information shed no light on Sarah's presence in the church.

'There was no reason for her to do that. So long as the shop is covered, I don't mind who's on duty. When I sent her a message back to thank her and ask if Louise is okay, she replied saying Louise was helping you with an event.'

'Louise isn't being disloyal to you,' Jennie was quick to say; the last thing she wanted was for Sarah to think badly of Louise. 'She's just helping me out of a hole, I promise. Please don't be mad at her.'

'I'm not mad with Louise,' laughed Sarah. 'When I dug a little deeper, Fiona told me it was Fran's wedding she's helping with. And since I was invited anyway, I thought I'd arrive a little early and get a sneak preview.'

'At the job you almost had,' said Jennie apologetically, remembering that Fran had gone to Sarah when Jennie had said she couldn't manage the increased numbers.

Sarah laughed. 'Trust me, Fran never wanted me to do the flowers. I've enough experience with brides to know when they're happy and when they're not. And she made it crystal clear she was not happy.'

'How?' asked Jennie, unable to imagine Fran showing dissatisfaction towards anyone or anything.

'She asked if I would employ you again to do her wedding.'

'Ah, but you said no?' asked Jennie, flattered but a little surprised that Fran hadn't stuck to her word about not talking to Sarah.

'I felt I had to remain loyal to the Arbuthnotts. I explained that to Fran and she understood, though she did ask if I'd buy your designs for the team to work from.'

'That's very flattering.' The idea of being a flower consultant rather than a mere florist still gave Jennie a buzz.

'And I can see why she wanted me to,' said Sarah, looking out to the body of the church at the designs, which were all in place. 'I realise now just how big a mistake I made the day I let you go.'

'It's working out okay though.'

'Maybe for you!' laughed Sarah. 'But I can guarantee you, after this wedding, you're going to be inundated with people looking for your designs. Which means work that won't come my way.'

'I never meant for it to happen this way,' said Jennie, hoping her eyes conveyed her sincerity. 'I only ever really aspired to work for you. My own company felt like too big a dream, someone else's life, and I don't think I believed I could ever be truly good enough.'

'But you are that good, Jennie. You really are.'

'I didn't plan it particularly, it just grew.'

'With your talent, it was always going to happen,' she said, taking a deep breath, bracing herself to say something, though Jennie had no idea what. 'Jennie, will you come back to me? Not as an apprentice, I mean in a full-time position, maybe as Creative Director? You could name your salary.'

'I don't know to say,' said Jennie, knocked for six by the offer. 'What about the Arbuthnotts, and all their friends?'

Sarah waved a hand dismissively. 'Forget about them, they're as fickle as the day is long. Once they see the work you're doing, they'll forget their loyalty to George. And besides, with the work you would generate from new clients, we'd barely notice if the Arbuthnotts and their cronies disappeared. So, how about it? Will you?'

'Sarah, it's extremely kind. I—'

But before Jennie could give an answer, the church door flew open and James dashed in, holding a yellow Van Beek bag aloft.

'You got them?' Jennie called, jumping up, so relieved and delighted that she impulsively rushed up to James and gave him a huge, all-consuming hug.

'I got them,' he said, at first not returning the hug, but as Jennie squeezed tighter, he wrapped his arms around her and slowly, tentatively drew her closer, in a way that told her he was open to forgiveness.

After a moment, Jennie pulled away, uncertain what to say, conscious that Sarah was standing just a few feet away.

'Let's talk later,' James whispered, his eyes locked on hers, smoothing a hair from her forehead. 'For now, we have work to do.'

'Right,' said Jennie, gathering herself, feeling adrenalin rising again. 'Can you take the bouquets, buttonholes, corsages and car flowers to Fran so that I can get on with the garland for the door?'

'Load me up, buttercup!'

Together they moved the items from the van to his car, Jennie alive with the synergy between them.

'I'll see you later,' he said, after everything had been moved.

'Yes,' said Jennie, wanting desperately to kiss him but knowing she shouldn't, not until they'd spoken properly and cleared the air.

'I'd better go.'

'See you later,' she said, waving him off, watching his car disappear down the country lane and praying it was all about to come good between them.

30

Jennie and Louise completed the arches round the doors just moments before the first guests arrived.

'That was close,' said Jennie, pouring cups of tea from her flask in the van.

'They don't know that,' said Louise, her feet up on the dashboard, a doughnut in hand that they'd bought from a petrol station on the way down.

They watched the guests saunter up the path to the door of the church, full of excited chatter, the ladies holding on to their hats and tugging at hemlines as gusts of fresh summer breeze blew through the graveyard.

Jennie laughed at the two of them, trying to be incognito in the cab of the van. 'We must look like we're on a stake-out!'

'But let's wait for the bride to arrive before we head off to the marquee,' said Louise.

'Of course!' Jennie reached for a doughnut. 'I'm not going to miss seeing Fran's big arrival.'

A few minutes later the car with the bridesmaids drew up. George got out in a powder – blue gown and jostled the flower girls and page boys around ineffectively, the six of them running rings round her in their excitement.

'Sarah just offered me a full-time position,' said Jennie, enjoying the sight of the kids running amok, and George chasing after them.

Louise put down her doughnut. 'You're kidding!'

'Nope, she came into the vestry, sat down and said she wanted me back.'

'Oh Jennie, I'm so happy. What did you say?'

'I didn't.'

Louise nodded knowingly, recognising Jennie was well on her way to creating her own brand without the help of Sarah. 'It would be great to have you back, but it's a big decision.'

'Mmm,' said Jennie, who hadn't had a moment to make sense of it all.

'Here's Fran now!' cried Louise, when the bridal car pulled up.

Fran's father stepped out of the car, followed by Buckley with his floral collar, and held out his hand to his daughter. Jennie gasped as Fran stepped out looking radiant in what looked like an antique dress in champagne tulle, with a V-neck, lace bodice and cap sleeves.

'Effortless,' said Louise.

'Classic,' sighed Jennie.

'Is she bare foot?'

'I think she might be,' said Jennie, straining to see. 'She told me she hates heels, so it wouldn't surprise me.'

'And the bouquet looks perfect.'

'It does work,' said Jennie, who had struck the balance between understated and feminine – velvety cream ranunculus, wild rose, grape hyacinth, forget-me-not, and lily of the valley, natural and relaxed, just like Fran.

'Your work is complete!' sang Louise.

'Almost,' said Jennie, screwing her cup back onto the top of the flask and packing away the doughnuts before turning on the ignition. 'We'd better check all's well at the marquee.'

*

Jennie walked into the biggest marquee she'd ever seen to find it bursting with luxurious cream ranunculus, filled with the heady scent of lily of the valley, and dancing with tiny blue forget-me-nots. Kat, Mary, Prisha and Zaynab had followed Jennie's instructions to the letter, setting the tone beautifully for Fran's informal-formal wedding.

'That's it, I'm done,' said Jennie, pulling a chair out from one of the tables.

'You look as if you could sleep for a year,' said Mary, coming to join her.

'That's exactly how I feel.'

'You've created something very special,' said Prisha, pulling a chair out next to her.

'We all did,' said Jennie.

'But it was your vision,' said Kat.

'Perfect,' said Zaynab, Mohammed suckling at her breast.

'She's pretty good,' said Louise, all six women now sitting round the table, tired but elated.

'You ladies deserve champagne,' came a voice from behind.

Jennie turned to see James, her heart skipping a beat at the sight of him.

'Champagne might finish me off,' she laughed, trying to play it cool.

'Speak for yourself!' said Mary, as James procured a bottle and glasses from the bar in the middle of the marquee, and brought them over.

'Shouldn't you be at the church?' Jennie asked as he poured the drinks.

'The service just finished, photos are happening. I've been sent ahead with Henry to make sure everything's in place this end.'

As James passed round the drinks a shout came from the entrance of the marquee, opposite the bar. 'Whose is this bag?'

'Bring it over, Henry,' called James.

Henry was dressed exactly as James but, in Jennie's opinion, his tall, thin frame didn't carry the outfit off with such aplomb.

'Looks like George's,' said James, unzipping the large leather tote after he'd introduced them all. 'Yup, the smell of Santal 33 definitely confirms it's hers.'

Jennie caught a whiff of the perfume and it took her straight back to Annabel's, when George had sped past her on the stairs and out to Sarah at the van. The moment her life changed for ever.

'Are you sure?' asked Louise, craning her neck to get a better look.

'Ninety-nine per cent.'

'It's just, why would she have a Van Beek carrier bag in there?'

Jennie sat up, her energy and focus returning surprisingly quickly.

'Would you mind pulling that out?' she asked James, pointing to the bag.

He handed her the bright yellow plastic bag.

Jennie looked at Louise who, like Jennie, knew precisely what the bag contained.

'Oasis garlands,' they said in unison.

James turned the bag upside down and the garlands fell on to the table, leaving everyone with the same simple question: why?

*

'I wonder what he's saying to her,' Jennie said to Kat and Louise, watching James standing under an old oak tree, grilling George. Guests spilled out of coaches onto the gravel drive in front of Brompton Manor, with its honey stone gables and lilac wisteria draped at its mullioned windows, and dispersed towards the marquee near the stable block.

'Looks pretty heated, whatever it is,' said Louise, from where the three of them were now seated in the van, to one side of the house.

James gesticulated furiously at George, and George was all limp limbs and doe eyes. Eventually, James threw his arms up in contempt.

'He's walking away!' said Louise, clutching hold of Kat's hand. George made no attempt to follow.

'We should get going,' said Jennie, putting the key in the ignition, though she wanted desperately to stick around to talk to him.

'Are you mad?' cried Louise.

'What?' she asked.

'We need to find out what she said,' said Kat. 'Why she stole the garlands.'

'I'm sure it's none of our business.'

'It's entirely our business, she almost ruined the church flowers,' said Kat. 'And look, James is heading over here.'

Jennie watched as he strode purposefully towards the van, admiring his swagger as he did.

'Think I'll go for a pee,' said Louise, getting out and disappearing.

'I need to stretch my legs before the journey home,' said Kat, and Jennie laughed at their transparent subterfuges.

James, on seeing Jennie, waved openly. Jennie gave a short, awkward wave back. It wasn't until he was right beside the van that she got out, grazing the horn as she did.

'Hi,' he said.

'Hi,' she replied, wiping her damp palms down the front of her filthy apron.

'It *was* George who took the garlands,' he confirmed.

'Any idea why?'

'Turns out she's been playing the influencer on Oli's parents. They're building a new lifestyle brand, and she convinced them that making the wedding bigger would be good publicity. I doubt it took much persuasion; like I said before, they're partial to a bit of a show.'

'That makes sense,' said Jennie, though she was still unclear as to exactly why George took the garlands. 'I couldn't understand why someone like Fran, so kind and unaffected, would be bound by Oli's family's desire for a big wedding. She seemed so keen on something intimate. But if she knew there was a broader purpose, I can see why she gave in. That's the thing about Fran, she'll do anything for anyone.'

'She said the same about you,' countered Jennie. 'But what was in it for George?'

'The same thing that always motivates George.'

'More followers?'

'A bit of cross-branding never hurts, but there was another reason, too.'

'What?' asked Jennie, sensing James was reluctant to say.

'She wanted to make the wedding so big that you couldn't possibly manage the flowers.'

'Why?' asked Jennie, the irony not lost on her that it was George who almost sabotaged her career at the last minute, rather than Stephen.

'I think she hoped you'd buckle and move on. But when that didn't work, she figured if you messed up this gig by not completing the church flowers, you wouldn't get another, not in these circles at least, and ultimately you wouldn't stick around the city, or me.'

'Why would George care about me being around you?'

James cleared his throat. 'Turns out, George has a thing for me,' he replied, his brow line nudging a little higher than usual.

'Oh,' said Jennie, hoping keenly that the feeling wasn't reciprocated. 'Are you—?'

'No!' he said quickly. 'No, no, no, absolutely not.'

'Good. That's a relief,' she exhaled, her body finally relaxing.

'Don't read too much into it. George has always been insecure, despite the larger-than-life persona. At least we now know why she's been *so* strung out recently. I promise, it'll all die down and you'll get to know the George we all know and love.'

'It seems like quite an extreme thing to do, to up-size a friend's wedding, and then sabotage the flowers,' said Jennie, trying to play it cool despite being acutely aware that James had just hinted towards a future together.

'I guess insecurity can trigger of all sorts of strange behaviour. She'll regret it in time.'

'True,' said Jennie, thinking of Stephen and Lauren, hopeful that both of them would learn something from losing the relationships they controlled, find greater security, and end up in happier places. She hoped the same for George, too. 'How did she even know about the garlands?'

James shook his head. 'Something about a phone call on the flower truck.'

Jennie remembered her conversation with Henrik when she called to ask about the garlands yesterday afternoon. She figured he must have gone straight from the tower to the flower shop. 'George must have been on the truck with either Sarah or Fiona.'

'I guess,' said James, Fran sneaking up behind him and putting her hands over his eyes.

'What's going on?' she asked.

'Fran!' said Jennie, kissing her on the cheek, not wanting to hug her in case she dirtied her dress with her florist's fingers and apron. 'You look sensational.'

'Thank you,' she said, doing a silly little curtscy. 'Everyone's talking about the flowers. They're incredible.'

'They almost didn't happen at all,' said James. Jennie shook her head discreetly, telling him not to bother Fran about George on her big day.

'What do you mean?' she asked.

James filled Fran in on George's real reason for influencing the size of the wedding, and then, when that failed to get rid of Jennie, trying to sabotage the church flowers.

'I'm so sorry if she caused you any trouble, Jennie,' said Fran.

'Aren't you angry?' asked James.

'I'm cross that she would try and sabotage Jennie's work, but mostly I just feel sorry for her. I'd hate to live the way she does, trying to please so many people, believing the world loves what you have and who you know, rather than who you are. I wonder how long she's felt this way about you.'

'You don't care that she caused you to have a wedding you didn't want, and almost one with missing flowers?'

'The wedding has turned out to be beautiful, I can't be mad about that, and I couldn't be happier that you'll get lots of publicity out of this,' she said to Jennie. 'And as for her trying to wreck the church flowers, it would have been disappointing, but still I would have been more upset for Jennie. It would have been her work that was compromised, not mine.'

'You're too nice,' said James, giving his sister a squeeze.

'I always have been the nicer of the two of us,' she teased as Sarah came to join them. 'We were just saying how everyone is talking about the flowers.'

'They're magnificent,' answered Sarah. 'I'm desperate to have Jennie back on the team. Have you had a chance to think about it?'

'I have,' said Jennie, who had decided to listen to her gut, to grab life by both hands and follow her most ambitious dreams, even if it did scare her half to death. She took a deep breath before replying, 'As grateful as I am, I think I'm going to pass.'

31

'I can't believe you turned Sarah's offer down,' said James, as he and Jennie strolled round the walled garden, listening to the sounds of the wedding – children shrieking, raucous laughter, glasses clinking – drifting over from outside the marquee.

'It was tempting,' said Jennie, thinking of all the hours she'd spent here, inhaling the heady scent, dreaming her life away. And now here she was with her own business, strolling through the garden with the owner's grandson. She wondered again how many times they might have literally crossed paths over the years: as children when James was climbing trees and building dens; as teenagers, drinking a sly beer or alcopop in the woods, or in their twenties, when strolling through the grounds with family or friends. It gave her a very great sense of 'meant to be'. 'But it's the easy option and I think the harder option might be more rewarding.'

'It usually is. That's certainly true of medicine,' he said, gesturing to the rickety bench next to the cold frames, where she'd perched with Tracy. Jennie sat and admired a perfect peach rose, its petals calling her to touch their silky softness. She could imagine the feel of it against her cheek, just as she could imagine the feel of James's hand. Both begged to be touched, but she resisted. 'I hope you know how grateful I am for what you did for Mum.'

'How is she?'

'She saw someone straight away, thanks to you,' said Jennie, remembering how her mum had gushed about James: how thankful she was for him, and how she was convinced everything would work out for Jennie and him in the end, even if Jennie hadn't been so sure. 'They started her on a course of hormones, so hopefully they'll help. We're just pleased it didn't turn out to be anything more sinister that might have needed surgery.'

'Me too,' he said, sincerity burning in his eyes, and a silence fell between them. Jennie ached to mention what had happened in the pub again, but she wasn't certain how to begin.

'Thanks for asking me out when you did,' she said eventually. 'Without you I wouldn't be here, and Fran would have ended up with very different flowers. You've made two people happy.'

'I was only really interested in making one person happy.'

'She's amazing,' said Jennie, following James' gaze to where he could just see Fran through an open gate, holding a glass of champagne and dancing in her wellies with one of her flower girls.

'I wasn't talking about my sister,' he said, turning towards Jennie.

'Oh?' she said, a shiver of hope surging through her body.

James released a long sigh. 'I'm sorry for how I handled the pub incident. My mind was on exams, so I shut you out until they were over. It felt as if I might combust if I tried to deal with both things at once.'

'Fran did mention you can't multitask,' she laughed lightly.

'I've been an idiot. I couldn't stand the idea of the flower guy having you.'

'Henrik?' Jennie asked, amused that James might still think that was even a possibility.

'I spoke to him when I was collecting the garlands from his truck. He set me straight. He told me he was into you, but you weren't into him. He told me you were all about "some doctor guy"!'

'He was right,' said Jennie, fixing her gaze on James's, hoping he could tell just how much she wanted to kiss him, how much she adored him.

'Can we go back a step? Pick up from where we left off?' he asked.

'I'd love to,' said Jennie, almost completely swept up in the moment, but something niggled at the back of her mind.

'What is it?'

'Do you think, with our different backgrounds and all, that it might be a bit of a gamble?'

'How do you mean?'

'I mean with you having all this,' she cast her gaze around the walled garden and gestured beyond, through the gate, towards the house, still unable to believe that James was the heir, 'and me from my working-class background.'

'I love that you come from hard-working roots, in the most part that's how I was brought up, too, despite all my friends coming from money. You know my parents are just teachers, nothing fancy, they don't even have a house of their own. Both the estate and the house in Notting Hill belong to my grandmother, and you've seen the state of the place, everything tired and old, it's a mess. So, I think we're pretty equal, don't you? You might actually be better off than me.'

'But one day you'll inherit all of this,' she explained, amused that she'd mistaken dilapidated for grandeur.

'Maybe, maybe not,' he shrugged. 'My grandmother's mad enough to leave it to a donkey sanctuary! There are no guarantees.'

'I suppose that's true,' laughed Jennie, who knew only too well, after the last few months, that life really can spin on a dime. She couldn't have imagined that three months ago she'd be the owner of her own business, surrounded by friends, and have the interest of a charming young doctor. She was her own woman now, happy and successful, living her dream. 'But why didn't you tell me? You must have realised when I kept talking about the walled garden.'

'I thought you were probably referring to here, but I wasn't a hundred per cent sure. And I was planning on bringing you, remember? But then things got in the way and . . . I don't know . . . if I'm honest, I find it a bit embarrassing. Like I said, it's my granny's wealth, not mine.'

'And there's no one else you're interested in?'

James laughed from his belly.

'What?' asked Jennie, the tiniest bit affronted. 'You did mention there was someone you had your eye on.'

'You're referring to the girl who "caught my eye", right?' he asked, locking his eyes firmly on Jennie's.

'Mmm-hmm.'

'That girl was you!'

'Excuse me?'

'That girl was you.' He reached out and took her hand in his. 'There was never anyone else. That first day at the flower market, I was gutted I didn't ask for your number. And then when you were there at the Arbuthnotts', and George was prattling on about how extraordinary your flowers were and how she had to have you for her thirtieth birthday party, all I was thinking was, forget the flowers, forget the party, the only thing I'm interested in is this girl in the apron with the flyaway curls. It's only ever been you.'

Jennie said nothing, but all the little pearls of wisdom her friends had given her about shared values and interests and family came flooding back to her, and she realised it was possible for them to make their relationship work, despite their backgrounds, especially now she had taken control of her own career and destiny.

'It's true,' said James, clasping his other hand securely over Jennie's. 'I went away and broke it off with Camilla immediately. I should have told you on our first date, I almost did, but I couldn't quite tell how you felt.' He paused, his eyes giddy with delight. 'Can you believe it? All these years, we could have met. We were meant to be.'

'Right,' she whispered, looking deeply into his sparkling eyes, honesty and desire radiating out of them. 'Wow.'

'Wow indeed,' said James, leaning slowly towards her and placing the truest kiss of Jennie's life tenderly on her lips.

*

In the end James invited Jennie to stay for the reception, so she said goodbye to her friends, who drove home with a crate of champagne and several plates of canapés in the back of the vans. After waving them off, Fran took Jennie into the main house and lent her a cocktail dress that had belonged to her

348

grandmother in the 1980s – a blue metallic fabric with one shoulder and a ruched bodice, which Jennie thought looked like something Princess Di might have worn. Fran even pulled her hair into an effortless up-do to complete the look.

At the top table, James and Jennie sat next to each other, drinking and kissing and giggling, and chatting to James's parents, who had flown in for the week from Sri Lanka, and were as sweet and gracious as their children.

'There's someone I'm desperate for you to meet,' James told Jennie after the speeches, and guests were making their way to the other end of the marquee to dance.

'Who?' she asked as he led her towards a centre table full of the older guests. One in particular immediately caught Jennie's eye – the old woman from the walled garden.

'Granny,' said James, going directly to the woman, almost unrecognisable in an elegant silk dress and bolero jacket. 'This is Jennie.'

Jennie thought James was going to add something more, 'Jennie the girl I've been seeing a bit' or 'Jennie the girl I've might have mentioned', to prompt the old woman's memory, but as soon as his grandmother saw Jennie her eyes sprang to life.

'We've met before,' she said, before Jennie could say anything herself.

'You have?' asked James, his eyes flitting between the two women.

'In the walled garden,' Jennie confirmed.

'When?' he asked.

'Now and then,' answered his grandmother, her eyes only on Jennie. 'Come, sit with me,' she said, patting the empty chair beside her. 'I've had a feeling about you from the start.'

'You have?' asked Jennie, who still couldn't quite tell if the woman felt she was a little too fanciful. 'Good or bad?'

'Oh, very good. You're a dreamer, like me,' she replied, her eyes dancing. And at that she took Jennie's hands and scrutinised them, turning them over several times. 'But you're not afraid of hard work, and a hard-working dreamer is a force to be reckoned with.'

'Thank you,' Jennie replied, overjoyed that it felt as if James's granny had always known her.

'I saw it the first time we met – the hint of green in your cuticles, the thorn scratches, the hardened skin from stripping flowers. Only a hard-working florist has hands like these.'

'How can you be certain she's a florist?' asked James, standing beside them, scrutinising his grandmother's face.

'Because her hands are just like mine,' she said, and she showed them both her fingers: green, scratched and callused.

'So they are!' exclaimed Jennie.

'And besides,' she giggled. 'Fran told me that her florist, Jennie, was courting my grandson. When I saw you together at the top table, my intuition was proved correct.'

'James told me you used to be florist, too.'

'An amateur. Not like you,' she said, admiring the pieces around the marquee. 'You are a professional of the highest calibre.'

'Thank you,' said Jennie bashfully, delighted by her praise.

'The last time we met, I thought to ask if you'd like to rent the walled garden and cottage from me, but I had a feeling you'd refuse. I could tell you were far too polite to accept such an offer. I went away regretting not asking, God knows I could use the help. In fact, each time I've been in the garden since, I've thought of you and hoped that we'd cross paths again.'

'Gosh,' said Jennie, blown away by the confession.

'It would be foolish for me not to make the offer again now.'

Jennie thought she must have imagined what James's grandmother had said, or misunderstood, that she couldn't possibly have just offered Jennie her fantasy. It was only when James placed his hand on her shoulder and asked 'Jennie, what do you think?' that she realised it must have been real.

'I, I don't know what to say,' she stammered, her eyes brimming with tears, her hands trembling.

'You take some time,' said his grandmother, patting Jennie on the knee and getting slowly to her feet. 'Let me know what you decide.'

'Granny isn't messing about. She really would like you to have the walled garden and cottage,' said James, sometime later on the dance floor, when Jennie had had time to absorb the offer, and James had spoken at length with his grandmother.

'It's such a generous idea, one I really appreciate, but . . .' she leant back in hold, in order to see James's face more clearly. 'Sarah once told me, "it's not what you know but who you know".

'That sounds like the sort of thing George would say,' laughed James, his head cocked to one side.

'Right,' Jennie chuckled, returning to her thought. 'In the context that Sarah said it, she was wrong. But in some ways, she was also right.'

'How so?'

'All the ladies, they want "Team Jennie" to continue. They're not 'connected', they don't have great skills, but they do have great spirit. You know? And that spirit, that love, that's what translates into the flowers.'

'It's not what you know but who you know,' James nodded slowly, getting it.

'It feels to me as if the business belongs at Primrose Tower,' she said, imagining all the fun she and her friends could have together, all their heart and laughter being channelled into the creations.

Jennie couldn't quite believe what she was saying, but in her heart, she knew it felt right. For all she still held onto her fantasy of the walled garden, the reality was that it would be lonely, and too much for her to run alone.

'Maybe one day the garden can happen,' she mused, a great sense of certainty and contentment flooding over her. 'But for now, the tower and my friends feel even better than the dream of dreams.'

'Are you sure?' he asked, placing his check on hers and pulling her body closer.

'I'm sure,' said Jennie, a little thought forming. 'But why don't *you* take it on instead. It could be a perfect project for you – a house to renovate with all those extra hours you're going to have when you become a consultant, a garden to redesign. I could visit on my days off.'

'You wouldn't mind?'

'It would give me the best of both worlds. My friends in London, and you here with my family close by; it would complete my big dream come true.'

'You're my dream come true, Jennie Treloar.'

'As you are mine, James Cavendish,' she said as they twirled round the dance floor, lights sparkling above them, Jennie safe in the arms of the man she loved.

EPILOGUE

'If anyone had told me last Diwali that this year I'd be working as a part-time florist, I'd have thought they were mad,' said Prisha, the five of them gathered round Kat and Jennie's kitchen table for their weekly team meeting, which this week included discussing a huge Diwali celebration banquet in the city for an Indian billionaire businessman.

'You can say that again,' said Mary. 'My sons can't believe I've retired from nursing and taken up floristry. And nobody at church can believe I've been put in charge of the flowers.'

Since Fran's wedding, not a week had passed that Jennie hadn't had at least one big event and several smaller ones. The progression of employing Prisha, Zaynab and then Mary, with Kat as driver at weekends, had been a natural one from paid occasional helpers to part-time members of staff. Business was so good that Jennie had bought her own vintage van, emblazoned with *Jennie Treloar Flowers*, and negotiated terms with the council to lease the tower's community hall as her workspace. Residents popped in all the time to see what she was up to, and Jennie had quickly become a key figure at Primrose Tower, leading a committee for building improvements, reinstating a shop, and setting up a community cafe. It felt to Jennie like a home from home, her own little slice of village life, right in the heart of London.

Louise, who continued to work for Sarah, kept her up to speed on developments at the shop. Sarah enquired often as to Jennie's employment status but knew, as everyone in the trade did, that she was doing exceptionally well on her own.

'I speak English and I have friends,' said Zaynab, with Mohammed, now six months old, sitting on her knee gnawing on a teething ring. Jennie couldn't quite believe just how much both he and Zaynab had grown. It was as if Zaynab was a different woman from the one Jennie had first met, frightened and alone. Now she was blooming, a confident mother, her English getting stronger through lessons, and thriving in London despite losing her husband, and raising her son without the support of her family.

'And I could not have imagined having the confidence to have a second job and a new relationship,' said Kat, who'd been seeing the lovely Leah for the last few months, having met at a wedding they'd been doing the flowers for.

'And who would have believed I'd have a man!' laughed Mary.

'None of us can believe that!' teased Jennie, who Mary knew was jubilant that she and Omar had become an item. They hadn't quite got to the stage of moving in together, but it was clear to everyone who knew them that they were both smitten, and it wouldn't be too long before they took the next step. 'Everyone's come so far.'

'Including you,' said Kat.

'When James marry you?' asked Zaynab.

Jennie blushed. 'It's too soon for that,' she said, though she'd be lying if she hadn't thought about it, and their wedding, which could only take place in one location – the walled garden, with all the bouquets and arrangements made from roses grown on site. And she thought too of how one day they might have a family, and how their children might run bare foot as Jennie looked after the cottage, and ran the business from the garden. But for now, she was more than happy where she was. 'He's so busy with his new post and all the work of renovating the cottage and garden,' she said, proud as punch that he was following his dream, too. He'd already made significant progress with the garden, clearing and pruning, and preparing for spring. He was confident there would be enough blooms for Jennie to use in some of her arrangements, and the thought thrilled her to the core.

'He'd be crazy not to jump at the chance of marrying one of London's most sought-after florists,' said Kat.

'Oh, please!' said Jennie, embarrassed by the praise.

'Did *Tatler* make it up when they printed that article about Jennie Treloar Flowers?'

'It was just luck that the editor was at Fran's wedding,' groaned Jennie, remembering the call she'd taken the following day from the editor, asking if she could write a feature on her. Jennie had thought it was joke, but then they'd met, and she'd been interviewed, and a photographer had come and taken photos of her and her friends in the tower. When the article was published, glossy and glowing, Jennie's Instagram following shot up overnight – people falling for her romantic, whimsical creations, set against the utilitarian backdrop and community of the tower. Sarah, and even George, had shared the story, resulting in Jennie's Instagram followers outstripping Sarah's – not by so many that she was 'famous', just enough to make her business lucrative. Her dad still couldn't make head nor tail of it.

'Luck and hard work,' said Mary. 'That's how anyone who's made it makes it.' And Jennie thought immediately of Granny Cavendish and how she'd said almost exactly the same in the woods the first time they'd met. She'd loved getting to know her these last few months, James gloating about how 'he'd always known they'd get along like a house on fire', and enjoyed, too, Granny's conspicuous pleasure at having James and Jennie around the estate, all three of them in their element, their sleeves rolled up, tending the land. A little luck having come their way.

'Success isn't the thing – friendship and happiness are,' she said, hoping she didn't sound too corny.

'Absolutely,' agreed Prisha. 'To friendship and happiness.'

'To friendship and happiness,' they chorused, their joy resounding for all to hear, throughout Primrose Tower.

ACKNOWLEDGEMENTS

I've been wanting to tell the story of Jennie and her friends at Primrose Tower for some time, so I'm delighted that it's now in bloom, something made possible by the dedicated team at Welbeck Fiction, my superstar agent, Juliet Pickering, and all at Blake Friedmann Literary.

In particular, a huge thank you to Rachel Hart, who is not only brilliantly efficient and insightful but also really lovely! And to Madeleine Feeney who has the ability to enhance my work with the lightest of touch. Thanks also to Joanna Kerr and Alex Allden for creating such a beautiful cover design, and to Jon Elek for giving me the opportunity to tell my stories.

As always, a big thank you to my family for all their support when deadlines loom – for mornings playing dinosaurs in the garden, and for pizzas and rhinos and bunkers – I couldn't do it without you.

And lastly, for friends and neighbours everywhere, who bring cheer in uncertain times.

ABOUT THE AUTHOR

Annie trained in London as a classical musician, then worked as an assistant for an Oscar winner, an acclaimed artist, a PR mogul and a Beatle. After several years of running errands for the rich and famous, she went to medical school where, hiding novels in anatomy textbooks, she discovered her true passion for writing. She went on to complete a Creative Writing MA with distinction. Annie now lives back home in Scotland, by the sea. When not writing, she enjoys swimming with her son, visiting antiques markets with her husband, eating cake with friends, playing the piano, and walking her basset hounds.

WELBECK

PUBLISHING GROUP

Love books? Join the club.

Sign up and choose your preferred genres to receive tailored news, deals, extracts, author interviews and more about your next favourite read.

From heart-racing thrillers to award-winning historical fiction, through to must-read music tomes, beautiful picture books and delightful gift ideas, Welbeck is proud to publish titles that suit every taste.

bit.ly/welbeckpublishing

WELBECK

ANDRE DEUTSCH

MORTIMER

MORTIMER

WELBECK

OH!